A KISS IN THE KITCHEN

"Have you ever made bread before, my lord?"

"Never, but I used to watch my mother's cook do it when I was a small boy. One had to take the dough and abuse it dreadfully, as I remember."

Belle laughed. "It's called kneading. I believe a gentleman like yourself can do it nicely, for it takes only strength and stamina."

He slapped at the dough, then pushed it out, folded it over, and pushed it out again. "Like this?"

"Perfect, my lord. You would make an excellent baker—although I think you would tire of such an enterprise, having to rise before dawn each morning so your wares would be fresh."

John's gaze locked on Belle as he continued to work the dough. "As you will of being our cook, Miss Hill. I want you to know how much I appreciate what you are doing for my friend's family. You are a remarkable young lady."

Belle blushed, but experienced a rush of pleasure at the compliment. "I must begin breakfast. Since you are here, you may have your choice of anything you wish."

At that moment, John suddenly wished he could kiss the sweet upturned mouth smiling at him . . .

—from "Cakes, Kisses and Confusion"
by Lynn Collum

SWEET TEMPTATIONS

LYNN COLLUM
WILMA COUNTS
JO ANN FERGUSON

Zebra Books
Kensington Publishing Corp.
http://www.zebrabooks.com

CONTENTS

CAKES, KISSES AND CONFUSION

by

Lynn Collum

ONE

John Burns, sixth Earl of Sedgefield, wandered into the library at Sedgely Park and strolled over to the man who sat at a small corner table, busily engaged in writing letters.

His lordship's secretary looked up, peering expectantly through thick glasses.

"Did you hear from Westings yet, Ballard?"

"Not yet, my lord, but it is early days. I only posted your offer for his bull three days past," the secretary replied patiently.

"Has the steward come this morning?"

"He only comes if there is a problem or he needs to ask permission for some change, my lord."

Sedgefield sighed. Then, noticing a small figure of Neptune draped with sea serpents on the edge of a nearby table, he picked it up. "Good heavens, this is ugly. Wherever did my late cousin find it?"

"The Burns family always had a fondness for nautical things, my lord. I believe he purchased that in Greece."

The earl muttered softly under his breath, "And their nautical leanings cost them their lives, to my regret."

He put down the piece and walked to the window, staring out at his newly acquired estate. Had it been two months since the letter had arrived at his barracks in

London announcing the tragic death of the fifth earl, his wife, and their two sons on their yacht at sea?

"Do you know, Ballard, I quite miss the hustle and bustle of army life. I was never intended to be a country gentleman."

The secretary again stopped writing. "Have you considered tasting the delights of the Season in London? 'Tis what most gentlemen do this time of year. It has been over six months since your cousin and his family died. 'Tis well past the proper mourning period."

John grimaced at the notion of attending the balls, routs, and musical evenings. "I'm neither a rattle nor a rogue, Ballard. London holds little to entice me."

The secretary nodded and went back to his letters.

John stared out at the well-manicured lawn stretching before him. He had been content with his life in the army. He'd earned his captaincy and the respect of his men while fighting in the Peninsula. Being a soldier was all he knew, but now this mantle of responsibility had fallen on his shoulders with that fateful accident at sea. It was a life he was neither prepared for nor wanted, but he had always done his duty. He just wasn't sure he could tolerate the boredom.

The first month he'd kept busy meeting tenants, watching the shearing of the sheep, the planting of crops—the normal everyday tasks performed on an estate of this size. But his late cousin had been an excellent fellow, hiring good people and a superior steward. There was little to keep an active man like John busy.

At the desk, Mr. Ballard shifted several papers, uncovering a letter addressed in a delicate feminine hand. "My lord, I forgot to mention you received a letter from your aunt, Lady Maxwell."

With little enthusiasm, John took the missive from his late father's sister. He broke the seal and read the lady's urgent request for him to come to Brixham.

As the new head of the family, it was his responsibility to oversee the most personal of matters, she declared. She went on to explain that his cousin, Sir Roger, was at that moment forming an alliance with a most unsuitable female who possessed neither birth nor fortune.

About to order his secretary to write a refusal, John paused. His old friend, Colonel Sampson Griffin, lived only half a day's ride from Maxwell Manor. John hadn't seen Sam since he'd been invalided out of Portugal nearly three months ago. That visit alone would make the trip worth the trouble.

It had been some five years since he'd been to Devonshire. The thought of some adventure, no matter how small, beckoned him. Still, the idea of interfering in his cousin's affairs was unthinkable. On the other hand, if he were to meet this female and find her truly inappropriate, he might be able to convince Roger to heed a caution from his old childhood playmate. And if he decided not to interfere, he'd at least have an opportunity to visit the colonel.

He requested his secretary write to inform his aunt he would arrive by the end of the week. As to Sam, John decided not to inform his old friend of his journey to Devonshire, since matters with Cousin Roger might take up more time than expected and possibly even prevent him from dashing over and visiting the Griffins. If he did make the trip, he was certain his former colonel would be happy to see him, even unannounced.

The earl had no doubt all would run smoothly at Sedgley Park in his absence.

True to his word, John rose early the following morning and set out in his curricle for the south coast with only his former batman, Flynn, in attendance, much to the distress of the valet John had inherited from the former earl. John decided to travel at a leisurely pace and enjoy the English countryside.

Some three days later, just before four in the afternoon, he arrived at his cousin's manor near the fishing village of Brixham. He'd scarcely brought his carriage to a halt when the double doors of the timbered manor house opened to reveal his aunt, much rounder and grayer than he remembered.

"You are come at last, my dear Sedgefield, and here is Roger gone off to Hillcrest Cottage to visit that woman and her daughter."

Lady Maxwell, standing only as tall as his shoulder, turned her lined cheek up for a kiss before leading him into the manor. She chattered of Mrs. Evelyn Hill and her daughter, Annabelle, and their plans to entrap Sir Roger in marriage. To John's mind, it seemed much of his aunt's distress was directed at the mother, not the daughter, but he listened patiently.

After some ten minutes, he tried to excuse himself to change from his travel dirt, but his anxious aunt wouldn't hear of it. She wished him to hear the worst. He let the lady have her say, which lasted all the way through tea, interrupted only by his occasional question.

In truth, he found little to concern him in what he heard. Miss Hill appeared to be of genteel birth, but somewhat impoverished, living with a mother whose ambition equaled Lady Maxwell's. The only bad thing said of Miss Hill was that her mother had thrown her into the path of every eligible and titled gentleman within the neighborhood, albeit with little success until Sir Roger had returned from Town for a visit which had become prolonged.

At last, putting down his teacup, John cleared his throat. "Aunt Jane, I appreciate that you have other plans for Sir Roger, but a man must go his own path."

Lady Maxwell reached out and took her nephew's arm in a surprisingly strong grasp. "Pray, do not dismiss my worries as those of an overprotective mother. That Hill woman is the most vulgar creature I have ever encountered. All I ask is that you meet this pair of . . . females. If then you do not think as I do, I shall say no more."

The earl patted the lady's hand, seeking to calm her. "Very well, dear aunt. I shall ride to wherever this cottage is and scout the lay of the land, as we say in the army."

All smiles, Lady Maxwell ordered a fresh mount for her nephew and gave him directions to the cottage. He set off to meet this temptress, convinced little would come of the matter. In the end, no doubt, he would spend a few pleasant days visiting with his cousin and then the colonel before returning to his own estate in Berkshire.

After riding several miles, he came to a stone fence line which marked the boundary of his cousin's property. Through the woods he could see the cottage perched on the cliffs, the vast expanse of ocean beyond. He dismounted, tied the horse to a limb, then scaled the fence.

As he came to the rise, John found himself intrigued with the view of the bay below. Instead of going to the cottage and knocking, as he had intended, he went to a spot at the top of the rocky precipice and gazed in admiration at the prospect below. He'd forgotten how lovely the south coast of England was. He watched a small sloop tack against the wind, and wondered where it was bound.

Once again he longed for his old life of never knowing what new adventure was around the corner, and he rued the nasty trick fate had played upon him.

"Oh, Miss Belle, they smell wonderful."

The maid closed her eyes and breathed in the sweet scent of cheesecake as Miss Hill lifted the tray from the oven. She quickly set the hot tin of finger-sized pastries on the wooden table in the center of the small kitchen.

Belle tossed aside the towel and began to place the small treats on a plate, knowing her aunt would be here any moment to shoo her up to her room.

Aggie, the Hills' maid of all work, glanced over her shoulder at Cook, who was busy preparing a tea tray, then blew on one of the cooling cakes a moment before she popped it into her mouth. Happily munching, she whispered, "If you ask me, miss, Mrs. Hill would do better to hire you as her cook as what she's got. Wherever did you learn?"

Belle smiled. In a conspiratorial voice, she said, "I should like that much better than the role of wicked niece I seem doomed to. As to my skill, my old nanny and I were much alone in Northhamptonshire when my father was at sea. She taught me a great deal."

At that moment the door opened and Mrs. Evelyn Hill entered the room, coming to a halt upon spying her niece still in the kitchen. She was a small, wiry woman, with beady black eyes that seemed to see everything. "Why do you linger here? I ordered you to your room some ten minutes past. You know your uncle has forbidden me to allow you any social encounters with young gentlemen, due to your late mother's scandal."

Belle straightened, a fire igniting in her blue eyes. "My parents' elopement was twenty-five years ago and has long been forgotten, Aunt. As I have said before, I believe you misunderstood what Uncle William meant in his letter. Surely there can be no harm in my taking tea with the family on such a proper occasion."

Evelyn Hill's eyes narrowed. She needed the money William Parks was paying her to take care of her niece, but she was aware her own daughter's beauty paled in comparison to this saucy chit's. "I cannot risk angering Mr. Parks, Belle. You must go to your room at once. Sir Roger is in the parlor. Aggie, escort my niece to her chamber and lock the door. I don't want to find her in the garden as I did yesterday where the baronet might have seen . . . er . . . encountered her."

Belle angrily took the plate she'd filled with the little cheesecakes she'd baked. "Aggie, might I have a pot of tea? Or do you intend I should go without food as well as companionship, Aunt Evelyn?"

The lady had the decency to blush. "Make a pot, Cook, and send it up after you have done with our tray."

Belle trudged up the steps to the small room which had been nearly a prison since she'd arrived at Hillcrest Cottage some three months ago. Within ten minutes, Aggie arrived with a small pot of tea. She announced the baronet hadn't brought his cousin, the earl, as he'd promised. With an apology, she backed out of the room and locked the door.

Belle had hoped her aunt might relent about her decree of not allowing her to join the afternoon tea when Sir Roger came courting. Ann had informed them the baronet might bring his cousin, Lord Sedgefield, who was coming for a visit. It seemed the gentleman had failed to arrive at Maxwell Manor.

She settled down and poured out tea, then took a small bite of one of the cheesecakes. The little pastry was delicious, and she felt pride in her unusual ability to cook. Few young women of her class could even boil water. Aggie's words about her cooking skills returned and seemed to take root in Belle's brain.

Why not work as a cook for some genteel family? It wasn't as if she could be a companion or governess without proper references. And at least as a cook she would have the freedom to come and go at will. She would be paid for her efforts—unlike here, where cooking was her only chance to escape her confinement from this room. She would only need to work for a few years. A position with a vicar's family or a well-heeled farmer might do the trick.

Her gaze swept the small room, made smaller by the large bed and oversized wardrobe against the opposite wall. She would go quite mad if locked in here much longer. But how the devil could she get away? Aunt Evelyn never seemed to allow her a minute on her own. Her excursion into the garden had been by mere chance while Cook was distracted and Aggie served in the parlor.

Belle's gaze wandered to the small balcony. It was her window to the outside world, where she often stood for hours staring at the ocean and cliffs in the distance. Could it also be a way to escape? She jumped up and went to inspect the old trellis, heavy with roses. The old wooden slats were widely spaced and pitched at varying angles.

Escape seemed impossible. Besides, how would she ever find transportation, even if she did manage the climb down? It was nearly five miles to Brixham, where she might catch the stagecoach, and her aunt kept neither horse nor carriage.

Daunted, she sighed and propped her elbows on the balustrade, then settled her chin on her hands, mentally lamenting her existence. If she didn't do something, there would be no change in her life for the next three years until she turned five and twenty. Then she would inherit the small but adequate fortune her father had left in Uncle William's control. She simply must come up with a plan.

A movement on the cliff caught her eye. Silhouetted against a blue sky, a gentleman in buckskins and a riding jacket stood gazing out at the ocean. Having caught a glimpse of Sir Roger, she was certain this was not him. The man on the cliff appeared taller and more athletically built than the baronet. There was something in the stranger's upright bearing which bespoke a disciplined life.

Belle puzzled over the identity of the man, for they

rarely had visitors out on this remote spit of land. To her surprise, he turned and surveyed the cottage, as if sizing up the residents. From where she stood, shadowed from the sun and protected by the leaves of the ivy which intertwined with the roses and covered the exterior of the cottage, she felt certain he was unaware she was observing him. He appeared to be wrestling with some decision. He drew off his beaver hat and ran his hand through his hair as he continued to stare at Hillcrest Cottage.

Suddenly the sun glinting off his neatly trimmed hair and its exact shade of auburn struck her as familiar. Sir Roger had just such sun-burnished curls, albeit longer. Was this the baronet's cousin, Lord Sedgefield? If so, what troubled him about the cottage?

There could be little doubt he was reluctant to come in as he stood gazing at the building. Was it the possibility of an alliance between her cousin and his? Lady Maxwell had made her dislike of the match well known, or so Aggie had told Belle after the maid's last trip to Brixham. Belle wasn't surprised, since her aunt was a pushing, vulgar woman.

At that moment, the gentleman on the cliff returned his hat to his head and seemed to come to some conclusion, for he strode back up the path, which ran parallel to the stone fence, instead of using the stepping stones which led to the front door. It seemed he had no intention of calling at the cottage.

In a flash, Belle realized if the gentleman had come to put an end to her aunt's ambitions about Sir Roger, the stranger might be only too happy to help Belle escape, thinking to create scandal. She might then flee to Exeter, the nearest large town. There she could take the common stage to some city and apply for a position as someone's cook.

Her first thought was to call out to him when he drew

near, but her aunt might hear her, for the drawing room
windows would be open on such a warm afternoon. She
waved her arms above her head, but the gentleman
seemed lost in thought. As he moved through the trees,
he looked neither left nor right.

Frantic he would pass her by without notice, Belle
looked about for something to catch his attention. Her
gaze fell on the small cheesecakes left on the plate. She
could just toss one across his path, and when he looked
up she would signal him to come to her.

She grabbed one small cake. It was much lighter than
the stones she and her father used to skip on the lake
where they lived. She would have to adjust her aim a
bit. The gentleman was nearing her vantage point. She
drew back and hurled the small pastry with gusto.

Down on the path, John dwelled on his presumption
at having come to judge his cousin's choice of female.
Head of the family or no, he had no business telling
Roger whom to marry. Out loud he said, "Aunt Jane
will just have to be content—"

At that moment, something soft and warm struck his
chin.

A startled gasp caused him to open his mouth, and
he tasted sweet, delicious cheesecake, still warm from
the oven. John stopped in amazement, wiping at the rem-
nants which clung to his face as he savored the small
amount he'd tasted. Why had someone hurled the small
cake at him? He looked up to see a beautiful young
female standing on a balcony of the cottage, a hopeful
expression on her lovely face.

What the devil? Could this be the Miss Hill with
whom his cousin was greatly enamored? The chit must
be quite mad to be tossing food at strangers—besides
its being a cursed waste of the best cheesecake he'd ever
tasted.

He opened his mouth to speak, but she suddenly put

her finger across her lips in a gesture of silence. Then
she motioned him to come to her, pointing at the trellis
as the means of entry to her balcony.

Appalled at the notion that a proper female was beck-
oning him to her chamber, John realized perhaps his
aunt's worries weren't unfounded. It seemed he needed
to know a great deal more about this female who had
captured his cousin's interest. What plot did she have in
mind that required his silence? Had *he*, a newly titled
earl, suddenly become her prey?

As she stood looking anxiously down at him, he was
struck anew by her beauty. Blond curls framed a delicate, heart-shaped face. Even white teeth appeared when
her full pink lips smiled tentatively. Her wide blue eyes
seemed full of mystery as she watched him.

John knew the lady on the balcony was perhaps the
most dangerous of women. She portrayed an air of innocence along with all that irresistible perfection, which
made one want to fulfill her every wish.

Using his handkerchief, he cleaned his face and determined how best to proceed. Until he knew what the
chit wanted, he would have to go up to her balcony.

With a quick glance about to make certain he was
unobserved, he climbed over the small fence that en-
closed the garden. Upon reaching the trellis, he inspected
the wood. With little difficulty, he scaled the structure
and arrived at the balcony, where the young lady moved
aside for him to climb to safety.

"You are Lord Sedgefield, are you not, sir?"

John bowed. "I am. Do you often throw pastries at
passing strangers to amuse yourself, Miss Hill?"

The young lady laughed. "Oh, sir, I do apologize. My
aim is much better when skipping stones on water."

"I shall have to take your word for that, but allow me
to say my face and I are quite glad that you chose to

throw a cake and not a stone." The gentleman rubbed his chin.

Belle blushed, but, knowing time was short, came straight to the point. "I am most delighted to meet you. Sir Roger said you were expected. I know you will think this most unusual, but I must ask your assistance."

The earl smiled, but eyed her warily. "How may I be of help, Miss Hill?"

Despite her brazen actions, Belle observed the gentleman with a mixture of caution and curiosity. His jade green eyes watched her with equal caution from a sunbronzed face with a wide generous mouth and aquiline nose. She saw inherent strength there, but she wasn't certain she should trust a man about whom she knew nothing save his name, no matter how intriguing he appeared. She decided to keep her own counsel, for who would truly believe she was nearly a prisoner in her aunt's home?

"I shall not bore you with any great details of my circumstances, my lord. I am not happy here at Hillcrest Cottage, and I wish to leave. I am of age, but, unfortunately, I have no transportation to take me to my destination. Would you be so kind as to take me to the coaching inn at Brixham?"

A flash of surprise crossed the earl's face, but he quickly seemed to get his shock under control. Then his eyes narrowed. "You want me to steal you away from your home just as darkness is about to fall, take you to a coaching inn, and leave you to fend for yourself? Really, Miss Hill, I could never consent to such a scandalous scheme." Nor would he be such a nodcock as to fall into her little plot. Was she that desperate to find herself a husband?

Belle laughed nervously. "Put that way, it does sound rather scandalous, my lord. But I had nothing quite so clandestine in mind. I was hoping you might await me at the bottom of the lane at noon tomorrow. I could make the two o'clock stage to Exeter, and you need not inform a soul you assisted me."

John's mind was racing. This chit was up to something, but what? Was she the schemer his aunt thought her, or did she merely wish to escape the designs of an ambitious mother? Did she think such a ploy as running away with him would force him to offer for her?

Yet another possibility entered the gentleman's mind. If she left Hillcrest Cottage in such an odd manner, his cousin's eyes might be opened to her unsuitability as a wife. All John need do was provide a chaperon for the chit to protect himself. "You wish to take the stage to Exeter?"

"I do, my lord."

The earl came to a quick decision. "Then allow me to take you to Exeter instead. 'Tis but twenty-five miles, and I would feel better if I were certain you came to no harm."

There was but a moment's hesitation. "I shall take you up on that kind offer, Lord Sedgefield, for my funds are quite low until I receive my inheritance."

The two settled on a meeting time. Then the earl climbed down the trellis, all the while telling himself such a reckless act was justified, since he would be saving his cousin from an imprudent marriage. But something about Miss Hill's demeanor didn't fit his notions of a conniving baggage. Still, what proper female would be willing to go off to a distant town with a virtual stranger?

With one last look at Miss Hill on the balcony, John felt certain that, no matter the impropriety, he was doing the right thing to spare his cousin. With that, he strode off toward his horse, his mind set on a plan of action. When he'd set out for Devonshire, he'd never had this kind of adventure in mind.

Belle watched the gentleman disappear into the trees. She found herself intrigued with the earl. Why had he been so willing to help her with so little information? Was he truly kind, or did he have some other motive?

Most would consider it dangerous for her to flee in the carriage of an unknown gentleman, but there was something about Lord Sedgefield that caused one to trust him, even like him, on short acquaintance.

Reason told her not to allow her attraction to his good looks to cloud her judgment. After tomorrow, she would likely never see Lord Sedgefield again. That thought left her unaccountably low, even as she went about packing her few belongings for tomorrow's escape.

TWO

Belle shredded her toast as she awaited her cousin and aunt in the small breakfast parlor of Hillcrest Cottage. She'd been unable to sleep due to a mixture of nerves and excitement at the possibility of at last escaping the confines of this cottage on the cliffs.

In the hallway, her aunt shrieked at Ann to hurry or they would be late. Then the door opened to reveal Evelyn Hill. Though she was dressed in a saffron yellow morning gown with an excess of cream lace at the collar, sleeves, and lower skirt, the lady's face held a pasty white pallor. Her small dark eyes immediately fixed on Belle.

"I hope you have no thoughts I shall take you to Brixham with us, Belle. If there is anything you need, give a list to Ann, and she will make certain to acquire the items . . . if they aren't too dear." Mrs. Hill swept into the room and took a seat at the table.

"Good morning to you, too, Aunt Evelyn," Belle said, with a touch of sarcasm which totally escaped her relative.

Mrs. Hill put her hand upon the teapot, then shouted, "Aggie, we shall require more tea! This has grown quite cold." Lowering her voice, the lady then directed her conversation to her niece. "Belle, you should have waited until we were down. We cannot afford to be wasting tea leaves."

"I was under the impression my uncle was providing you with adequate compensation for my room and board."

The lady sniffed. "What William Parks considers adequate wouldn't keep a milkmaid from starving, much less a lady of quality. We must economize until Sir Roger comes up to scratch."

Aggie entered the breakfast parlor with a new teapot and removed the old. As she was leaving the room, Miss Ann Hill entered, looking like a frightened lamb.

Belle gave the girl a reassuring smile. She liked her cousin excessively, but knew Ann's life was far more difficult than her own. The girl carried all the burden of her mother's great ambition.

"Good morning, cousin."

"Good morning, Belle." The girl glanced nervously at her mother, then slipped into her seat. "Cannot Belle be allowed to go shopping with us this morning, Mama?"

Mrs. Hill opened her mouth to deny the request, but her gaze fell upon her daughter's attire. "What have you done to your gown, Ann? You must remember your father was a gentleman. You should dress as a gentleman's daughter."

Ann's pale cheeks flushed. "Belle said . . . that is . . ."

Hoping to save her cousin, Belle forged into the conversation, but she must tread lightly. Her aunt believed a vast amount of ribbons, lace, and furbelows trimming a gown showed the owner's elevated station. In that lady's mind, there was no such thing as excess.

"Aunt Evelyn, dear Ann is so beautiful I think it a pity one's attention is always engaged by the intricacy of her gowns. We removed the lace at her collar so Sir

Roger could admire the swan-like beauty of her neck. The ribbons always fluttering in the breeze at her waist draw his attention from her lovely figure, and I am certain I read in *La Belle Assemblée* that one should never exceed three ruffles on the hem of any gown."

Mrs. Hill's eyes narrowed as her mouth puckered in thought. "But 'tis so very plain. I cannot like my daughter to appear in the village dressed no better than the miller's daughter."

Ann, sensing her mother might be convinced, said, "There can be no danger of that, Mama, for this is the finest muslin one can purchase at the local modiste's. Why, Hattie Martin's gowns are not only cheap calico, but homemade as well."

"Well, we haven't time for you to change, so I guess it will have to do. 'Tis not likely you will see the baronet today anyway, since no doubt that tardy cousin of his has arrived by now. But you are not to alter any more of your gowns until I have given permission. Eat your breakfast so we may go."

Ann grabbed a slice of toast from the rack and began to butter it as Belle put her plan of escape into action. "Aunt Evelyn, I was hoping to gather some flowers from the garden while you are gone to the village. It would brighten up the parlor for Sir Roger's next visit."

The lady contemplated her niece's request for a moment, then nodded. "I suppose you cannot get into trouble in our own garden, and you have been looking a bit pale of late. I wouldn't want your uncle to pay a surprise visit and think I have not been taking good care of you." Aunt Evelyn took a sip of tea, then added, "But you are not to go beyond the stone fencing."

"I understand, Aunt." Belle had no intention of giving a promise which she fully intended to break. She would not only go beyond the fencing, but all the way down the narrow path to the main road, where she hoped and prayed Lord Sedgefield would be waiting as promised.

Within ten minutes, Aunt Evelyn and Ann had donned their bonnets and climbed into the ancient carriage sent from the local inn for their trip to Brixham. As the hired vehicle pulled away, Belle could hear her aunt admonishing her daughter for having chosen a poke bonnet instead of her chipstraw with the new ribbons.

Belle, nerves fluttering in her stomach, announced to Aggie, "I shall go up and retrieve my bonnet and shears. I am going into the garden to gather flowers for the parlor."

"Do you need me to help, miss?"

"You have too much to do, Aggie. I can manage nicely. Should I find I need assistance, I shall call you."

The maid was relieved, for Mrs. Hill had insisted all the furniture in the parlor be given a new coat of wax— as if that would make it look less worn. The servant marched off to the kitchen.

Belle dashed up the stairs to her room. She pulled two small portmanteaus from under her bed, then went to the balcony. She searched the area for a servant or passerby.

Convinced no one was about to observe her, she dropped the bags to the ground one at a time.

Returning inside, she placed the letter she'd written to her aunt the night before on the bed. It explained her intention of seeking employment since she was of age, but gave no specifics. Then she donned a simple gypsy-style bonnet and grabbed up the shears as if she truly meant to cut flowers.

The voices of Cook and Aggie, busy in the kitchen, echoed in the foyer as Belle stole down the stairs. Without a word, she slipped out the front door and dashed round the cottage to her bags. After glancing nervously about, she opened one and shoved the shears inside before she removed her reticule and tan leather gloves.

Once ready, she picked up the two portmanteaus and hurried through the front gate. As she turned onto the lane which would take her to the main road, trepidation surged though her. This plan was fraught with danger. She had no employment and little money, plus she would have to manage to slip away from Lord Sedgefield once she reached Exeter. But there was no going back to her confined life at Hillcrest Cottage.

Trudging up the path with the burden of her bags, she suddenly disturbed two swallows in a bush. Belle paused to watch them fly away, then realized she was quite as free as they were. With a new energy to her steps, she proceeded down the path to her new life.

"Can you drive this old monstrosity, Flynn?"

Lord Sedgefield stood in front of an ancient traveling coach which his cousin had given him leave to use on his visit to Colonel Griffin. John had experienced only a twinge of conscience at using the former soldier as an excuse, for in truth he was doing Roger a favor by revealing Miss Hill's flighty—nay, even fast—nature. Besides, he would stay the night with Sam once he'd seen the young lady to her destination.

The former batman, short and lean, with gray hair fringing a lined face the shade of a saddle, snorted. "They ain't made the conveyance I can't drive, Cap'n." The older man had tried to remember to call his longtime employer by his title, but after several days of stumbling over the two names, Lord Sedgefield had given Flynn permission to continue to call him by his military rank. Somehow he wasn't ready to sever that last connection to his former life.

Flynn ran his sharp gaze over the vehicle before

bringing his attention back to the earl. "This rickety old coach ain't what's got me in a fidget. I'm thinkin' you might want to come up with some other notion than runnin' off with Sir Roger's female to prevent the pair from gettin' buckled."

The earl had explained what he was about to Flynn, since he needed the man's help. "The lady requested I help her run away from her mother. Clearly she isn't happy with her situation. Besides, it would be ungentlemanly if I didn't at least offer to take her to the nearest coaching inn, for there was just such a look in her eyes as to say she intended to go whether I aided her or not."

John didn't mention her eyes were a pair of the prettiest he'd ever seen.

"Cap'n, has it occurred to you that this female is tryin' to get herself compromised by a titled gentleman, askin' you to run off with her and all?"

John frowned. "Of course. I'm not some greenling, Flynn. What I need is a chaperon for the chit. If you'll take the box and cease giving me a jaw-me-dead, I want to stop at the small hedge tavern just on the main pike and hire one of the innkeeper's daughters to act as Miss Hill's maid until we arrive in Exeter and find out just what her game is."

Flynn rubbed his gray-bearded chin. "That takes care of the female's ambitions, but what about Sir Roger's dashed hopes?"

"My aunt will help calm those waters. I have left him a note informing him of Miss Hill's request for transportation to Exeter. I even asked him to inform Mrs. Hill of her daughter's request. I want no misunderstanding on anyone's part. Now we must hurry, or we shall be late for our rendezvous with Miss Hill, and she might take a ride from some unsuspecting fellow."

Flynn chuckled. "That ain't likely, Cap'n. Not every day does a chit have an earl offer to run away with her."

John made no comment. Instead he climbed into the ancient traveling coach, trying to ignore the musty odor that lingered despite the liberal use of linseed oil. As Flynn called to the team of horses, the earl knew he didn't like the idea of Miss Hill's being anything but an innocent miss in the clutches of a scheming mother. Yet he'd been a man of the world long enough to know most things were very often what they appeared.

Within a matter of some ten minutes, they were at the Golden Fleece tavern. John and his cousin had often stopped there as boys on their many jaunts through the countryside. The innkeeper's wife was a former maid at Maxwell Manor.

Mr. Millet was delighted to oblige the earl, who promised to have the girl back by the end of the week. Meg Millet, a plump-cheeked country girl with brown curls, was the envy of her sisters as she packed to go off on a high adventure with Lord Sedgefield.

The carriage arrived some five minutes before noon at the narrow path at the crossroads Miss Hill had mentioned. John climbed down, and within minutes spied the young lady hurrying up the overgrown path. He was struck anew with the girl's innocent beauty. Was she really a scheming adventuress?

He strode to her and tipped his hat. "Good morning, Miss Hill. Pray, allow me to help with your bags."

Belle gladly surrendered her heavy load. She'd been delighted to see the waiting carriage, but her gaze had riveted on Lord Sedgefield, handsome in a blue coat over a gray-striped waistcoat and gray buckskins. His green eyes seemed to hold a curious yet shuttered look as they swept over her face. She really couldn't blame him for being wary of some female who'd thrust herself upon him in this forward manner.

"My lord, you cannot know how grateful I am for

your help. I hope this has not greatly inconvenienced your visit to Sir Roger and Lady Maxwell."

"Not at all, but are you certain you wish to go to Exeter? To leave all behind?"

"I am quite certain I will regret little I leave behind."

The young lady spoke with such determination that it surprised John.

Upon arriving at the coach, the earl introduced the servants to their newest passenger. Belle found herself in a quandary. While she experienced a flood of relief that the gentleman had taken the time to find her a maid, as was proper, she knew escaping from the fresh-faced Meg likely would not be as easy as disappearing from Lord Sedgefield.

At the moment, however, she was so delighted to be free from Hillcrest, she didn't dwell on the problem. Instead she gave herself over to enjoying her first trip in a carriage in over three months.

John found himself puzzled by Miss Hill. Her conduct was totally at odds with her reputation. True, she'd run off with him, but since entering his carriage she'd been nothing but polite and ladylike. She'd questioned Meg about her family, appearing politely interested in the maid's endless chattering about her sisters.

Determined to find out what the young lady was up to, John waited for the right moment and, at a lull in the conversation, inquired, "What exactly are your plans, Miss Hill?"

"Plans, my lord?"

"After we reach Exeter."

The lady's gaze dropped to her hands, now clasped together in her lap. "I thought I would stay the night at the posting inn, then take the stage to my final destination."

The earl frowned. "I thought Exeter was your final destination."

The young lady shook her head. Then she looked up at the earl, who nearly gasped at the intensity in her blue eyes. "Exeter is far too close to Hillcrest, my lord."

John grew quiet. Perhaps he'd paid too much heed to his aunt's slander. This young lady truly seemed intent on getting away from her mother and not on entrapping him, as he'd first suspected. He wondered what her plan was—employment as a governess or lady's companion?

He didn't want to embroil himself in her affairs any deeper, but he suspected her funds wouldn't sustain her for long, and he didn't want her on his conscience. He gave the matter due thought, then offered the lady an alternative to staying the night at an inn.

"I was planning on visiting an old friend from my army days who lives near Exeter." He prayed Sam would be in residence. "Shall we stay at his estate near Ashton? It would save you the expense of a room, and Flynn can drive you to catch the stagecoach the first thing in the morning."

Belle eyed the gentleman closely. She wondered how much he suspected about what she was doing. His intelligent eyes seemed to miss little. The truth was she didn't have funds to throw away on a night's lodging if it wasn't necessary, so at last she nodded her head. "If you don't think your friend will object."

"Sampson Griffin object to being host to such a lovely lady? That will be the day I should like to see."

Griffin Manor, which lay some two miles beyond the town of Ashton, was a neat Georgian home of red brick. There was a sturdy plainness to the structure which reassured Belle about the owner. The grounds on which

the house sat were dotted with apple trees, and the immediate park around the house was well maintained.

When the coach came to a halt, John remembered
only Flynn was driving, and he couldn't leave the team.
The earl opened the door, kicked down the stairs, and
then, after getting out, helped the other occupants to the
ground. The problem with running off with a female was
that one didn't bring a lot of servants along, leaving one
to fend for one's self.

John knocked on the door as Belle and Meg remained
near the coach. After what seemed like an extended
length of time, the door opened to reveal Colonel Sampson Griffin himself.

"John!" The gentleman appeared less than pleased to
have a visitor. Then, seeming to gather his wits, he
stepped out and embraced his old friend.

As the men caught up on their news, Belle took note
that one sleeve of the colonel's gray coat hung empty
just below the elbow. The excess material of the sleeve
had been folded under the arm and sewn. Her gaze
moved to the gentleman's face. He was quite handsome,
despite the three red scars that ran from his left ear to
his mouth. He stood as tall as the earl, but his physique
was leaner. His blond hair hung rather shaggily about
his face, as if he took little note of his appearance.

The earl, suddenly remembering his companion,
stepped back and gestured at Belle. "Sam, may I present
Miss Annabelle Hill, whom I am escorting to Exeter as
a favor. We are hoping to take advantage of your hospitality tonight."

Belle was a bit startled when his lordship used her
full first name. No one called her Annabelle these days,
especially since she now lived with her cousin, who was
only months younger and named Annabelle as well. But
the younger Miss Hill, also named for their grandmother,
had always been called Ann by one and all.

The colonel turned slightly so his scarred face was hidden from her view, then bowed. "Miss Hill, delighted." He straightened and looked discomfited. "John, you know you are most welcome here at any time. Unfortunately, we are at sixes and sevens at the moment. Mother has taken to her bed with the ague, as well as Cook, the maid of all work, and Batters. I haven't a single servant to see to your needs, and my sister hasn't the least notion what to do about the house or the meals."

The earl mentally swore as he stood pondering what they would do. Miss Hill stepped forward. "Colonel Griffin, might Meg and I be of help? I am accounted a very good cook and I'm certain Meg knows a great deal about housework. Her family runs an inn."

"I do, miss." The young maid grinned at the two men.

There was such a look of hope in the colonel's brown eyes that Belle nearly laughed.

"Miss Hill, if you would be willing to help, you would have my eternal thanks. I am at my wit's end and Letty . . . well, she is very young and not the least help. She is vowing to go to an inn tonight rather than stay here to starve and play nursemaid to the servants."

Removing her tan kid gloves, Belle stepped forward. "Then, sir, show me the kitchens. I shall make certain there is food for the ill as well as the robust. Meg and I shall manage very well tonight."

The colonel, his face a study in relief, gestured for the women to enter his home. In an undertone to John, the gentleman said, "You've made a lucky choice of traveling companions, old friend. Once I show Miss Hill and her maid to the kitchens, you must tell me where you found such a treasure."

John swore under his breath. He'd been so determined to keep Miss Hill under his watchful eye, he'd given little thought to anything else. How could he tell his old friend he'd run off with the woman his cousin had been courting? Things were going to be more complicated than he'd anticipated.

THREE

The main kitchen at Griffin Manor was painted bright yellow, giving it a warm, inviting feeling. It looked much like other kitchens Belle had seen, though larger than the one at Hillcrest or her father's.

The cavernous chamber had windows high against the ceiling, and rows of cabinets held plates, crystal, and copper pots. In the center of the room stood two long work tables. On a far wall, a large black cookstove filled one fireplace. Beside the modern convenience was an old-style spit rack in front of an open hearth.

What made this country kitchen unusual was its present state. Nearly every surface in the room was covered with dirty pots, pans, dishes, or cups. The floor hadn't been swept or mopped in days. A light dusting of flour ringed the tables, bread crumbs littered the floor, and blotches of spilled milk created irregular patterns on the slate flooring.

Belle's heart plummeted at the sight as she stood beside Colonel Griffin. Although confident in her skills as a cook, a great deal more would be required to manage this kitchen than the ability to remember and execute recipes.

Colonel Griffin stopped just inside the room, then turned to her, a sheepish expression on his face, which he kept turned slightly from her view. "I do apologize,

Miss Hill, but I warned you we were at sixes and sevens."

"So you did, sir." Belle hoped Meg was strong and efficient, since they would be doing far more cleaning than cooking in the beginning. But this would be a test of her ability to perform the duties she'd chosen for herself as a means of support until her inheritance was hers.

A moaning sound echoed in the room. A matronly woman in a white sack apron over a gray dress tried to rise from a chair at the far end of the room, but after a moment she abandoned the effort and slumped back in the seat.

"Cook!" the colonel said. "I thought you were already abed."

"Hoped I might find the strength to do a bit of cleanin'. I'm frightfully sorry for this mess, but the pot boy and the scullery maid done took ill, and I'm too weak to go to me own room."

Belle, seeing the look of defeat on the gentleman's face, took charge immediately. "Colonel, if you and Lord Sedgefield will see Cook to her room, Meg and I shall take care of the kitchen. Then we'll begin to prepare something for those who are ill. How many are there?"

The colonel put his lone hand to his forehead as he thought. "Let me see. There is my mother, the butler, two footmen, the upstairs maid, and three kitchen servants."

Belle nodded her head as she removed her pelisse and hat, finding a clean place to put them aside. "Eight ill people can be managed with a little organization, I'm certain. While you gentlemen assist Cook to her room, Meg and I shall make something light for the invalids to eat so they may recover their strength."

John, who'd remained standing at the door surveying the disastrous state of the kitchen, watched Miss Hill open drawers until she found aprons. His respect for the young lady's pluck was growing by the moment. She certainly wasn't faint of heart, nor did she appear in any way the scheming chit his aunt had described.

As Belle tied the sash on the white apron, she looked at him. "Will you help the colonel with Cook, my lord?"

The earl suddenly felt the fool as he looked up and saw his old friend struggling, with only one arm, to manage the ill woman. He'd been so lost in his admiration of Miss Hill's determination he'd forgotten he and Sam needed to take the ailing woman back to her room. Hurrying across the room, he realized there was a great deal more to Miss Annabelle Hill than just a pretty face.

As the gentlemen departed with Cook hoisted between them, Belle set her mind to the task at hand. "We need lots of hot water, Meg. We must scrub this place from top to bottom before we can begin preparing dinner for the others."

Meg, removing her own bonnet and cape, rolled up her sleeves saying, "I'll fetch the hot water from the boiler, miss, if you'll move some of them dishes into the wash area."

Within a few hours, the kitchen was spotless. Meg stood basting the hens Belle had decided to roast for supper. Leek soup simmered on the stove, and apple tarts were baking. Belle stirred the chicken soup she'd prepared for those who would be dining in their rooms.

After determining all was in readiness, Belle set out bowls and teacups on trays to take to the ailing. Just as she finished the task, she looked up to see Lord Sedgefield watching her from the doorway.

He'd changed his clothes, and she thought him decidedly handsome in a dark blue coat over a pale blue damask waistcoat and gray pantaloons. She guessed she looked a fright, and straightened to push an errant curl back from her cheek, inadvertently smudging flour from the pastries on her cheek.

"Was there something you wished, my lord?"

John stepped into the kitchen and looked around. "You are a wonder, Miss Hill. I cannot believe this is the same kitchen Sam and I departed from a few hours ago."

Belle felt her cheeks warm from his praise. " 'Tis nothing anyone else couldn't have done, my lord. In truth, Meg did most of the work while I prepared the food."

The earl's brows rose. "Meg, I shall increase your pay twofold for all this work."

The large country girl bobbed a curtsy and grinned before going back to her job.

John came to stand beside Belle, impulsively taking her hand. "I don't know many genteel young ladies who would have the skills to do what you have done here, Miss Hill." He gestured toward the cook pots, where wisps of steam filled the room with enticing aromas.

Belle blushed, then tugged her hand free, uncertain about the strange sensation his warm hands caused. She found it odd that her mind didn't work well with the handsome gentleman so near. She moved back to the stove to stir the broth, hoping to cover her disquiet. "Well, sir, perhaps you should save your praise until after you have dined. You may find I have more good intentions than true culinary skill."

John laughed. "As you wish, but I—"

"Lord Sedgefield! I have been looking all over the manor for you." A young lady with auburn locks, a heart-shaped face and a tilt-tipped nose stood in the kitchen doorway, dimpling at the earl. Dressed in a simple white muslin gown trimmed with blue ribbons the color of her eyes, she looked a vision, and it was evident by her saucy manner she was well aware of that fact.

John turned to see his host's young sister, looking quite grown up since the last time he'd seen her. But his mind was so full of Miss Hill that he paid scant heed to the young lady's beauty. To him she was still the colonel's flighty little sister, whom he'd met on his visit some five years ago. "Ah, Miss Griffin, do come and allow me to introduce you to my traveling companion."

At seventeen, Lettice Griffin was the acclaimed beauty of the neighborhood. Like many pretty young females, the excessive praise had gone to her head, and she was quite puffed up with her own consequence, convinced any man was hers to conquer. The news of the arrival of Captain Burns, now the wealthy, titled Lord Sedgefield, had sent her into alt. Her one wish was to go to London and cut a dash.

Since Sam had returned from the wars injured, he'd repeatedly refused to take her to Town. She noted his lordship's broad shoulders and manly legs, and decided maybe she might go as a countess—if she could make the earl fall madly in love.

Her gaze flitted to Belle, and her delicate brows rose at the sight of a seemingly genteel lady draped in an apron doing such a menial task. Who was this woman with flour on her cheeks and dressed like the manor's cook? And why was she traveling with Sedgefield? Miss Griffin pasted a false smile on her face and came to stand beside the earl.

"Allow me to present the colonel's sister, Miss Lettice Griffin. Letty, Miss Annabelle Hill, my cousin's neighbor in Brixham, whom I was escorting to Exeter." John noted the odd look in Letty's blue eyes as they swept Miss Hill and added, "It is fortunate for us she graciously agreed to come to your brother's aid."

Letty didn't offer her hand to the guest. Instead, she looked around at the now clean kitchen. "You cook *and* clean, Miss Hill. How quaint."

John knew a sudden urge to shake Letty until her teeth rattled. When had she become such a spoiled brat? "And how lucky for us—but then, Society always adores an original." With that he turned his back on the colonel's sister, ignoring her stunned expression.

"Is there anything we can do to assist, Miss Hill?"

Belle had taken Letty Griffin's measure in an instant, but she cared little about the chit's condescending manner. The girl was young and had a lot to learn about life. "Mayhap Miss Griffin would kindly take some soup and tea to her mother?"

Letty opened her mouth to protest *she* didn't do a maid's work, but Lord Sedgefield was before her. "I am sure she would. Come, Letty, we must pitch in and help, just as Miss Hill has so bravely done. You take a tray to your mother. I shall take one to your butler."

The young beauty gave the earl a bright smile and nodded her head agreeably, for she was no fool. Yet the second the gentleman turned his back, she glared at this strange female who'd invaded Griffin Manor and had them all acting like lackeys.

Belle stifled a laugh as Miss Letty Griffin picked up the tray and practically stomped from the kitchen in the earl's wake. This little adventure Belle had embarked upon was going to be very interesting—in more ways than one. In truth, she preferred to deal with the spoiled Letty than to continue her life of near incarceration at Hillcrest.

Dinner that evening proved to be a rather simple affair with only three courses, but Colonel Griffin and Lord Sedgefield behaved as if it were the finest meal they'd ever enjoyed. They praised the cook's efforts until Belle found herself blushing.

Conversation then grew general, and that led to remi-

niscing by the two former soldiers of life in the Peninsula. Their experiences had formed a strong bond between the two men. Letty quickly grew tired of war
stories and began to flirt with his lordship.

Belle was more tired than she'd imagined. She sat
quietly while the young miss simpered and dimpled at
Lord Sedgefield, noting he treated the girl like an an-
noying child as he tried to converse with his old friend.

When dinner at last ended, John rose and bowed to
Belle. "Miss Hill, you have acted as Cook. You must
allow us to act the footmen for the evening and remove
the remains of our feast."

Belle's brows rose and she nearly laughed at the horrified expression on Letty Griffin's face. "I think, my
lord, Mrs. Griffin might like all her china and crystal in
one piece. Perhaps Meg should handle things."

John shook his head, a determined set to his handsome
chin. "Sam and I were soldiers. We've had to wash up
after ourselves before. I think we can manage without
fear of destroying Mrs. Griffin's lovely things. Meg must
be as exhausted as you are."

Letty complained, "Well, I certainly haven't the least
notion of how to scour anything!"

The colonel rose, frowning at his sister. "Then perhaps it is time you learned. One never knows when another crisis like this might arise. We might not be so
lucky as to have so skilled and generous a lady as Miss
Hill at hand."

"There is only a crisis, dear brother, because you refuse to go to town and hire a few temporary servants.
As if anyone cares about your scars or—"

"Enough, Letty. If you don't wish to help, go sit with
Mother."

There was an uncomfortable silence. Then the chit
sighed. "Oh, very well, I shall help."

The colonel bowed to Belle. "I feel certain you would

like to retire after such a long day, Miss Hill. Allow me to show you to your room."

As Belle left the room on the colonel's arm, she heard the earl trying to coax Letty into a better mood.

"Come, child, I shall wash and spare those lovely hands. We cannot have the prettiest lady in Ashton with hands as prickly as a hedgehog."

The last thing Belle heard before the door closed was Letty's delighted laugh, and it was perhaps the most grating sound Belle had ever detected. She didn't know why, but Miss Griffin's incessant flirting was becoming bothersome.

Hoping to take her mind off the tiresome girl, Belle engaged in polite conversation with her host as he led her up the stairs. "How long were you and Lord Sedgefield in Portugal?"

"We went in with Moore in the year '08. John was but a lieutenant then, and I a captain. He hadn't a thought in his head that he'd ever inherit from his cousin. Mad for the army the lad was, and a better soldier for it. He studied all the great conquerors—Hannibal, Caesar, and Alexander. He'd have made an excellent general, but fate seemed to have other plans for him, no matter his wishes."

"Fate is said to be quite cruel, I believe."

The colonel stopped in front of a door and opened it for Belle. With an effort he smiled sadly, then tugged at his empty sleeve. "As I well know, Miss Hill. But we must all learn to deal with our disappointments in time." With that, he bid her good night.

Belle wondered whether Colonel Griffin truly had learned to deal with his disappointment. The marked sadness in his eyes seemed to say no. And Letty intimated he was refusing to go to town, ashamed of his scarring. He was a hero! Surely none would turn away from such a man.

Putting thoughts of her kind host from her mind, Belle found her portmanteaus sitting unpacked on the bed. As she removed her clothes, her mind dwelled on the irony that each man had lost his chosen career for different reasons. Yet they both had other options due to inherited property which weren't open to her.

As a female, her life was a bit more complex. There were a few choices of occupation for a genteel woman, but she had no one to write her a character for any of them. Therefore, she was forced to find employment in the less exalted realms and take what she could.

Yet after only half a day's work, she was exhausted. How would she ever manage as a full-time cook for some family? She wished she could stay here at Griffin Manor, but within a few days her help would no longer be needed.

She had to go in search of employment and manage to do so without the earl's knowledge, for no doubt if he discovered her plan to take a menial position somewhere, he would escort her straight back to Aunt Evelyn.

On that gloomy note, she changed into her nightrail and crawled into bed.

The following morning, John rose early, with the intent of offering his help to Miss Hill in the kitchen. His domestic skills were few, but he was certain she could use some assistance—at least that was what he told himself he was doing.

He found the young lady in the kitchen, up to her elbows in flour. "Good morning, Miss Hill. Where is Meg?"

"Good morning, my lord. She is taking tea and toast to Mrs. Griffin and seeing to the other patients' needs."

"Am I late reporting for kitchen duty?"

The young lady eyed him thoughtfully, surprised to see

him at such an hour, then remembered as a soldier he would often have been up before dawn. Clearly he'd not fallen into the leisurely ways of an earl as yet. Not wanting to look a gift horse in the mouth, she smiled. "Not at all. Have you ever made bread before, my lord?"

"Never, but I used to watch my mother's cook do it when I was a small boy. One had to take the dough and abuse it dreadfully, as I remember."

Belle laughed. "It's called kneading. I believe a gentleman like yourself can do it nicely, for it takes only strength and stamina."

"And that I have in abundance." With that, he took off his coat and rolled up his sleeves. He found an apron in the drawer where he'd seen Miss Hill find one the previous day.

Belle floured the table, out rolled the ball of dough, and began the kneading process to demonstrate the method. Then she turned the task over to his lordship.

He slapped at the dough, pushed it out and folded it over, then pushed it out again. "Like this?"

"Perfect, my lord. You would make an excellent baker, should you decide being an earl is a dead bore."

"Quite an idea. I could sell bread to the *beau monde*. Shall I call it Burns's Buns? Better yet, The Earl's Oven. That way I could make all kinds of bread, not merely buns."

Belle laughed. "I think you would soon tire of such an enterprise, having to rise before dawn each morning so your wares would be fresh."

John sobered, and his gaze locked on the young lady as he continued to work the dough. "As you will of being our cook, Miss Hill. I want you to know how much I appreciate what you are doing for my friend's family. You are a remarkable young lady."

Belle blushed, but experienced a rush of pleasure at

the compliment. "I must begin breakfast. Since you are here, you may have your choice of anything you wish."

John suddenly wished he could kiss the sweet up-turned mouth smiling at him, then wondered where that thought had come from. "Buttered eggs and ham will do for me, with lots of black coffee."

With that he thumped the dough, concentrating on the bread instead of the young lady. He wondered what he was about to be having such feelings for a female he knew little of save she'd run away with him in a clandestine manner and on very short acquaintance. Why, he didn't even know where she was going on this flight from her home. Might it be to meet some man of whom her mother didn't approve? That thought made him strike the dough with excessive force.

Belle hurried about the kitchen gathering the things she would need for his breakfast. She washed her hands, then set about cracking eggs into a bowl for scrambling. As she whipped the mixture, she looked up to see Lord Sedgefield's intense gaze on her.

She looked a question at him.

He hesitated a moment, then asked, "Do you need to send a message to someone that you will be delayed, Miss Hill? I know you were intending to catch the stage-coach at Exeter to complete your journey."

Her blue gaze shuttered at once, then dropped back to the bowl where her hand had paused. Suddenly she worked all the harder at whipping the eggs. "My plans were rather indefinite, so no one is awaiting my arrival. I shall be able to remain at Griffin Manor as long as the colonel has need of me."

He had little doubt the lady was keeping her destination a secret. Where was she going, and why didn't she want him to know? Did she fear he would return to Hillcrest and tell her mother of her plans? Hardly likely, since Mrs. Hill was determined to wed Roger to the girl. But would that be such a bad thing?

His gaze moved back to Miss Hill, who'd turned to the stove and poured the eggs into a skillet. He'd never met Mrs. Hill, but of one thing he was certain: His aunt was completely wrong about the daughter.

By the time his breakfast was prepared, the young lady declared the bread ready for the pans. He watched her shape the loaves as he sat at the table enjoying his eggs and coffee.

"They must rise once more. Then they're ready for the oven."

He put down his cup. "Is there anything else I can do for you?"

She shook her head. "There is little to do until the others are awake. I thank you for your kind help. For now, I shall take tea to Cook and see how she fares this morning."

John watched Belle disappear down the hall off the kitchen. He owed her a debt for what she was doing for his friend. With a sigh, he decided to go find Sam, for if anyone needed his spirits bolstered, it was his former colonel.

Upon reaching the front hall, John found Lettice Griffin with a letter, which she was turning over in her hand as if she were trying to read the contents through the paper. Spying him, she blushed and extended the sealed message. "This just arrived for you, my lord."

She surrendered the missive, then stood watching him.

"Is there something I can do for you, Letty?"

"I was hoping you might ride with me this morning." She dimpled at him and fluttered her dark lashes.

"Another time, perhaps. We cannot leave Miss Hill in the lurch, for you know she can use our assistance with the simpler tasks."

Lettice frowned. "I haven't the least knowledge of cookery or cleaning."

John grinned. "I just made bread, with our gallant Miss Hill's instruction. If you hurry, I'm certain she will teach you something equally valuable."

"I cannot imagine why you and Sam seem to think I should learn how to cook and clean. *I* intend to marry very well and shall have twice the servants of Griffin Manor." Putting her chin up, Miss Griffin disappeared down the hall toward the breakfast parlor.

John laughed as he watched the indignant miss march away. She certainly was determined and ambitious. He lifted the letter and noted his cousin's seal, then broke the wax wafer, fully expecting the baronet to be furious with him for having made off with the woman with whom Roger seemed enamored. As John read the missive, he uttered an oath at the information within.

The earl lowered his hand, crushing the letter. It couldn't be true. He hadn't run away with the scheming Miss Ann Hill, as his cousin had called her in the letter. He'd made off with the chit's cousin, also a Miss Hill, but called Belle. What the devil was he to do now?

FOUR

"John, you look quite ill." The colonel paused at the top of the stairs watching his friend, who stood frozen like a statue. "I shall never forgive myself if you or Miss Hill are felled by this dreadful sickness."

The earl, coming out of his distracted state, looked up and gestured with the letter crushed in his hand. "I've received some bad news from Brixham, old friend."

He paused a moment. Sam had always given good advice on military matters. Perhaps he might help with this problem.

Or would he? His former colonel seemed so much less assured here at Griffin Manor than he had in Portugal. Had his severe injuries changed him?

Still, John had no one else to turn to with his problem. "Do you have a moment? There is something I would discuss with you."

Colonel Griffin descended and led his friend to the library. Thankfully the weather was fine, and no fire was needed, since none had been set by the still ailing staff. He gestured at the brandy decanter, but John waved off the offer.

"Then tell me what has happened to put you out of kilter," Sam said.

Sedgefield moved to the window, folding the disturbing missive. "I came to Devonshire at my aunt's request to keep my cousin, Sir Roger Maxwell, from making an imprudent match. I was hesitant to interfere, but certain events after my arrival convinced me to intervene in the matter. Against my initial instincts, I became involved. It now appears that instead of aiding my cousin, I may have done Miss Hill a disservice due to a simple misunderstanding."

Sam settled into one of the leather wing chairs beside the cold hearth and eyed his friend thoughtfully. The colonel was embarrassed at how little thought he'd given to the fact that the earl had arrived traveling with a lovely young woman. The problem was, Sam thought, he was too involved with his self-pity, and that needed to stop.

What had John said that day? Ah, he had explained he was doing a friend a favor. Clearly there appeared to be some mystery as to why Miss Hill was in the earl's company.

Curious, the colonel remarked, "I can understand Sir Roger's being enchanted with Miss Hill. She's smart, genteel, and one must own she's a dashingly handsome woman. What I don't understand is why Lady Maxwell objects to such a match. Is there a lack of funds or some unsavory connection?"

John looked back at his friend, a chagrined expression on his face. "Truth be told, it wasn't this young woman Aunt Jane objected to, but her cousin . . . and that young lady's mother. As to fortune and connections, I believe Miss Ann Hill lacks both."

The colonel's blond brows furrowed as he tried to understand. "I must be a bit thickheaded this morning. Pray explain how our Miss Hill comes to be here with you if the cousin was the problem."

The earl shrugged, then came to sit opposite his friend, realizing the whole story would have to be told, which would take some time. He spoke of his aunt's

tales of a dreadful female and her daughter living out
at the cottage and their designs on Sir Roger. He re-
counted his visit to the cottage, deciding at the last moment against meeting his cousin's paramour.

As he was about to depart, Miss Belle Hill had pelted
him with cheesecake and beckoned him to her balcony,
making her unusual request to be taken to a posting inn.

At this point, he looked down at the missive still in
his hand. "I mistook her for Evelyn Hill's daughter.
There she was on the balcony of the cottage. I didn't
know a cousin was residing there as well. I agreed to
help her run away, thinking it would open Roger's eyes
to Miss Ann Hill's unsteady nature."

Sam stared at the earl for a moment, then threw back
his head and laughed. "You mean you mistook our Miss
Hill for the scheming daughter and absconded with her
to spike her guns, only she's not the jade you were after?"

"Exactly." The earl sighed at his own folly. "As you
can imagine, my cousin is furious at my conduct and is
comforting the very lady I was trying to keep him from.
I've certainly made a mull of things. But the worst of
this fiasco is now Miss Hill's aunt has declared her
niece's—and, by association, her daughter's—reputations
in ruins due to my actions. Marriage is the only solu-
tion."

The colonel sobered. "Poppycock! You've had that
maid with you from the beginning, haven't you?"

The earl nodded.

"Then don't be bullied by some scheming old Tartar.
Sounds to me as if our Miss Hill had good reason to
be gone from under her aunt's roof."

"Very likely, but here is the problem. I'd always assumed Miss Ann Hill would return to her mother once
she realized she couldn't trick me into marrying her. By
then, Roger would have known what she was. But Miss

Belle Hill truly wants to leave Hillcrest, and I don't feel right about my role in her departure. I've damaged the lady's reputation, however inadvertently." The earl's fist knotted as he spoke about his actions.

The colonel sat in silence, tapping a slender finger against his compressed lips. At last he suggested, "As I see it you have several choices. You can take the girl back and quiet the aunt's accusations by showing her Meg."

"Out of the question. Having come to know the young lady a little, I'm convinced she wouldn't have left unless there was good reason. I won't force her back to whatever injustice she ran from."

Sam unknowingly stroked the scar on his cheek as he watched John closely to see his reaction to the second option. "Then your only other choice is to offer for her."

The earl pondered the suggestion for a moment as if it wasn't that distasteful, then shook his head. "What respectable female wants to gain a husband in such a manner? She knows she's not been compromised and would likely refuse me."

Colonel Griffin slapped the arm of the chair with his hand. "Well, my suggestion is you remain here for the remainder of the week. My servants will all soon be back at their posts, and I strongly desire that the lady be my honored guest after all she has done for us. During that time, you might find out what Miss Hill truly wishes. She must have had a plan when she ran away from her aunt. Then you can aid her in any way she desires, whether it be to return to Brixham, go to London, or whatever."

Sedgefield agreed to the plan, knowing that delaying any decision at the present was good advice. He'd rushed into this foolish plot against Sir Roger's paramour only to have made a dreadful mistake. He would take his time to find out what the young lady truly wished. "I should be delighted to accept your hospitality for the remainder of the week. But, Sam, make certain you don't mention my mistake to Miss Hill. I'd prefer she not know what a fool I've been."

The colonel rose. "As you wish. Now, have you breakfasted?"

"Earlier, in the kitchen."

Sam merely arched one golden brow.

"Don't give me that look. I didn't want all the work to land on Miss Hill when I knew I was fully capable of assisting with the burden of cooking. After all, 'twas I who brought her here."

The colonel agreed his friend did own some responsibility to the lady. The men departed for the breakfast parlor. Soon the top of the sideboard was filled with a delectable selection served by Meg.

John drank coffee as his friend dined, but his mind continued to wrestle with the problem of what he could do to help Miss Hill. He was determined to see her safely settled and away from her scheming aunt.

Later that morning, Belle knocked on Colonel Griffin's library door. Upon being bid to enter, she discovered the earl within, as well as her host. The men appeared to be looking at a map of the Peninsula. She suspected both missed army life, since the subject seemed to be a favorite with them.

The colonel, who'd been hunched over pointing out something, straightened and asked, "Was there something you needed, Miss Hill?"

"Forgive me for interrupting you, but I just spoke with Cook—who is feeling better, by the by. She is vowing to return to the kitchen on the morrow. But she informs me today is normally the day the second footman goes to Ashton for weekly supplies. She's given me a list of what's needed. Since none of the household servants are yet up and about, I shall do the task. I was hoping you would be so kind as to provide me an escort."

Colonel Griffin's face paled. "I cannot drive to town–"

The earl, watching his friend and seeing his distress, stepped from behind the desk, hoping to cover Sam's agitation. "If the colonel here will loan me his curricle, I should be delighted to drive you to town, Miss Hill. You deserve an outing after working so diligently in an overwarm kitchen."

Pleasure filled Belle at the idea of Lord Sedgefield's offering his time for such a domestic matter. She'd fully expected to go with a groom or Colonel Griffin, but that gentleman seemed reluctant to go. Had he not yet mastered the feat of one-handed driving, or did he merely not wish to be the object of pitying eyes in the town?

Covering his earlier surliness, Sam insisted they use his carriage, instructing Miss Hill to put all purchases on his account at Hamlin's. The earl requested the young lady meet him at the stables as soon as she donned her bonnet.

A few minutes later, as Belle hurried back downstairs from her room, the sounds of Miss Griffin and her brother arguing in the library echoed in the foyer.

Through the door, Lettice's shrill voice shouted, *"I want to go to town with his lordship. I can do the shopping just as well as she."*

The colonel's voice was quieter. "Nonsense. This is nothing like shopping for fabrics or ribbon. You would likely purchase flour with vermin, so busy you are flirting with John. Cease your foolishness and go see how Mother fares."

Belle exited the front door of the manor, not waiting for Miss Griffin's response. The warm spring air smelled of roses and wild thyme.

She made her way to the stables, where the grooms were rolling out a bright yellow curricle which looked as if it hadn't been used in some time. One groom jumped into the carriage to wipe the dust from the black leather seats as two grays were strapped into the traces. The earl watched the whole process as he stood in conversation with Flynn. An older man in a stained leather jerkin vest, slouch hat in hand, stopped what he was saying to them and barked orders at the others, alerting Belle he was in charge of the stable staff.

Keeping a watchful eye on his men, the head groom shook his head as he looked back at his lordship. "Like I was tellin' your man, the colonel don't never go anywhere since he came back wounded. It's like them Frenchies took more 'un the gentleman's arm. He just mopes about his library. Don't even usually greet visitors what come from hereabouts."

Just then the earl glanced around and saw Belle. His welcoming smile sent a thrilling tremor through her. "Shall we take a bit of a tour of the neighborhood before we go to Ashton? Patrick here tells me there is a lovely old ruin of a castle between here and town."

Belle happily agreed. She hadn't enjoyed the freedom of such an outing in a very long time.

When the carriage was deemed ready, the two climbed in. With the earl's smart snap of the whip over the heads of the team, they were off. The day was pleasant and the pair made polite conversation about the passing countryside as they bowled along the road to the nearby town.

At last the earl drew the carriage to a halt at the top of a rise which allowed them to survey the valley below. He pointed to the left, and Belle's gaze was drawn to what appeared to be only large stones and rubble.

"The groom swears it's an old Norman castle, but I've seen far more impressive ones in Portugal and Spain."

Belle had to agree there was little to see from their vantage point, but she noted a certain wistfulness in the gentleman's tone as he spoke of his former life. "I believe you miss the army a great deal, my lord."

He relaxed against the leather seat, but kept his team in check. "I cannot deny being a soldier was the one thing I always wanted. There would always have been some new adventure awaiting one."

Belle was much struck by his words. "You sound like my father. He never could stand to be home for more than a few weeks at a time before he was longing to be off once again at sea, especially after my mother died."

The earl turned his emerald gaze on her. "Was he in the navy?" When the lady nodded, he added, "I once thought of going to sea, but I knew it wouldn't do."

Belle tipped her head to one side, the better to see his amazing eyes. "Seasickness?"

"Not a bit of it. I was assured I look much better in red than in blue," the earl teased.

They both laughed. Then his lordship sobered as he stared at the young lady beside him, looking quite lovely in her unfashionable blue dress and straw bonnet, her soft blond curls ruffled by the light breeze. "Do you not think I might be trusted a little, Miss Hill?"

Belle licked her lips nervously, having no idea the sensation such a gesture created within his lordship's chest. "I—I do trust you, my lord. Have I not left my home in your company? I assure you I would not have done so with just anyone."

Forcing his gaze back to meet hers, John asked, "Then tell me, why have you run away from your aunt? Where are you going? Is there anything I can do to aid you?"

She twined her fingers together as she pondered what to tell the earl. In truth, he'd been everything a gentleman should be, never prying into her affairs, merely taking her at her word. Surely he wouldn't betray her plans to her aunt if he knew the truth.

"Very well, my lord. I shall tell you all, but you must promise what is said here stays between us."

Lord Sedgefield agreed, then listened with growing indignation when he learned of Belle's mistreatment at the hands of her aunt, and all because of some long ago scandal by her parents. At that moment he was glad he'd mistaken the two cousins.

After Miss Hill finished, he asked, "Pray, what do you intend to do until your inheritance is released by your uncle?"

"Why, just what I have been doing at Griffin Manor, my lord, cooking. Do you not think I am capable?"

John turned, staring out at the green fields of Devonshire, in shock at the idea of this beautiful and genteel woman slaving in some small country kitchen for ungrateful employers. Looking back at her, he reached out and took her hand. "Very capable, none more so. But surely you cannot wish such a lowly position. Your father was a gentleman."

"My lord, my mind is quite made up. I won't return to my aunt and live as a prisoner. I must support myself, and cooking is all I truly am suited for."

"My dear Miss Hill, don't make any rash decisions at the moment. Sam wishes us to remain after his servants are well, to at least the end of the week. Pray enjoy the remainder of your time here as an honored guest. That should give us time to think of some other alternative to your dilemma."

Belle had considered all the alternatives and knew there was nothing else. Still, she was quite touched at his lordship's concern. His offer was too enticing to turn down. "I am perfectly content to remain at Griffin Manor as long as the colonel deems us welcome."

The earl grinned at her, making her heart misbehave

in a dreadful manner. "Good girl. I shall say no more on the matter at present, but I am certain we can come up with something other than your toiling as a cook until you are five and twenty. Besides, we cannot have you rushing off after all your hard work. You need time to rest and retrench before beginning any new adventure. Now, shall we go to town and purchase the things on Cook's list?"

The thought suddenly occurred to Belle that Lord Sedgefield was exactly like her father. Everything in life was looked on as an escapade.

Would the earl be forever gone on some adventure, leaving his own family very much in the lurch? She knew her father had loved them, but he'd been too restless to stay in one place for long. No doubt whoever married Lord Sedgefield would find herself alone a great deal.

After dinner that evening and without an invitation to the others, Letty dragged Lord Sedgefield off to the music room to show off her skill at the pianoforte. There was little the earl could do but allow his host's sister this indulgence. Colonel Griffin, hoping to make amends for his brusque treatment of Miss Hill in the library that morning, offered to take her for a walk in the fading light in the gardens. Belle agreed, glad to be out in the fresh air after being cooped up in the kitchen much of the day.

As they strolled through the rose-scented evening air, Belle knew she wouldn't mind staying here. Unfortunately, the colonel had a very competent cook who was determined to resume her post in the morning. If Belle could only find a situation this pleasant, she would be content, if not happy.

They walked along in companionable silence for a

while. The sounds of the pianoforte echoed softly in the distance, with only random sour notes. Letty Griffin's enthusiam far surpassed her skill. Belle suspected the colonel would be delighted to have his headstrong young sister off his hands in the spring. She'd overheard the girl tell the earl that was the time for her comeout in Town.

"You have a lovely estate here, sir. You shall miss it when you are in London for the Season."

The colonel drew back in surprise, his hand flying up to cover the scar on his handsome face. "Whatever gave you the notion I was for London? I've no intention of going to Town in the spring—or ever." He gave a bitter laugh, then stared at the distant apple orchard. "I wouldn't want to frighten any of those young ladies who flood Town every year looking for husbands."

"Frighten! Sir, I think you are mistaken. There is nothing more romantic to a young female than a dashing hero with a war wound." Belle gently smiled up at him.

"Wounds heal, Miss Hill. I shall never again have my arm back. How could I ask Cara . . . that is, how could I ask a female to ally herself with someone who isn't whole?"

Belle's female intuition told her Colonel Sampson was in love with this Cara. "Please call me Belle."

"I should be honored. Pray, call me Sam."

They once again began to stroll. " 'Tis my belief the loss of your arm will impede you only as much as you allow it. Our groom lost an arm to a cannonball with Nelson in Egypt, but there was nothing he couldn't do that he put his mind to. My father never worried about us when March was around."

The colonel looked skeptical. "He drove a carriage?"

"To an inch."

"Hunted?"

"His aim was deadly."

The gentleman stopped and used his boot to move a stone from the gravel path. "And did he . . . marry?"

"Not only married, but became the proud father of five."

The colonel turned away. "You don't understand, Belle. The first time Cara saw me on the street in Ashton just after I returned, she actually gasped and stepped back."

Belle suddenly wanted to shake the unknown lady, but she knew some females were more fragile than others. If the woman truly loved the colonel, the sight might have been wrenching. "No doubt it was from shock at how severely you were injured, not that she was frightened. I might have reacted in the same way if someone had failed to warn me of a dear friend's severe injuries." She stepped in front of him, placing her hand on his arm. "Have you seen her since?"

He shook his head. "I couldn't bear it if she told me this had changed everything."

"You should have more faith in yourself . . . and her. You are both, no doubt, stronger than you think. Remember, your actions hurt more than you and the lady. My guess is your family is very much affected as well."

The colonel smiled at her, then tilted her chin upward and kissed her cheek. "Belle, I must say you are the best thing to arrive at Griffin Manor since my father planted these apple trees. You have almost convinced me that, like you, I am up to any task, no matter my circumstances."

She laughed and began to stroll along beside the heartened former soldier. She asked him about the orchard, hoping to improve his spirits.

Back in the music room, John stood propped against the open door, staring out at the pair having an intense conversation at the edge of the apple orchard. He straightened at the sight of Sam kissing Belle's cheek.

What could Sam be about, taking such a liberty with her?

The strains of Mozart flowing behind the earl barely penetrated his thoughts. His brow wrinkled with worry. Had Sam been smitten with the lovely Miss Hill? More importantly, had Belle developed a *tendre* for his former colonel? After all, it was said that female hearts were often touched by the sight of a man who needed tending, and Sam certainly needed someone to take him in hand and make him see little had changed, despite his injury.

The very thought that his best friend and his traveling companion were falling in love filled John with despair. He was the one who'd met the beautiful Belle first. He didn't want to surrender her to Sam. In truth, he didn't think he could.

He straightened suddenly. By Jove, he'd fallen in love with Belle Hill. How was that possible? They'd met only days before. But John knew that she was the only woman for him.

FIVE

By the following morning, most of the staff of Griffin Manor and its mistress, Mrs. Myrtle Griffin, were recovered enough to resume their normal activities.

The lady of the house came down to breakfast looking a bit pale, but eager to greet her son's old friend and newly elevated earl, Lord Sedgefield, as well as the young lady her son had praised so highly for her efforts at keeping the manor running over the course of the last few days.

Mrs. Griffin was a short, plump, gray-haired woman with an easy disposition who paid little attention to household matters. Batters, the family butler, and Cook had always seen that the house ran efficiently without troubling their indolent mistress. Still, the lady was properly appreciative of what Miss Hill had done for them.

The earl, having come down early to spend some time with Belle, watched his friend introduce the young lady to his mother. John was struck by the informal, light-hearted manner in which Sam performed the introductions, as if they were old friends–or new lovers. Was Belle responsible for the colonel's renewed spirits? If so, how could he destroy that by declaring his love for her? Those dark thoughts left him quiet throughout the morning meal.

After breakfast, Mrs. Griffin ordered everyone to go

about their morning amusements save Miss Hill, with whom the lady of the manor wanted to speak.

Lord Sedgefield found few of the suggested activities to his liking but at last, realizing he couldn't linger in the room all day, agreed to the colonel's suggestion they go to the stables to see the new foal, born the previous day. Letty rose at once, announcing she would accompany the gentlemen.

Alone with her hostess, Belle had a comfortable coze, hoping to learn something more about the colonel and the unknown Cara. His admission of lost love last night in the garden had sent Belle on a mission to set his unhappy life to rights.

Unable to escape the inevitable, Belle gave an edited version of her own life, stating finally that Lord Sedgefield was accompanying her to a friend's. It would never do for Mrs. Griffin to be scandalized with the truth that her guest had run away with the earl in a clandestine manner.

As Belle hoped, the colonel's mother began to speak of her worries about her son and daughter. "I tell you, Miss Hill, I know that you think being without close family at your age is quite the worst thing, but you shall eventually marry and have little ones of your own. Then you will know what true worry is, my dear."

Belle said what was proper and waited for the lady to continue.

"I had thought Sampson would be happily married by now, and I would be making plans to take Letty to London in the spring for the Season. But nothing has gone as planned since my dear boy came home from the war. He seems to grow more morose by the day, and Letty only becomes more difficult with passing time." Seeming to realize she was criticizing her only daughter to a near stranger, she added, " 'Tis not that she is truly bad, only bored and angered that her brother keeps vowing he won't take her to Town."

Belle bit her lip a moment before she plunged into the colonel's affairs. "Was he engaged to this Cara of whom I've heard him speak?"

Mrs. Griffin shook her head. "Not engaged to Mrs. Campbell, for it would have been unseemly for a widow to become betrothed before her year of mourning was complete—not but what everyone didn't know Giles Campbell treated the poor woman dreadfully, and she didn't shed a tear when they brought him back from the hunt dead. But Sam was there for her in the months after the funeral, advising her about the estate and such matters—that is, until he had to report back to Portugal." The older woman sighed. "I don't understand what went wrong. They both were clearly in love before he left. After Sam returned, he wouldn't even come out of his library to greet her when she came to call. Finally she ceased coming to call altogether due to his repeated snubs."

Clearly Mrs. Griffin didn't know about Sam's unexpected meeting with Cara Campbell in Ashton and the lady's reaction to his wounds. All Belle knew for certain was that she liked Colonel Sampson Griffin and wanted to do something to help him and his Cara, no matter if the lady deserved her help or not. "May I make a suggestion, Mrs. Griffin?"

Her hostess nodded eagerly.

"Perhaps a dinner party might pull the colonel from his self-imposed isolation. You could say the dinner is in honor of his lordship's visit. Invite several of the neighbors, including Mrs. Campbell. That way your son and the lady must come face to face." Belle hoped to gain a positive result, but since she didn't know the widow, she had no way of knowing if she were inadvertently setting Sam up for more heartache.

Myrtle Griffin tugged nervously at the fringe on her

gray paisley shawl. "I don't know, Miss Hill. Sampson has been reluctant to see anyone since he returned so badly injured. He thinks himself horribly disfigured, and nothing we say can convince him otherwise."

Belle's hands closed over the lady's fidgeting ones. "I know it must be difficult for a handsome, athletic man to realize a woman would love more about him than his physical looks and agility, but if Mrs. Campbell cannot overcome such a minor thing, I am sure there are hundreds of women who could. The colonel must move on with his life. Until he has resolved matters with the widow, that cannot happen."

Seeing the confident look in her guest's blue eyes, Mrs. Griffin smiled. "I think you are right, my dear. Shall we make out the invitations and have one of the grooms deliver them at once? That way Sampson cannot object after the project is set in motion."

Belle prayed they were doing the right thing. She suspected the colonel wouldn't be happy that his mother was forcing him to reenter local society, but he'd seemed to become more relaxed with her over the course of the past few days, hiding his scarred face less and less. He would soon realize having a full life was more worthwhile than sitting in his library and letting the world pass him by due to his fear of being rebuffed.

She debated whether to inform Lord Sedgefield of what she and Mrs. Griffin were doing, then decided against involving him. No doubt he would think she was overstepping her bounds, since she hardly knew the colonel. But in truth, while she'd only just met Sampson Griffin, she liked him and wanted to help.

With that thought firmly in mind, she sat down to write the invitations as Mrs. Griffin wrote the names and directions.

* * *

John hurried down to the drawing room that evening hoping to finally have a moment alone with Belle. All day she'd been as elusive as a rainbow after a summer storm. Since his personal revelation of last evening, he wanted to know the lady's feelings. Did she like him a little, or had she succumbed to the neediness of Sam?

Sedgefield experienced a twinge of guilt at his rancorous feelings for his friend when he thought of Belle. There could be little doubt Sam's spirit was as wounded as his body, and something must be done. But did it have to involve the woman John had come to love?

He opened the drawing room door and checked on the threshold. The room was full of strangers dressed in their country fashions for dinner.

Mrs. Griffin hurried forward, flushed pink with the success of her party. "I hope you don't mind, but I've invited the neighbors to meet you and Miss Hill. I didn't want your visit to be so dull you'd never return. I do believe everyone I invited has come."

"It would seem so, madam." His eyes scanned the room and stopped on the female form he'd been looking for. Belle stood on the opposite side of the room, dressed in a simple powder blue silk gown trimmed with white lace and ribbons. She looked beautiful despite the fact her dress wasn't the height of fashion.

As Mrs. Griffin chattered about those in attendance, the earl took note of the intimacy of Belle's situation. She stood in conversation with Sam in a far reach of the room, away from the other guests. His friend looked as if he would far rather be anywhere but in his own drawing room, since his back faced the guests and his hand clutched the green velvet drapes as if he were holding onto his control by a thread. The earl suddenly wondered if this little party was as big a surprise to his friend as it had been to him.

John felt a hand slip round his arm. He looked down

to see the tiresome Letty smiling up at him. "Oh, Mama, allow me to introduce the earl to our friends. They have all been anxiously awaiting you, my lord."

He very much doubted that, but he allowed her to escort him to the nearby group, knowing he couldn't escape the ritual. But even as the young lady preened and dimpled at him as she made the introductions, John's gaze kept wandering to the pair still in intimate conversation near the window.

Across the Gold Drawing Room, Belle's attention was centered on Sampson Griffin. His shock upon discovering his mother had managed to pull together a party on such short notice was severe. He'd known immediately Belle must have been behind the arrangements for the party, for his mother was far too indolent to have planned and executed even such a simple event so quickly. But he was too much the gentleman to rail at his lovely guest.

Glancing back over his shoulder, he said, "Great heavens, did you invite the entire town of Ashton?"

"Only those friends your mother vows have been longing to see you since your return. Are you very angry with me, Colonel?" She smiled up at him, a questioning expression in her blue eyes.

His gaze swept the room as he watched John being dragged about by his sister, who had come very close to making a cake of herself over the earl on this visit. "Well, I must own it was a bit of shock when Mother informed me of her plan when I entered the drawing room. But in truth I am determined to take your good advice of last evening. I must once again join the neighborhood society—for Letty's sake." The gentleman paused a moment to watch the guests, then gave a half grin. "But I'm not sure John won't be wishing your head on a platter after he's had to make polite conversation with Squire Fairmont or Mr. Applegate for an evening.

They are perhaps the two most boring people in Devonshire."

Belle cast a long glance at Lord Sedgefield, surrounded by several elderly gentlemen who were barraging him with questions. He was devastatingly handsome, and she felt the strangest feeling in the pit of her stomach when he glanced up and smiled at her. She suddenly wished she hadn't taken on this task of aiding the colonel and could spend the evening in company with the earl, as if she were any fashionable young lady with expectations of marriage.

Hearing a sigh beside her, she returned her attention to the colonel. "I have no fear for his lordship, sir. After a man has faced down a French column, how could he not survive the onslaught of several gentlemen farmers determined to wrestle away his lordship's secrets on drainage and on breeding prime cattle?"

Sam laughed. "You are right, Miss Hill." Then he paused and his gaze searched the room. Seeming not to find what he was looking for, he sighed again, his gaze veering to the oriental carpet.

Belle instinctively knew who he was searching for. "Mrs. Campbell was invited and sent an acceptance."

"Was I so very obvious?"

"Only to me." She put her hand on his arm, and he smiled at her, causing a certain gentleman across the room to frown.

"I know I'm behaving like the veriest schoolboy. But, Belle, I've never known a woman like Cara. While I lay in the surgeon's tent after Salamanca, all I could think about was surviving to return to her."

Before Belle could respond, the drawing room doors opened, and Batters intoned, "Mrs. Cara Campbell, Miss Dorothy Campbell."

The colonel's arm tensed beneath Belle's fingers, and he half turned away, shielding his scars from the newest guests. Belle closely observed the women and discovered Mrs. Campbell to be an elegantly tall woman with dusky curls and a heart-shaped face more handsome than beautiful. But there was a strength of character in the lady's countenance at odds with the story of her rejection of the colonel in Ashton.

Mrs. Campbell's companion stood beside her, her ruddy cheeks aglow in the light. Her plump face held a sour look as she surveyed the gathering. For some reason, Belle suspected, this lady was no friend to the colonel. Had she grown comfortable in her role of companion to the widow and disliked the idea of being supplanted by a husband?

The widow's gaze roamed the room and halted immediately on the colonel. Then her cool stare locked on Belle. An immediate hostility flared in the lady's large topaz eyes, giving Belle confidence that some tender emotions for the colonel still filled the woman. Hopefully, with a little nudge these two could be brought together.

Sam stood paralyzed, staring at his true love, but Belle didn't know if it were to admire the widow or to worry about the outcome of their long-awaited encounter. Fearing he might bolt or merely avoid this fateful meeting, Belle locked her arm with his lone remaining limb. "Come, you must introduce me to the lady."

Sam looked down at Belle, his expression dazed for a moment. Then, smiling reluctantly, he placed his hand over hers. "Has anyone ever told you you would make a wonderful company commander, Belle?"

"It comes from having a father who was a captain in the navy. Barking orders comes naturally to the Hills. And, as you know, the acorn never falls far from the tree." Belle grinned and tugged him forward.

Across the room, Cara stiffened. Was this lovely creature the reason Sam had avoided her company since his return? Had he developed a *tendre* for this beautiful young woman on his arm? Her heart sank.

Then a touch of anger filled her breast. She'd spent so many sleepless nights after behaving so stupidly in Ashton on seeing Sam that first time scarcely two months ago. She hadn't heard he was back, let alone severely injured. The shock had been great. She'd come to the Manor to explain, only he'd refused to come out of his library and greet her. And now it appeared it had all been about another woman and not her *faux pas*.

Cara loved Sampson Griffin with all her being, but she'd had one disastrous marriage. She wouldn't try to compel him to honor his words of love uttered nearly a year ago, especially not if this chit had captured his attention.

"Good evening, Mrs. Campbell, Miss Campbell. Welcome to Griffin Manor. Please allow me to introduce one of our guests, Miss Belle Hill." There was a cool reserve in Sampson Griffin's greeting none could mistake. Belle cursed the gentleman's pride. She thought the widow's smile so brittle that her face might crack.

"Do you stay long with the Griffins, Miss Hill?" Mrs. Campbell asked, but there was an edge to her tone.

"Only until the end of the week, when his lordship shall take me to Exeter."

Sam, surprisingly nervous with Cara, turned to Belle, who seemed to give him strength with her reassuring smile. "Unless we can convince you to stay longer. I think you must rest longer from all your efforts on behalf of us all."

Just then Mrs. Griffin arrived and swept the ladies into the room to introduce them to the earl. Belle watched the colonel's gaze follow the widow.

Thinking it best to allow him to circulate on his own to gain some confidence, Belle excused herself and went to make conversation with Mrs. Fairmont, a faded ma-

tron in a dreadful puce gown who sat alone on a sofa
against the wall, not bothering to socialize with her
neighbors.

Dinner was announced some ten minutes later, to
Belle's relief, for she'd discovered her companion had
little to say other than to remark that the colonel was
quite changed and what a pity about his disfigurement.

The party moved into the dining room. Belle, as an
honored guest, found herself seated beside Sam at the
head of the table. A young man named Tibble sat to her
right, but she soon discovered his conversation was limited to his latest purchase, a racehorse.

Cara sat to Sam's left, but was as frosty as a winter
morn in her responses when the colonel made tentative
efforts to converse. She seemed to find Squire Fairmont's farming advice more to her taste when she spoke
at all.

Tired of trying to cover the lapses in conversation between the two estranged lovers, Belle's gaze drifted
down the table to where Lord Sedgefield sat at Mrs.
Griffin's left. To Belle's chagrin, Letty was to his left.
Belle suddenly envied the young lady as she heard her
laugh gaily at something the earl had said. If only her
life could be as it had been when her father had been
alive, with plans for a Season and no thought of employment for Captain Hill's daughter. She might have
met Sedgefield as an eligible *parti,* not one he must aid
in finding a position in someone's kitchen.

Putting her past dreams from her mind, she determined to concentrate on bringing Sam and Cara together.
At least she would try to make certain they were happy.

When the servants served the dessert, Sam leaned
close to tell Belle that her cheesecake of last evening
had been far superior to Cook's pudding. He begged her
to give the woman her recipe. She agreed.

Then her gaze drifted down the table, locking with

Sedgefield's. That gentleman frowned back as if he were angered at her in some manner. What had she done to displease him? Did he not realize she was doing her best to help his friend? As the colonel again drew her attention, she wished the evening were over.

After dinner the ladies withdrew, leaving the men to their port. They'd scarcely entered the drawing room when Letty pulled Belle aside.

"Whatever do you mean by flirting with my brother in front of Cara Campbell? They are practically engaged."

Shock caused Belle's blue eyes to widen. "I wasn't flirting, I was trying—"

Letty angrily shook her head. "I know flirting when I see it, Miss Hill. I'm certain it seemed the same to Cara. I think it is horrid of you."

With that, the young lady flounced off, leaving Belle with her mind in a whirl. Had she given the widow a misconception about the relationship between herself and Sam? That would never do. But before she could decide what was best to do, Lord Sedgefield was at her side as the gentlemen returned, having agreed to dispense with drinks and join the ladies.

"Are you enjoying your evening, Miss Hill?"

Belle smiled up at the earl. "It is a long time since I have been to a social affair. I do find it enjoyable, my lord." As she admired his handsome face, she decided in order to help Sam, she must convince Mrs. Campbell she was merely a hardened flirt. Who better than Lord Sedgedfield on which to practice the art? Then she realized it would be no difficult task.

A slight crease appeared in the earl's forehead and Belle wondered what she could have said to displease him. Perhaps he was remembering what she'd told him about her life at Hillcrest. Not knowing which, she set out to make him smile. "And are you now fully conversant with all the ways to plant and harvest wheat properly? Raise exceptionally fat pigs? Have hens that lay legions of eggs?"

John couldn't resist the twinkle in her blue eyes, and he laughed. "Of course. As to the pigs and hens, I have little need for such information, but you forget I shall need a great deal of wheat to make flour for my bakery project. I am still quite determined to open The Earl's Oven."

"So you intend to charge into a new profession and take the *ton* by storm. Shall you sell your baked wares from a cart on the street or from a store?"

The earl appeared to consider the question seriously, then said, "Oh, I think from a cart. That would lend such an air of distinction to my earldom, do you not think?"

As the pair bantered on for a while, the guests began to depart. It being a farm community, most of the gentlemen announced they had much to do in the morning. John noted Belle's gaze followed Sam about the room as the colonel escorted his departing neighbors to the door.

Then a disturbing notion slipped into John's thoughts. Had she been flirting with him to make his old friend jealous? The very idea was contemptible to the earl. Furious, he grabbed the lady's arm, saying, "Come out to the terrace a moment, Miss Hill. There is something I wish to say to you."

To her utter amazement, Belle found herself marched across the drawing room and out a set of open double doors to a darkened terrace. His lordship roughly dragged her down the stone steps to a small bubbling fountain bathed in silver moonlight. At last he stopped and stared down at her, but the darkness concealed his expression from her.

"Is there something you wished, my lord?" Belle

peered up at the gentleman, wondering why he wanted her alone. Her heart beat faster at the possibilities.

"Have you been deliberately flirting with me?"

Belle's cheeks warmed. What must he think of her? "Well, I was, but—"

Before she could explain, the earl crushed her to him, kissing her angrily. The embrace was punishing, but as she surrendered to his touch, the kiss became one of mutual passion. Sensations surged through her, making her tingle from head to toe as she melted into his strong embrace.

Suddenly, John pushed Belle away, staring down at her upturned face. "I won't be a pawn in your game to make Sam jealous. Despite my own feelings for you, I shall leave you to the man you want. But I warn you, don't toy with Sam. He's been through too much already."

The earl turned and strode rapidly back to the manor, leaving Belle trembling with emotion in the darkness.

SIX

"He loves me!" Belle uttered the words with astonishment. She'd been drawn to the earl from the moment she'd seen him on the cliffs at Hillcrest, but had tried to resist his charms. Her circumstances at the time did not lead her to believe a wealthy, titled gentleman would pay her the least heed, and yet he had.

A door snapped shut, bringing Belle out of her musings. The remainder of his statement penetrated her joy. He mistakenly thought her in love with Sam, and intended to leave her at Griffin Manor.

In that moment, Belle knew she loved Lord Sedgefield with all her heart. She couldn't bear the idea he had misinterpreted all her efforts on behalf of the colonel and Mrs. Campbell. She must go to him at once and correct the mistake.

Belle lifted her skirts and ran back up the path his lordship had taken. The glow of the full moon lighted the white gravel on the path, keeping her from doing herself an injury in the darkness. She discovered the door Sedgefield had entered was to the dimly lit library. No doubt he wished to avoid the few remaining guests in the drawing room.

She entered the chamber, only to discover the earl had gone elsewhere. Belle slipped out into the hall and dashed up the stairs, suspecting the gentleman had sought the privacy of his own rooms. As she turned the corner, she caught a glimpse of John's back as he strode rapidly down the hall, his rigid posture speaking volumes of his anger and unhappiness.

She wanted to call to him, but she heard the voices of the remaining guests as they exited the drawing room to retrieve their wraps and hats for their journey home. She didn't want the entire house to know she was about to do something scandalous—go to his lordship's room.

The earl arrived at his chamber and, without pause, opened the door and entered. Belle hurried down the hallway, determined to speak with him at once. Scarcely a minute after the earl disappeared from her sight, a loud feminine shriek filled the upper hallway.

Belle halted in her tracks, puzzled at the cry. It had come from John's room! She dashed to the door, which remained open. As she clutched the door frame, she saw Letty Griffin, her auburn curls tumbled about her shoulders, sitting on the bed eyeing Lord Sedgefield triumphantly.

Spying Belle in the doorway, Miss Griffin suddenly became all weepy. "Oh, thank goodness someone has come. I don't know what came over Lord Sedgefield, Miss Hill. He has used me in a dreadful manner."

John crossed his arms angrily. "That is a great clanker, Letty, and well you know it. If you don't remove yourself from my room at once, I shall give you the spanking you have needed since I arrived at Griffin Manor."

The young lady's eyes narrowed. "My brother will never allow it. He will believe me, sir."

Belle recognized Letty's scheme. "Not when I tell him I saw Lord Sedgefield enter this chamber alone but a moment ago."

Just then the sound of rapidly approaching footsteps echoed in the hall. The colonel, Mrs. Griffin, Mrs. Campbell, and her companion appeared at the door.

Sam entered the chamber and looked at his disheveled sister, then at his friend. "What is going on here?" His tone held no accusation, only curiosity.

Letty slid down from the earl's bed and dashed to her brother, repeating the lie about John. Then she threw herself upon his chest, weeping.

Mrs. Griffin twisted her handkerchief, half hopeful there was truth in her daughter's words, for there could be little doubt the earl would be a prize catch for any girl. "Can this be true?"

"Positively scandalous," Miss Campbell remarked, peering over the shoulder of the widow, who quickly shushed her.

Belle moved to his lordship's side, determined to defend him against such slander. "Miss Griffin's story is a total fabrication."

Letty turned to glare at Belle. "She would defend him, for she wants him for herself. I tell you he brought me here and tried to kiss me."

The colonel's face was full of doubt. He'd known John for years and knew him for an honorable man. Still, he had a responsibility to protect his sister's honor. Sam looked to Belle for help. "How do you know Letty is being untruthful?"

"Because his lordship was with me in the garden. We . . . had a misunderstanding. Before it was resolved, he decided to return to his room. I followed him, hoping to clear up our disagreement. He was from my sight for only a moment before I saw him enter this room alone. Your sister was in here waiting for him. I fear she has made up this story for her own purposes."

John, delighted at Miss Hill's fierce defense of him, turned her to him, oblivious to the watching faces at the doorway. "Why did you follow me, Belle?"

"To tell you that you have it all wrong. It's you I love,

and I don't want you to leave on the morrow without me." Belle held her breath, waiting for his reaction.

"Dearest Belle, I wouldn't think of doing such a foolish thing." The earl slid his arms around her, drawing her toward him.

But the embrace was halted by a woman's angry voice. "Well, I never." From the doorway, Cara indignantly pointed at Belle. "Miss Hill, *you* are a horrid flirt. How dare you lead Colonel Griffin on in such a dreadful manner only to throw him over for a title? The colonel is the finest man who ever was called a gentleman! To have him so shabbily treated—"

A smile lit Sam's face, pulling his scarred skin into a half moon. "Cara, my darling, do you still love me?" He put his sister from him and took the seething widow in his arms, crushing her to him.

The lady blinked at the colonel a moment, startled to find herself exactly where she wanted to be. Her face softened. Then she shyly replied, "I have loved you faithfully since you left, dearest Sam. How could you doubt it?"

"I did after our encounter in Ashton, even when Belle assured me you were just startled. She's been encouraging me to try and win your heart anew. In truth, while I've faced legions of soldiers without fear, I was frightened of one beautiful widow and what she might say."

The widow put her hands to her rosy cheeks. "That is what the two of you have had your heads together about all evening. Oh, Miss Hill!" Cara turned to Belle, her eyes full of contrition. "I said such a dreadful thing. Can you ever forgive me?"

Belle stepped forward and took the lady's hand. "I can, for it seems everyone misunderstood our friendship."

Seeing she was *de trop,* Belle returned to the earl's

side as the colonel again drew his lady into the curve of his arm.

Watching from the hallway, Miss Dorothy Campbell placed her hands on ample hips. "Don't do anything rash, Cara. My brother has hardly been dead a year."

Mrs. Griffin suddenly turned on the lady. "Do be quiet. I am quite tired of your sour attitude. Sam and Cara love each other, and Giles Campbell is dead and gone." Common politeness forbade her from adding, "and good riddance."

Miss Campbell sniffed, then said, "I will not be spoken to in that manner." She turned and left—heading where, no one knew or cared.

Despite the lack of privacy, Sam kissed Cara. Across the room, John took advantage of the distraction and smiled at Belle. He tilted her chin up and his mouth captured hers. This kiss was far more wonderful than the one in the garden, for their hearts were as one.

Letty stamped her foot as she glanced from one blissful pair to the other. "Ooooh! Everyone is happy but me. What about *me?*"

The two distracted couples ceased their embraces, eyeing the petulant miss who stood with her hands on her hips, pouting. Sam looked across at his friend. "Well, John, what do you think I should do with this slandering, spoiled baggage? I think locking her in her room for a couple of months might cure her from telling tales."

"Months!" Letty stared at her brother in horror. Then she turned to her mother. "You cannot let him do that. It would be cruel." When her mother made no comment, Letty's shoulders sagged in defeat. "I know I did wrong, but I was desperate. Sam was refusing to take me to Town, the earl was ignoring me, and Squire Fairmont was suggesting I consider an alliance with that dreadful spotty nephew who is his heir."

"That is no excuse for your conduct, young lady." Mrs. Griffin showed signs of weakening, but the look on her son's face told her now was not the time to discuss the matter. "We shall decide your punishment in the morning. For now, apologize to his lordship, then go to your room."

Letty was all contrition. Then, with dragging steps, she exited the room.

Belle, so content with her own happiness, couldn't bear for others not to know the same. "I hope you will not be too hard on her."

Cara, her eyes shining as she stared into the colonel's, agreed. "Sam, she is young and headstrong. In truth, she only misbehaved because you were being stubborn about her Season . . . and other things."

Sam made a face, then looked at his friend. "John, if you can forgive her prank, I shall find some lighter punishment for her." He was more interested in gazing at his love than in planning any reprimand for his errant sister.

Lord Sedgefield, wanting to be alone with Belle, smiled. "I think a good dressing down is all that is needed after a night of wondering what her fate shall be."

Mrs. Griffin, overjoyed that her son seemed more like his old self and was at last to have his Cara, turned, gesturing for the others. "Come, everyone. We must have Batters bring champagne to celebrate this happy occasion."

Following behind, his arm around Cara, Sam could be heard to say, "But there is no occasion yet, Mother. I haven't had a moment alone to ask Cara to marry me."

"Pshaw, as if there is any doubt. Am I not right, my dear?"

"Well, madam, a lady always likes to be asked—even

when the outcome is assured." The widow's response echoed back up the hallway.

That was the last thing Belle and John could hear as the Griffins and Mrs. Campbell headed for the celebration in the drawing room. The earl's arms tightened around Belle as she made to follow.

"Is Mrs. Campbell right?"

Belle nodded, her heart pounding.

The earl grew quiet for a moment, releasing her, and allowing his arms to drop back to his side. "There is one thing I must confess before I offer you my heart."

Her delicate brows rose in surprise. She was suddenly nervous. "You have a dark secret?"

"I helped you escape Hillcrest because I thought you were Ann and that I would be thwarting her relationship with my cousin, Sir Roger."

"Why would you do such a thing to dear sweet Ann?" Belle stepped back, shocked at his admission.

"Because I thought Ann was a beautiful madcap chit who tossed delicious cheesecakes out windows and asked strangers to run away with her."

With a delighted laugh, Belle stepped into the earl's arms. She couldn't be angry when she'd suspected his motives all along. "So you did it because I am so incorrigible? It had nothing to do with Ann?"

John kissed her smiling mouth, then sobered. "I know little of your cousin. But I must tell you my aunt is determined to stop their romance."

Belle laughed bitterly. "That is no secret. It is the gossip of the neighborhood. But, John, despite my dreadful Aunt Evelyn, Ann is a wonderful girl. She would make Sir Roger an excellent wife, although I must own he will have a formidable mother-in-law, with whom he must be firm."

"Well, I am glad the confusion is ended. Sir Roger must do what is best for him. As for me, I want nothing more than a lifetime with you. Will you marry me, dearest Belle?"

Belle drew back, a teasing light in her blue eyes. "Even if I continue my dreadful habit of tossing cheesecakes at you to draw your attention?"

"I can think of nothing I should like more than your cakes and kisses coming my way." With that, Lord Sedgefield lowered his head and availed himself of the latter.

Northhamptonshire Cheesecakes

2 oz currants	1 pt milk
1 oz butter	1/2 tsp almond extract
1 1/2 oz sugar	Grated lemon rind
1 egg	1/4 tsp nutmeg
Some small flaky pastry cups	

Stir the butter, sugar and eggs in a saucepan over low heat until thick. Take care not to let it boil. Boil 1 pint of sour milk (or new milk with half a dessertspoonful of vinegar or lemon juice to curdle it) until it separates into curds and whey. Strain off the curds, press well, and when cold add them to the cheesecake mixture along with the currants, spice, etc. Pour into the uncooked pastry cups and bake at 350 degrees F about 10 minutes, or until top is golden brown.

THE WAY TO
A MAN'S HEART

by

Wilma Counts

ONE

"Did Almack's live up to your expectations?" The Honorable Edward Jamison directed his question to his cousin, Miss Nicole Beaufort, as he helped himself from his mother's breakfast buffet.

"Stale cakes and watery beverages are not my idea of proper fare to offer guests," Nicole responded.

"Trust Nikki to criticize the food at the marriage mart!" Catherine, Edward's sister, laughed.

"Well, she's French, don't you know? They're like that." He winked at his sister and grinned at Nicole.

Catherine sighed. "She is only *half* French, and one would hope twelve years in the Jamison family would have enhanced her English heritage."

"I see no reason for the *ton*'s leading hostesses to tolerate such inferior food, English or no. Besides"— Nicole gestured at the laden sideboard—"I do not see the Jamisons living up to—that is, *down* to—what is typically served in English homes."

"Lillian, my dear." Uncle Jamison, Viscount Leighton, spoke in mock seriousness to his wife as he rose from the table. "What is this talk of food? It was my understanding you were taking these young ladies to Almack's to find husbands. I shall be in the library expecting hordes of suitors to present themselves." He patted his wife's shoulder as he left the room.

"Leighton is right," Aunt Lillian reproved mildly as she rose to follow her husband. "You girls would do well to look to the future. At two and twenty, Nicole is nearly on the shelf already. And nineteen is none too soon for you to be seriously looking for a husband, Catherine."

"I presume that means you should spend more time in ballrooms and less time in the kitchen, Nikki," Edward said as the door closed behind his mother.

"But Nikki *prefers* the kitchen to the ballroom," Catherine said.

"I would not say that exactly," Nicole protested, "but I have certainly learned enough from Perkins—and in France earlier—to know most of the people in charge of feeding the *ton* are incompetent, to say the least."

"Oh, really?" Edward gave a hoot of laughter. "And I suppose you could do ever so much better?"

"Yes, I could."

"Nikki, you cannot mean that," Catherine declared.

"I certainly do." Nicole raised her chin firmly.

Edward and Catherine looked at each other, their identical blue eyes sparkling. *Uh-oh,* Nicole thought.

"Come now, cousin dear," Edward mocked. "Ladies of the gentry simply are not found supervising kitchen staffs."

"Perhaps not, but I *could* do it—and do it better than most who have those responsibilities now."

"Prove it," Edward challenged. "I will wager ten guineas you would not be allowed near a gentleman's kitchen."

"Make it twenty and you have your wager," Nicole said, her brown eyes flashing.

"All right. Twenty. But you must find a position and manage to keep it for, say, six weeks."

"Done."

"You are both quite mad," Catherine said. "Papa

would never approve, and Mama would have the vapors. And what about Nikki's guardian? Monsieur Thibaud would have some say in this nonsense."

"They need not know," Edward said airily. "Nikki was away last year for three months at the Bensons' estate in Durham. Besides, she is of age now."

The three of them continued to wrangle just as they had about many an escapade in the last decade and more. As usual, she and Edward, who were of an age, engineered the adventure, overriding the doubts of the younger Catherine.

Nicole admitted privately to some doubts herself this time, but she could hardly back down now. What? Have Edward call her craven? However, she did have qualms about deceiving Aunt Lillian and Uncle Jamison.

And Monsieur Thibaud? she asked herself. *Oh, Papa. How I miss you.*

Nicole had been born in a village near Paris during the infamous Reign of Terror. Her father lost his parents, two older brothers, and a younger sister to the insatiable appetite of Madame Guillotine, not to mention the loss of all family property and wealth.

He had taken his wife and baby to seek refuge with a childhood friend who owned a restaurant in Reims. Unable to take his place in French society as *le comte* D'Arcy, and unwilling to live off the largess of his wife's family in England, he had joined his friend's business venture and eventually became a chef of great local acclaim.

Nicole's memories of her early childhood were happy ones. Although the family lived modestly, her parents loved each other and their daughter. Her mother taught Nicole to read and write. Later, she attended a local girls' day school. In her free time, she enjoyed nothing more than being in the restaurant kitchen, where she was allowed to spell the boy turning the spit, chop vegetables, or stir a sauce.

When she was seven, her mother died, bearing a stillborn son. For a time the laughter was gone, but neighbors and friends stepped in to help the grieving husband. For three more years, life had gone on much as it had previously, though with an aching void her mother had once filled. Nicole was ten when her father sat her down to announce the decision that changed her life.

"I am taking you to England to live with your mother's people."

"But, Papa, I do not want to go to England!"

"Nor do I, my love. But you cannot stay here to grow up a mere chef's daughter. There is no future for you here. Your mama was a nobleman's daughter. You must have a proper place in society—even if it is *English* society," he said sadly.

"Very well." She agreed reluctantly. "As long as you will be with me."

"Well, I will and I won't be with you." When she turned frightened, tear-filled eyes to him, he added, "I must take you to the Jamisons, but I will not, cannot throw myself on their charity. Your mama had a modest legacy which is to be yours one day. I must make my own way."

"Shall we not live together anymore?" the child asked plaintively.

"No, my love. You must live with the Jamisons. Your mama loved her brother very much. I am sorry we never knew the English family. You will go away to school and become a proper English lady and marry a rich, handsome young man." He hugged her to him. "I will see you as often as I can."

"Must I do this, Papa?"

"Yes, my dear." His eyes, too, glistened with unshed tears.

And then had come the hard part. Papa would make his way in England as a chef, but it would spoil his daughter's chances in society were it known her father was little more than a servant. He swore her to secrecy as he became "Monsieur Thibaud," trusted family retainer of *le comte* D'Arcy, given the task of conveying the "dead" *comte*'s daughter to her English family. She had spent months learning to address him automatically as "Monsieur Thibaud."

In the ensuing years, he had been true to his word, seeing her as often as possible. Twice a year, during the summer and at Christmas, her unofficial guardian was invited to the Leighton country estate to visit his one-time charge.

The family knew he was employed as head chef in White's, one of the premier gentlemen's clubs in the city, but this was not a fact discussed with other houseguests. The agreeable, kindhearted Jamisons understood the girl's need to maintain this tie with her childhood. Monsieur Thibaud was, after all, they noted, a man of refinement and education. 'Twas unfortunate the Revolution had ruined so many lives. . . .

A few days after the breakfast table challenge, the younger members of the Jamison household sat in the drawing room waiting for the viscount and his wife to come down to dinner.

"Edward," Nicole said, "you will be interested to know I have learned of an available position as cook. I hope you have set aside my twenty guineas."

"Your guineas? Oh, no. Quite the reverse. Unless you want to cry off—we can forget the wager, you know."

"Having second thoughts, Edward?" asked Catherine.

"Well, yes . . ." His tone was reluctant. "I would not want Nikki harmed in any way."

"Oh, no. You do not squirm out of our wager so easily," Nicole said. "Not after I have just discovered the perfect position."

"And that is?" he prompted.

"Cook at Thornwood Manor in Surrey. Perkins happened to mention it when I was helping her with a béarnaise sauce this afternoon. Her sister is the housekeeper at Thornwood, and they've not had a reliable cook there in some time."

"Why?" Catherine asked.

"Apparently the earl came into his title in 1813 when he was serving with Wellington in the Peninsula."

"Yes," Edward said. "His brother was killed in a duel, and there was a huge scandal."

"The present earl returned to Thornwood at the end of the war last year, but he had scarcely taken hold of the reins when Napoleon escaped from Elba. He rejoined the army and was wounded last month at Waterloo."

"That does not explain why there was no cook at Thornwood," Catherine said.

"It was over a year before he came home, you see, and when he did come back, other matters took precedence. Evidently, the women of his family preferred to live in town, so they reduced the staff at Thornwood."

"He's back now and they need a cook," Edward stated rather than asked.

"Yes." Nicole laughed. "Seems they had one, but she did not stay long when his lordship sent his food back to the kitchen saying he would not eat such swill."

"How can you be sure he will not do the same thing to you?" Edward challenged.

"I shall not serve him swill."

"Thornwood is a single man. You cannot join such a household," Edward said simply.

"Thornwood is an invalid," Nicole said, "wounded in the war. Besides, his mother, his grandmother, and a maiden aunt are presently residing there. And the wager is only for six weeks."

"You must give up this plan, Nicole," Catherine admonished. "You will be ruined if it ever comes out."

"But it will not. I am not so well known in society that any chance visitor would recognize me in a *kitchen*. I have never met the earl or his female relatives."

"It is not a good idea. Something could go wrong," Catherine worried.

"I shall insist on taking Milly with me."

"Your maid?"

"She will be my cook's assistant. She has agreed, so long as it does not become a permanent change of status for her."

"You told her of this harebrained scheme?" Catherine was appalled.

"Yes. She thinks it will be a lark."

"Peagooses, both of you." Catherine threw up her hands in resignation. "You, too, Edward," she added, ignoring the conspiratorial wink between her brother and their cousin.

TWO

It had been surprisingly easy, Nicole thought as she climbed into bed on her second night at Thornwood. The housekeeper, Mrs. Hankins, was so eager to fill the position she scarcely glanced at the letters of recommendation Nicole and Edward had so painstakingly fabricated.

Nor had she demurred when Mrs. Buford, widow of a soldier, insisted on bringing her own cook's assistant with her. Hankins, who had been forced to fill in as cook, acknowledged herself to be mediocre at the task. Her only concern when the new applicant presented herself at the servants' entrance was Nicole's apparent youth.

Nicole assured the woman she looked much younger than she was and, after all, the proof of her worth as cook would be in the pudding, would it not?

Hankins caved in with a sigh of relief.

The next hurdle was the family matriarch, the present earl's grandmother, Mrs. Hankins explained as she conducted Nicole to the library. The Countess Thornwood, widow of the seventh earl, had managed her grandson's affairs in his absence and did so now in his incapacitation. She insisted on interviewing new employees.

"But . . . I understood his mother lived here. Wouldn't she . . ." Nicole was clearly confused.

"She rarely visits here. Came now because of Master Adam's infirmity. *She* is now Marchioness of Moresland. Married the marquis some three years after the eighth earl's death. Her eldest son succeeded, of course, but he died in that duel in '13. His lordship"—she pointed upward—"was in Spain at the time."

"His brother—the ninth earl—had no children?"

"Never married. Ah, here we are." Mrs. Hankins knocked on a great oaken door and stepped aside to allow Nicole to enter. "Mrs. Buford, my lady."

The large, book-lined room exuded elegance with its heavy brocade draperies and deep-piled oriental carpets. A diminutive white-haired woman was nearly swallowed by a great wing chair near the fireplace.

"Mrs. Buford. Please have a seat." The old woman stared at Nicole speculatively. "Oh, my. Hankins told me you were quite young."

"Yes, my lady." No point denying the obvious, was there?

"Are you sure you are capable of handling this position?"

"I believe so, yes. I am accounted a good cook. My father was a chef in France."

"You are French?"

"Only half. My mother was English."

"I see. Your accent suggests more education than is usual."

"Yes, my lady. I was very fortunate in that regard." Nicole hoped this noncommittal reply would divert the countess's attention and avoid the need for a more elaborate lie.

"You are aware my grandson is gravely ill? He was wounded at Waterloo."

"I had heard that, yes."

"His injuries are on the mend, but the boy refuses to eat. He lies up there wasting away—dying before our eyes." The old lady's eyes filled with tears, and Nicole felt a surge of sympathy for her. Then the countess added fiercely, "He must not be allowed to do so! It will be your job to make him eat."

"I shall do my best, madam."

"Others have tried and failed. He does not respond to the pleas of family members. I—we are at wits' end on this matter. You shall have free rein to do whatever it takes to keep him from starving himself into the grave."

"I shall try, my lady."

"Do whatever it takes, Mrs. Buford. Whatever it takes."

Nicole had been nervous about directing the kitchen staff, but they all accepted their appointed positions and tasks. It took only two meals to win them and the rest of the earl's servants over. Several declared they had never eaten so well. Mrs. Hankins reported the ladies of the house were pleased, as well.

There was not a word from his lordship. However, Nicole was not best pleased to find his trays regularly returned to the kitchen barely touched. She took a natural cook's pride in seeing people appreciate her art—and this man was totally disinterested!

"I'm sorry, ma'am. He just don't eat much these days," said Rogers, his lordship's one-time batman, now his valet, as he returned the lunch tray one day. "I'm that worried about 'im, I am. He gets thinner and weaker ev'ry day."

"Was he injured internally, then? Or does he suffer from fever? What does the doctor say?"

"His wounds be healin' right proper, methinks. Lost an eye, 'e did, and took a deep one in 'is upper leg. Doctor says the fever's gone now."

"He is completely bedridden, then?"

Rogers reddened. "Well, if'n I help 'im, he gets up for the necessary, but 'tis slow 'e is. He mostly just lies there staring at the ceiling."

"But his wounds *are* healing?"

"Yes, ma'am—the outer ones, anyways. But there's wounds and then there's wounds, if'n ye get my meaning."

"Yes, I think I do. It must be difficult for a strong man to find himself so weakened—but is that not all the more reason to try to regain his strength?"

"I don't believe he much cares anymore, you see?"

"It is true, then, that his fiancée jilted him? One of the kitchen maids said as much." Nicole could see Rogers was uncomfortable about discussing his employer, but she felt an urgent need to know as much as she could about the man.

"Well, it's sort of true. He made it easy for 'er to cry off when he saw how his damaged face affected her. He used to be quite a ladies' man, 'e did. But I think Mason's death eats away at 'im more."

"Mason?"

"Lieutenant Mason was his best friend. Mason got the infantryman wot bayoneted 'is lordship's leg, but the cavalryman that slashed 'is lordship's face ran Mason through."

"Oh, my goodness." Nicole felt tears stinging her eyes. "Still," she said decisively, "he must be made to eat to regain his strength."

"Yes, Missus. The ladies been tryin'. The countess comes and reads to him reg'lar and tells 'im all that's goin' on, you see. His mum mostly weeps and begs 'im to get better. The other one—sister of the countess, she be—she looks in now 'n' then, too. Proper worried they all is—'n' with due cause, methinks."

"Hmm. Mrs. Hankins managed to purchase a whole

salmon at the market today. Perhaps a tasty soufflé and apple cobbler would tempt his appetite."

"Mebbe." But Rogers did not sound hopeful.

Nicole considered herself fortunate to find one of her predecessors had established an herb garden. It was sadly overrun with weeds, but she and Milly had already begun to remedy that problem. The use of parsley, thyme, sage, mint, rosemary, and chives would enhance the flavors of usually bland English dishes. Soufflés were her father's specialty, and she prided herself on having learned his skill well. *The secret is in the egg whites.* She remembered his tone as she beat.

Later, the meal prepared, she arranged the plate attractively, serving asparagus and buttered potatoes with the salmon soufflé. She consulted the butler, Jenkins, on just the right white wine to complement the meal. At the last minute, she added a tiny crystal vase of primroses and a pot of tea to the linen-lined tray.

"There!" Proud of her results, Nicole placed a silver cover over the warm plate.

"Looks fine," Mrs. Hankins said, and others in the kitchen agreed. All felt they had a vested interest in persuading his lordship to eat—as, indeed, they did.

Rogers looked approving and hopeful as he carried the tray out of the kitchen. Ten minutes later, he returned with the tray, looking crestfallen.

"Says 'e ain't hungry, ma'am. Kept the wine and bade me bring the rest back."

"Did he even *see* the food we prepared?" Nicole asked.

"No, ma'am. Just said to take it away."

"Well! We will just see about that! Let me have that tray, Mr. Rogers."

"Now, Mrs. Buford, you can't go barging uninvited

into his lordship's chamber. 'Tain't proper." Rogers's shock was reflected on the faces of the entire kitchen staff.

"Proper or not, he will see me," she declared. "I am tired of trying to please that impossible man. Come along, Milly. You will lend propriety. You, too, if you please, Mr. Rogers."

Rogers grinned. "Wouldn't miss it, ma'am. I'll carry the tray meself."

Nicole fumed as they made their way up the back stairs to the second floor and down the hall to his lordship's chamber. Rogers knocked and announced, "You have a visitor, my lord."

"I want no visitor—as you well know," a disembodied voice growled.

"Sorry, my lord. Mrs. Buford insists. Best be prepared."

Nicole, watching from the open door, waited with Milly at her elbow as Rogers set down the tray and straightened the bedcovers.

"Who the devil is Mrs. Buford? Tell her I am not at home to anyone," the voice growled again.

"She's the new cook, sir. She's come about your supper."

"The cook? If she is employed in this household, she will damned well obey my orders. Tell her to be gone."

"Not quite yet, my lord," Nicole said firmly as she approached the bed.

An oil lamp on the table nearby gave ample light for her to see him clearly. What she saw took her breath away momentarily.

He was a big man with an unruly shock of dark brown hair and a stubble of dark beard. A narrow bandage circled his head at an angle, covering his left eye. The other eye was a raging pool of blue. He was half sitting against a stack of pillows, his chest and shoulders exposed. A mat of dark hair on his chest extended beneath the covers.

His face was gaunt, the cheekbones standing out prominently on either side of a straight nose. His mouth was wide, his lips well-defined. Despite his weakened condition, he was a handsome man, radiating power, strength, and control.

What her eyes conveyed might have been very pleasing to any female were he but cleaned and shaved. What her nose detected was not at all pleasing. Along with the rankness of mending flesh, the combined odors of sweat, medications, and stale brandy assaulted anyone entering the room.

"Good God, woman! What is the meaning of this?" He grabbed the covers, jerked them to his chin, and glared at her.

In for a penny, in for a pound, she thought. *I may lose my wager with Edward after all.* Aloud, she said, "I have come to ask you directly just what you find so objectionable about the food I have prepared."

"What food? I do not want any food! Now go away."

"I was told you liked salmon, and that apple cobbler was one of your favorite dishes. The least you can do is taste them. You have not even looked at them." She lifted the dish cover and a more pleasant aroma assailed the senses.

He glanced at the tray of food, then glared at her again and reached for the glass of wine at his bedside. "There. I have seen it. Now take it and yourself out of this room immediately."

"So. You've no appetite for nourishing food, but you do not hesitate to swill down the drink. Is that it?"

"You have the right of it," he said sarcastically. "And it is of no concern whatsoever to you."

"Oh, but it is." She removed the glass from his hand and the bottle from the table. "It is my job to see this household well fed. *All* of this household. No more drink—except water—until you eat a decent meal."

"Why, you impertinent wench! You would do well to remember your place." He was shouting now.

"As would you, my lord," she retorted. "You lie there feeling sorry for yourself while hundreds of people who are dependent upon you valiantly try to carry on without proper leadership." This much she had learned since her arrival.

"Get out," he said through gritted teeth. "You, madam, are dismissed. Collect your wages and get off my land."

"I'll go for now, but I will return in the morning with your breakfast. Your grandmother hired me. Until you are capable of managing your own affairs, it will have to be she who dismisses me. Meanwhile, do eat your dinner, my lord."

As she turned to leave the room, he picked up the pot of tea and hurled it in her direction. It crashed to the floor, and the stain spread across the light-colored carpet.

"What is going on here?"

"Adam, darling, what is the matter?"

"Poor dear."

Three older females crowding into the room spoke simultaneously. The youngest of the three had to be his mother, Nicole thought. She was a slightly plump blond woman who appeared to be waging a moderately successful campaign against the ravages of age on beauty. The other two were his grandmother and her look-alike sister, Miss Wainwright.

"Adam, what is the meaning of this display?" His grandmother's tone was severe.

"Oh, sister, do not berate the poor boy. Can you not see he is distressed?" Obviously, the aunt possessed little of the strength of the dowager countess.

"There, there, my dear." His mother rushed to his bedside and caressed his forehead. He twitched away from her ministering hand.

"Gran." Addressing the countess, he pointed at Nicole. "I want that woman off the premises tomorrow."

The aunt twisted her hands and looked accusingly at Nicole. The mother murmured soothing noises.

"I am afraid not, my dear," his grandmother said firmly.

"What?" Three voices spoke at once, one of them a surprised growl from the bed.

"Well, you see," the dowager explained patiently, "we had a dreadful time replacing the last cook. And Mrs. Buford is quite good, you know. Perhaps when you are better, you will be able to find a suitable replacement."

While his lordship sputtered, his grandmother took Nicole's elbow and steered her gently toward the door, trailed by Rogers and Milly. In the hall, Lady Thornwood said, "Well. That is more real emotion than we have seen since his return. Anger is at least healthier than despair. This is a step in the right direction."

"Whatever it takes, my lady. Whatever it takes."

Half an hour later, when his mother and aunt had finally left his chamber, Adam Jefferson Prescott, Earl of Thornwood and holder of several lesser titles as well, thrashed around in the bed as much as pain from his leg wound allowed.

Damn that woman! Feeling sorry for himself, indeed. What did *she* know of the situation?

The accusation he was shirking his responsibilities rankled, though. He had always prided himself on doing his duty to king and country. Had he not given up his commission after the Peninsular War when he would rather have stayed with his regiment? Had he not hastily answered the call to return to arms when Boney went on the rampage again?

And for what? Here he was, a disfigured, repulsive shadow of what he had once been. His best friend had perished on the field in Belgium. God! how he missed Mason. And he had lost the woman he was to marry— though, in truth, the *reason* for that loss hurt more than the loss itself.

And this . . . this *woman*—little more than a servant—had the audacity to accuse *him* of miring himself in self-pity! He tried to turn away from the image of brown eyes filled with challenge . . . and something else.

Understanding. That was it. She seemed to have understood instantly. Instead of taking comfort from this discovery, he resented having a stranger read him so well.

The rest of the image refused to go away. She was rather small, only slightly taller than Gran. She had deep auburn hair with glints of fiery red in the lamplight. When she bent over to take the wineglass, he had caught a whiff of roses and jasmine. If she were not such a termagant, she would be a damned attractive woman.

Now, where had that thought come from?

She said she would be back in the morning. A trace of a smile flirted about his mouth. *I will be ready for you, madam. Forewarned is forearmed.*

He glanced at the laden tray and picked up a fork. The soufflé was cold, but its flavor tantalized. He sampled a few bites—the cobbler was delicious—then lay back, exhausted.

He was asleep when Rogers came later for the tray.

THREE

The next morning, Nicole hummed as she prepared Thornwood's breakfast tray. At least he had taken a few bites of last night's meal. That brought a self-satisfied smile to her lips.

On impulse, she decorated his bowl of porridge with a smiling face of raisins. She set the bowl, along with milk and sugar and other condiments, on the tray with a plate containing a rasher of bacon, eggs, and muffins. Adding a small bowl of late strawberries, she indicated its readiness to Rogers.

"The coffee, ma'am?" Rogers asked. "He likes coffee in the morning."

"I shall carry it up myself," she said, ignoring the raised eyebrows around her.

Rogers entered the room first to ensure Thornwood was presentable before motioning Nicole and Milly in.

Thornwood sat up and eyed the tray as Rogers set it over his lap. "Where is the coffee?"

"Right here, my lord." Nicole stepped around Rogers to show herself, pot in hand. "Promise you will not throw it at me, and I shall pour for you."

"You! I might have guessed. I told you to stay away."

"You did?" she asked in mock innocence. "Funny. I do not recall your saying that at all."

"Insubordinate wench," he muttered under his breath,

but he held out the cup for her to pour. She thought she detected a twitch of his lips as she carefully set the pot out of his reach on the bedside table.

He wore a nightshirt this morning, and his hair was combed. Had he expected her, then? The dimly lit room smelled stale and close. Nicole wrinkled her nose, strode over to the windows and, throwing aside the draperies, opened two of the panels of glass.

"What the devil are you doing?" he demanded.

"There is a gorgeous summer day out there, my lord. Frankly, the air in this room is a trifle stale. And I might add that your swearing at me is most impolite."

"I'll swear if I want to. If your delicate nose is so offended, take it elsewhere," he snapped.

Nicole schooled her features so as not to smile at this fit of little-boy stubbornness.

"You swear at me again and you'll get no more coffee," she said. "Now eat your breakfast." She removed the silver covers meant to keep the food warm.

He looked at the food and scowled. "I am not hungry."

She ignored him, buttered a muffin, and prepared the porridge.

"I . . . am . . . not . . . hungry." The words came through gritted teeth.

"Nevertheless, . . . you . . . will . . . eat." She imitated his tone as she picked up a spoonful of cereal to shove into his mouth. He turned his head away petulantly.

"My lord," she said sweetly and calmly—she might have been conversing in a *ton* drawing room—"you may either eat this or wear it. If you do not open your mouth, I shall pour the entire bowl over your head."

"You wouldn't d—" The rest of his tirade was lost as she shoved the spoon into his mouth. He had to swallow before he could continue. "Now, see h—" She shoved in another spoonful.

He grabbed her hand. She was surprised at the strength in his grip. Lord, what would that power be like normally?

"Madam, you go too far. I am perfectly capable of feeding myself."

"Then do so," she said bluntly. "You will never get out of that bed if you do not regain your strength."

"And would that be so bad?" he sneered.

"Yes, it would indeed. Now eat. I shall stand right here until you have done so."

He gave an exaggerated sigh, picked up a fork, and made a stab at a strawberry. In complete silence, he ate about half the food on the tray. Then she could see him visibly tiring.

"Enough." He pushed the tray away.

"Very well." She motioned for Rogers to take the tray. "Is there anything special you would like for lunch, my lord?"

"Other than your absence, you mean? No."

"I shall come back then." She ignored his rude snort. "Meanwhile, you should get some rest. And then, my lord, you might consider allowing Rogers to attend your toilette."

"Damn your impertinence!" he yelled.

"You are swearing again." She quickly left the room, leaving Milly to finish scrubbing at the tea stain from the night before.

"Nicely done, Mrs. Buford," Rogers said, accompanying her back to the kitchen.

"He requires fresh air, sunshine, and more nourishment. And he needs something to think about besides his losses," she said thoughtfully.

"Yes, ma'am."

They briefly discussed what might spark some interest in the man lying above.

Adam's leg wound had not healed sufficiently for him to stretch out in the bathtub as he would have liked, so he stood patiently leaning on Rogers's shoulder as the valet poured cleansing water over him. He had earlier submitted to being shaved and having his hair washed.

"I must admit it feels wonderful to be really clean again," he said, donning a newly laundered nightshirt and returning to a freshly made bed. But damned if he would admit as much to that female.

He wondered briefly what she would serve him for lunch. Then it occurred to him this was the first time he had thought specifically about his own creature comforts since before the Battle of Waterloo, more than a month ago.

Rogers brought his lunch tray, but Mrs. Buford was not with him. Just as Adam was deciding whether he was, indeed, disappointed, she breezed into the room carrying two books. Milly was right behind her with a chessboard and a box from the game room he recognized as containing chessmen. A surge of pleasure at seeing Mrs. Buford again startled him.

"Good afternoon, my lord. I hope you like the rabbit stew," she said, chattering as though it were quite a common occurrence for a woman to invite herself into a gentleman's bedchamber.

"What is that?" he asked suspiciously, pointing his knife at the books and the items Milly carried.

"I have brought you some diversions. Two novels and a chess game." Mrs. Buford held up first one book and then the other. "This one is called *Pride and Prejudice.* It is by the same lady who wrote *Sense and Sensibility* a few years ago. And this one is called *Waverly.* It's about an army officer serving in the North. I think the anonymous author must be a Scot."

"Why?"

"He is *very* sympathetic to the Scottish view of events."

"Am I to understand you are *not* sympathetic to the Scottish view?"

"No. I mean, yes. I am sympathetic to their view— and so is this author, whoever he is."

"I will consider the first book. I have had quite enough of soldiering for a while." The last statement held a rueful note.

"And I have brought a chessboard," she said, stating the obvious with resolute cheer as he continued to eat.

He swallowed a bite before asking scornfully, "And who will oppose me? Rogers does not play." He had tried to teach Rogers the game, but the valet had no heart for it. Adam had spent many happy hours over a chessboard with Mason, though.

"I shall."

"I beg your pardon?"

"Me. I play the game. Actually, I am quite good at it."

"That is certainly not surprising," he said, grinning wickedly, "but I was speaking of chess."

She looked startled, then blushed furiously. "So was I, my lord. So was I. However, if you fear being bested by a woman . . ." She shrugged dramatically.

"Hah! Most unlikely."

"Well, shall we see, then?"

"Do you not have kitchen duties that demand your attention? Do I not employ you to *cook?"*

"My duties are fulfilled for the moment. Besides, by the terms of my employment, I have two hours free every afternoon."

"Indeed?"

"Indeed. So if you should care for a game of chess, I stand ready to accommodate you."

He shrugged. "Why not?"

When he had finished eating, another table was placed near the bed for the chessboard and a chair was drawn up for her. They played in silence for some time. After a while, she made a small noise of sympathy as she captured one of his knights.

"All right. I concede your point. Who taught you to play chess?" he asked, truly interested in the answer.

"My father. And I grew up with cousins who play very well."

"And your husband? Did he play?" He wondered what sort of man had attracted this woman.

"My husband?" she asked absently. "Oh. No. He had little interest in this game."

"He probably had other games in mind."

"He preferred cards." She deliberately ignored his double *entendre,* Adam thought.

He felt himself tiring even as he wanted to continue the game, but she must have perceived his fatigue.

"My goodness. Look at the time!" she said. "I must prepare dinner. Perhaps we can finish this tomorrow?"

Rogers helped her move the table carefully so as not to disturb the pieces. Then she was gone, taking with her the ubiquitous Milly, who had sat near a window mending linens the whole time.

That puzzled him a bit. A cook—a widow, at that—in need of a chaperon? No, probably not, though Mrs. Buford did seem to possess very refined sensibilities. What did she think him capable of in his present state, for heaven's sake?

She did not come with the evening tray, but he smiled to see that red wine in a fine crystal decanter accompanied the roast beef. However, his grandmother—his favorite relative—came to keep him company, and he found himself really listening to her tidbits of estate business and local gossip.

Mrs. Buford did not accompany Rogers and the breakfast tray the next morning, either. His disappointment annoyed him. After all, what did her appearance or nonappearance matter to him? What did anything matter anymore?

About midmorning, there was a knock on the door. Rogers being out of the room at the moment, Adam called out, "Yes?"

The door opened a crack.

"May I come in?" Mrs. Buford asked.

"One moment," he said, sitting up and hastily pulling the covers over his exposed legs. "All right."

"We have brought you a bit of the outdoors," she said as she came in carrying a large vase filled with wildflowers. Behind her marched Milly, with a smaller vase of roses he surmised came from the garden outside the library.

Setting the roses on a chest of drawers, Milly took up her position near the window. Mrs. Buford brought the wildflowers to the nightstand and made room for them. She smelled of sunshine and the outdoors.

"I have never had a woman bring me flowers before," he noted. "Thank you."

"Really? Hmm. I think it was Hamlet who said some customs are best observed in the breach—or something of the sort. Shakespeare, anyway."

"You are woman of surprises, Mrs. Buford. A cook who quotes Shakespeare!"

"Oh. Well . . ." She looked down, avoiding his eyes, and clasped her hands. "Do you need anything? Will you have something special for lunch, my lord?" She seemed confused.

"No. Surprise me," he said.

"As you wish, sir."

She gave a slight curtsy and then was gone, leaving him already somewhat surprised. Surprised at his pleasure in her brief visit. Surprised at his joy in the flowers and that whiff of the outdoors. And, now that he considered it, surprised at a cook's quoting Shakespeare and being aware of popular novels. There was more to Mrs. Buford than any of them knew, he thought.

FOUR

Nicole found her work as a full-time cook challenging—and far more exhausting than she had anticipated. She planned menus with Mrs. Hankins, who then consulted Lady Thornwood. Occasionally the other two ladies made a suggestion or request. Then Mrs. Hankins would shop for those items not supplied by the home farm. Nicole reflected that she was fortunate to have entered into her wager in summer, when there was an abundance of seasonal vegetables and fruits.

She arose early each morning. Only a maid charged with tending kitchen fires rose earlier. Soon the kitchen became a beehive of workers, some preparing and serving breakfast to the Quality, others doing the same for the servants' hall. Still others started on luncheon and advance preparations for the evening meal, or the baking, which was a major undertaking every other day or so. As the queen bee in this hive, Nicole coordinated activities, assigned specific tasks, and, of course, ensured the results would be tasty.

Perhaps queen bee was the wrong image, she thought. A general commanding disparate elements on a battlefield might be more apropos. Then she giggled to herself. The object of this war was to make the enemy stronger!

For several days, Nicole's forces had waged a successful campaign. The earl's trays were no longer returned untouched, though no one would yet describe his appetite as robust. He steadily gained strength, to the point of rising and being dressed to sit for a few hours in a wing chair by the window.

The new cook found herself spending more and more of her free time in the sickroom. Telling herself she did so only to carry out the countess's orders, she nevertheless could not deny her attraction to him. Shaved and groomed, the man was a breathtaking example of the male species! Nicole had had her share of would-be suitors and others interested in dalliance, but never had she responded in such a purely physical way to a man. She felt an inner tightening of anticipation whenever she was near him—but anticipation of *what?*

She thought his continued grumbling about her presence in his chamber and his grudging acceptance of her as an opponent in the chess games to be at least partly sham. His one good eye held a hint of merriment as he tossed out his challenges. The first real smile from him turned her all squishy inside.

During the third game—he had handily won the first one and she managed a win on the second—both were concentrating heavily on the board. The game had taken on a sort of presence and importance in and of itself, with each player concentrating on the hands moving the pieces on the board.

"Aha! Mason, I've got you!" he crowed triumphantly. "You tried that move once before . . ." His voice trailed off and he looked up to meet her surprised gaze. "I . . . I . . . am sorry," he stammered. "I, uh, quite forgot myself."

"Pleasantly so, I hope," she said lightly, wanting to ease the pain she saw.

He cleared his throat. "Mason and I used to play. He once tripped me up with the same move you just made."

He smiled in sad remembrance. "It worked only once, though."

"Tell me about Mason," she urged. He was silent for so long she thought she had offended him, but then he spoke quietly.

"Mason was, quite simply, the best friend anyone could ever have. We were school chums—met at Eton and immediately became inseparable. Spent all our holidays together, too."

"Really? Your parents did not object?"

"Neither set of parents was particularly sorry not to have us underfoot, so we alternated our holidays. We were always in some scrape or other. One time . . ." He launched into a tale of putting a sheep in the headmaster's office and an aborted plan to run away to sea.

"Mason had a very fertile imagination." He laughed—a genuine, carefree bit of laughter that quite charmed her. Was this a glimpse of what he had once been? Then he sobered. "We had good times, Mason and I." He turned away.

"How wonderful to be able to look back on happy memories," she said gently.

"Happy." His tone was bitter. "I am not happy. I am angry! Most of all, I am angry at Mason for leaving me as he did. Can you believe that? The man saved my life and I am furious at *him*." He paused and looked at her with a bleak expression. "I've not said that before, even to myself, but it's true."

She wanted to take him in her arms and comfort him, but of course that would be most unseemly conduct. Instead, she patted his hand and said, "Yours is a natural reaction, my lord. I was only seven when my mother died, but I remember being very angry at her for leaving my father and me."

"I did not react so to other deaths—not even my father's. And a soldier sees an uncommon lot of death."

"Perhaps you were not so close to any of the others."

"Perhaps."

And with that, the conversation was over. It was time for her to return to the kitchen. She rather imagined he felt he had already said too much.

Neither referred to that discussion in the days following, though Nicole continued to visit him at least once a day. He began to relax and even shared some amusing anecdotes of his Peninsula campaign. She was delighted to find his sense of the ridiculous paralleled her own.

Then one day Rogers brought the lunch tray back virtually untouched.

"Off 'is feed again, 'e is." Rogers sounded worried.

"He ate a hearty breakfast, though," Mrs. Hankins observed. "Maybe he just wasn't hungry."

"He's awful quiet-like, too," Rogers said.

"Let us see how he fares with the evening meal," Nicole said.

But the evening meal proved no different.

"He's in a right terrible funk, ma'am," Rogers reported confidentially to Nicole. "Went to bed with a bottle of brandy. And here's the reason why, I'm a-thinkin'." He pulled a folded newspaper from under his arm. "The countess, she brought 'im the paper this morning as soon as it arrived. She didn't read it, or she never woulda let 'im 'ave it."

"Why? Is the news of the occupation of France so dreadful, then?"

" 'Tain't that at all. Look here." He folded the paper back to a society column and pointed at a particular item.

"Viscount Bentham's announcement of his daughter's forthcoming marriage to the Marquis of Henniton? Is that the one?"

"Yep. Bentham's daughter Victoria was the one betrothed to his lordship hardly a month since."

"Oh, my." Nicole felt a surge of sympathy for Lord Thornwood, and a simultaneous spurt of contempt for the woman who had thrown away such a prize for Henniton. Nicole knew Henniton to be a middle-aged roué whose life of dissipation was often remarked upon by people who did not shock easily.

She did not pause to ask herself just how she came to view Thornwood as such a "prize."

"Didn't let no grass grow under *her* feet, she didn't," Rogers said bitterly.

"Was Thornwood so very much in love with her, then?" Nicole asked, suddenly aware she did not want to hear a positive response.

"I dunno. Who knows how the Quality really feel about such things? It was considered a good match."

"I understand she followed him to Belgium. She must have cared for him to have done that."

"I wouldn't put too much stock in her goin' to Brussels. Half the *ton* was in Belgium before the battle. 'Twas the place to be."

"So what happened? Why did she cry off?" Nicole hoped she did not sound morbidly curious.

"Well . . ." Rogers's reluctance to divulge information must have been one of the reasons Lord Thornwood valued him so, Nicole thought. But the man also genuinely cared for his employer and wanted to help him. Rogers gave a resigned sigh. "I ain't rightly sure I know, but I *think* she were put off by 'is wounds. Her father brought 'er to visit his lordship about three days after we brought 'im back to his quarters."

"That was good, was it not?"

"Yes—and no. You see, his lordship was a right handsome man before that saber took 'is eye and left a scar. When she come to visit, most of 'is face was covered in bandages. Guess she thought it was worse than it really was. Kept saying things like, 'Oh, my poor darling,' but she couldn't look at 'im." Rogers imitated the woman's supersweet tone.

"How terrible for Lord Thornwood."

"He knew, all right, despite bein' real sick with fever just then. *He* tried to comfort *her.*"

"And?"

"An' she came 'round a bit. Then the surgeon told her and her pa as how he was worried about his lordship's leg. Said he might hafta amputate an', anyways, he'd prob'ly always limp some."

"Oh, dear."

"Yes. That done it. She looked real shocked-like, an' cried, an' said, 'You mean he can no longer dance at a ball?' Then she run outta the room. One of the maids overheard 'er in the hall tellin' her pa as how she wouldn't be tied to an invalid, even if 'e was an earl." Rogers snorted scornfully. "Got herself a marquis now, so she done herself real good."

"How did her behavior affect Lord Thornwood?" Nicole's heart wrenched for the injured man. His fiancée's rejection must have aggravated his other losses.

"He just got real quiet-like. Didn't say much at all. A few days later she came back, an' they was alone for a little while. When she come outta 'is room, she wasn't wearin' the Thornwood betrothal ring anymore."

"Now, just weeks later, she is marrying someone else."

"Yes. If'n ya ask me, 'e's well outta it with that one."

"But perhaps he truly cared for her."

"Could be . . ."

Nicole wondered why the doubt in Rogers's voice pleased her so.

At midmorning the next day, the object of their concern awoke in a foul mood. Adam glanced at the brandy bottle on the nightstand. Empty. Just as well. Why in hell had he allowed the news of Victoria's betrothal to plunge him into such a fit of the dismals?

It was not, after all, as though theirs had been a great love match. Her father and his mother had promoted the union of properties. Thornwood needed an heir. Victoria, Adam's mother had pointed out, had excellent blood-lines. And besides, his mother continued, the two of them were quite the handsomest couple in the *ton* that Season. Her blond alabaster beauty complemented pre-cisely his dark good looks.

"Oh! To see my pretty child, now such a handsome man, wed to the Season's reigning beauty!" his mother had gushed.

"Please, Mother," he had protested, but she had gone on and on in the same vein.

Not even his grandmother's, "Handsome is as hand-some does" had diverted his mother's focus from their physical beauty.

And why, he asked himself now, should that be so surprising? His mother had talked often enough about how her beauty alone had captured two very eligible husbands for her. About how she had passed her beauty on to her sons, "the handsomest boys in Christendom." Other parents bragged of their children's scholarship or horsemanship, but not his mother. For her, looks were paramount.

And what about you, *Adam, old boy?* he asked him-self. Had he not agreed to marry Victoria largely because his prospective bride was so beautiful? Had he not ig-nored the fact he was often restless and bored in her company? And what did that matter so long as she pro-duced a suitable heir?

So he had chosen a wife largely because she would be a beautiful porcelain doll. Never mind that she had a brain and heart to match. Why should he now condemn her for rejecting him because he no longer possessed the same qualities he'd valued in *her?*

He started to rise and fell back with a groan. Lord, his head hurt. Rogers came in with a tray.

"Take it away," Adam ordered.

Rogers set the tray down, plucked a glass from it, and thrust it toward the groaning specimen on the bed.

"Mrs. Buford said ta tell you this would help. She says drink it all down at once."

Adam looked askance at the concoction and smelled it. "Good God! That woman is trying to poison me!"

"She said it smells vile, but it works."

"If I die, you be sure she is brought up on charges."

"Yes, sir." Rogers grinned as Thornwood took a deep breath and downed the drink. "I've brought you some breakfast, too."

"Ugh," was all the response he got as Adam lay back and closed his eye. Amazingly, his stomach seemed to settle quite rapidly. In a few minutes more, his head stopped throbbing.

"I believe the wench has worked a miracle," he said, "but I want no food just now."

Later, he settled for some soup for lunch. By the evening meal, his appetite had returned enough that the kitchen staff breathed a collective sigh of relief.

FIVE

The next afternoon when Mrs. Buford and Rogers entered the sickroom, Adam was dressed and sitting on a leather settee, surrounded by his female relatives.

"Oh, Adam, darling." His mother patted his hand. "I am so sorry you learned of Victoria's betrothal in such a manner. I should have told you, of course, but . . . well . . . it is a shame. You were *such* a handsome couple. Why, when the two of you entered a room, it quite took my breath away. Your papa and I were like that. I remember once—"

"Enough, Mirabelle," his grandmother said. "The past is past. His *and* yours." She turned to her grandson. "Jenkins tells me you were not exactly yourself yesterday. True?"

"True," he said ruefully, "but Jenkins has no cause to carry tales."

"He did not. I asked him why you refused to see us. He merely answered my questions."

"Gussie, please do not abuse the poor boy. He has endured so much," his aunt pleaded.

"That's it, Aunt Jess. You protect me." He winked at her.

"Are you truly feeling better today, my dear?" his mother asked. "Or are you still feeling such pain? Should you not still be in bed?"

"Yes, Mother, I *am* feeling better. No, Mother, I am not in pain. And no, Mother, I should not still be in bed." His voice conveyed exaggerated patience.

"Well," the marchioness replied defensively, "it is just that I would not wish you to overextend yourself, love."

"Here, Adam," Lady Thornwood said. "Overextend yourself a bit on this." She handed him a ledger. "This will bring you up to date on estate matters. There are some decisions to be made."

"But, Gran, I have told you whatever you and Kendall decide is fine with me." He handed the book back to her, but she refused to take it. "I am not ready for this."

"An old woman and a steward have no business taking on all the responsibility for Thornwood when you are here and capable of doing it yourself," Lady Thornwood replied sternly.

"Perhaps it *is* too soon," Aunt Jess ventured. His mother nodded, her eyes clouded with concern.

"Nonsense," his grandmother said. "Ah, Mrs. Buford. Perhaps you can persuade his noble lordship here to forego his chess game to devote some time to estate business. Come, Mirabelle, Jess." She swept from the room with the others in tow.

"I shall try," Mrs. Buford said to her ladyship's retreating back. She turned to Adam and said, "Sir, I have brought you something."

"What?" he asked, suspicious.

"It is . . . well . . . it is an eye patch." She pulled from her pocket a swatch of black material from which dangled two black grosgrain ribbons.

"I beg your pardon?"

Her nervousness seemed to increase. "Well . . . I asked Rogers . . . he said your facial wound is healed, but I noticed you continue to wear the bandage and I thought . . . perhaps you . . . here it is. Rogers will help you put it on." With that, she thrust the bit of cloth into his hand and nearly ran from the room.

Caught totally off guard, he sat there nonplussed for a moment. His first instinct was to resent her drawing attention to his missing eye. Too nervy by half.

But then it occurred to him she saw a need and set about fulfilling it in a practical way. Certainly her recognizing and accepting his injury was more honest than his mother's delicate and ostentatious avoidance of the topic.

He examined the patch. It was fashioned of two layers of black fabric, a soft inner layer to go next to the skin and a more serviceable outer layer. He was moved by the thought and effort she had put into it.

"My lord?" Rogers asked.

"Here. Help me put this thing on, Rogers, then hand me a glass to see how it looks." This quickly done, he turned his head this way and that before the glass. "Hmm. Not too bad, eh? I mean, given the circumstances . . ."

"It looks fine, my lord."

"Get her back in here, Rogers, please."

She must have waited in the hall, for she returned almost immediately, though she was visibly nervous.

"Well, what do you think?" he asked brusquely, raising his head to give her a clear view.

"Truthfully?"

"Truthfully."

"I think you look very dashing, my lord. It lends a certain . . . roguishness, if you will."

"You mean I look like a pirate, do you not?"

She laughed. "Not exactly. But it *is* more fashionable than that bulky bandage."

"I thank you," he said softly. "I appreciate your thinking of this."

" 'Twas such a little thing, my lord."

"Not to me." He held her gaze for a long moment.

"How would you like to sit in the garden for a while?" she asked, in an apparent attempt to lighten the mood.

"The garden?"

"Yes. You know, that lovely place of trees, shrubs, and flowers. 'Tis really quite glorious, and it is a beautiful day. The sky is incredibly blue for a change, and the sun is warm."

"I do not think so," he said. "Too much trouble getting me down there." In truth, the idea of being on display for the entire staff unnerved him.

"No one will take any undue notice of you there," she said, almost as if she had read his mind. "You negotiate this room well enough now with your walking stick. Rogers can help you on the stairs. Or"—she looked at him archly—"we could get a footman to help carry you, if need be."

"That will not be necessary," he said stiffly.

"You will come, then? Surely you would enjoy the fresh air."

"Why do I have this feeling I am being manipulated?"

She smiled and batted her eyelashes in an exaggerated show of innocence. "Perhaps because you are."

He gave in. "All right. Being outdoors is a great temptation. But you knew that, did you not?"

She merely nodded and, grabbing up the ledger left by his grandmother, preceded him and Rogers out of the room.

Comfortable wicker chairs and a glass-topped table had been placed in a shady nook. When he had seated himself, Mrs. Buford handed him the ledger.

"I shall send your tea out directly, sir," she said. "Should you require anything, Peebles is just behind that hedge there, trimming roses."

He tried to concentrate on the ledger, but his mind kept drifting to anchor itself repeatedly on laughing brown eyes, sun-drenched brown hair with hints of red, and a serviceable gray gown that revealed more delectable curves than any mere cook should lay claim to.

How long had she been here? Less than three weeks, was it not? Yet he felt comfortable with her. It was almost as though he had been searching for and found a friend who could serve in Mason's place.

But that was nonsense, of course. One did not find that sort of friendship with a woman, and certainly not with a servant.

After that, it became routine for Lord Thornwood to spend much of each day in the garden, even taking his lunch there occasionally, though in general he now joined family meals in the dining room. He was walking more each day, despite some difficulty in negotiating stairs.

At first he stumbled often in walking even the simplest routes—not because of his leg injury, but because losing his eye had robbed him of depth perception and the ability to judge distances. He longed to go riding, but knew his leg had to be stronger before he dared face mounting his beloved black, Vulcan.

Mrs. Buford often joined him when she was free from her duties. Had he been so obtuse as not to know it was unusual for a peer of the realm to spend so much time with a cook, his mother's pointedly unsubtle remarks would have made that very clear to him. However, it had long been his custom to respond noncommittally to his mother's opinions and then do just as he pleased.

Now if *Gran* had said something, that would have been a different story. But he doubted he would give up Nicole's company even then. Having learned her given name, he now thought of her privately as Nicole, though he maintained strict propriety in her presence.

They sometimes played chess. At other times, she would read aloud to him when he suffered strain in retraining his one eye to do the work of two. They walked and talked and talked. He found himself telling her things he had not thought of in years and asking her view of certain estate matters. He loved to hear her laugh—loved the fact she made him laugh.

He rather thought their laughter was the real reason his grandmother made no objection to his attentions to a woman who, in ordinary circumstances, would be considered unsuitable. And what made her unsuitable? The mere fact that she earned her living as a cook?

He found her a delightful companion whose manners and behavior would have been agreeable in any lady of the *ton*. She carefully diverted most queries about her own family, background, and education, but her very conversation indicated she was well read in a variety of subjects. Unlike many of the so-called belles of Society who invariably deferred to male opinions, Nicole had her own views, and never hesitated to make them known.

Gran was like that. Perhaps this was another reason Lady Augusta turned a blind eye to a growing friendship that had no chance beyond the gates of this estate.

In any event, when it came to anyone's being unsuitable, the label had to apply to himself, he thought bitterly. Once considered a very attractive catch on the marriage mart, here he was—scarred, maimed, and already rejected by one of Society's chosen. Oh, no doubt there would be some sort of match eventually—his fortune would ensure that—but it would probably be an infelicitous affair for both parties.

Was he, indeed, just feeling sorry for himself? No, he

decided. There was such a thing as facing reality. But he wanted to postpone such reality as long as possible.

To this end, he continued to refuse all visitors, much to the consternation of his female relatives, who felt obliged to entertain any callers. Most who called were local gentry, but occasionally someone came from farther away, despite his having ignored all mail of a personal nature for weeks now. Even such distant callers were turned away.

He and Nicole were sitting on a bench in a far corner of the garden one afternoon, laughing over a disaster in the kitchen, when Jenkins approached with a salver bearing visitors' cards.

"My lord, there are two gentlemen and a lady asking to be presented. Say they are staying with Baron Fitzgibbons." Fitzgibbons was one of Thornwood's neighbors. "A Captain Marsten and his sister, and a Lieutenant Wilson."

"Why did you not simply tell them I do not receive guests?" Adam demanded harshly.

"They were most persistent, my lord, insisting in no uncertain terms you *would* see *them*."

"Well, go back and tell them again I am not at home to *anyone*." Angry at the would-be visitors, he also recognized that the source of his anger was his own reluctance to appear before any but the very limited circle he found it necessary to accept. In fact, the prospect of dealing with others' pity and sympathy caused him a measure of inner panic.

Caught up in his own emotions, it was several minutes before he became aware of the unusual silence of his companion.

"I take it you do not approve." His tone held a challenge.

"It is not my place to approve or disapprove, my lord."

"Oh, come now, Mrs. Buford. 'Tis not like you not to have an opinion."

"Well, all right." Her tone and expression carried an unspoken warning. "Are you sure you want to hear my opinion, sir?"

"I am sure."

"I think your continued rejection of your friends is an act of cowardice." The words tumbled over each other like brook water over pebbles.

"I beg your pardon! *Cowardice?*"

"That is my view. I know about the letters you do not deign to answer and all the visitors who have been turned away at the door."

"So what is that to say to anything? If I do not want to communicate with certain people, or have them impose on my privacy, have I not a right to reject them?"

"I doubt very much this is about your right to reject impositions," she said.

"Oh? And just what *is* it about?" he demanded sarcastically. He dreaded her answer, which was sure to be honest, but he was too angry not to hear it.

"I think you are afraid they will pity you," she said softly. "And *that* you just cannot stand. Your pride—and perhaps a bit of vanity?—simply will not allow anyone to feel sorry for you."

He was not angry with *her*, but he lashed out at her all the same. "Pity, disgust—what is the difference? And who cares? Why should I subject myself to becoming a freak show attraction?"

"Why should you *not* allow your friends to show you their support? They care about you. Of course they are sorry about what happened to you."

"Marsten should bring his sister in to cluck and coo over this shell of the man who was, is that it? Then she can turn her back and shudder in revulsion."

"How can you know she would react in such a manner?"

"Believe me, I know. Victoria was nearly ill seeing me. Even my own mother rarely looks at me directly."

"So you think everyone who comes in contact with you is disgusted by your appearance. Is that not an indication of extreme self-absorption?"

He gave a strangled snarl of impatience as she went on.

"And what about me? Do you suppose, in your infinite wisdom, I am sitting here feeling repulsed and disgusted? Not so, my lord!"

"Well, have a *real* look. Then tell me how you feel!" Furious, he jerked off the eye patch and thrust his face toward her.

She stared at him. Was she afraid? Appalled? No, she seemed to gaze at him with more curiosity than horror.

Then she placed a hand gently on either side of his face. Her touch sent spasms of warmth through him. She pulled his head closer and softly kissed the ravaged flesh.

Shocked and totally incapable of stopping himself, he clasped her tightly to him. His mouth closed on hers in a kiss that was deep, savage, and searching. At first she seemed stunned, but then, amazingly, he felt her responding, giving back an equal measure of passion and, yes, acceptance.

He pulled away first and stared at her.

"Oh, God, Nicole. I'm sorry. I never meant . . ."

"No. Don't. Don't apologize."

"But—"

"Please—don't." She was obviously shaken, but was it by anger or something else? "I . . . I . . . have to go. The evening meal . . ." She rose hastily and left.

"Wait," Adam called, but she was already gone.

Oh, good God! Now he had done it. He had just destroyed the best thing in his life lately, perhaps the best thing in his life ever—his friendship with this extraordinary woman.

SIX

Overwhelmed by her own reaction to Thornwood's kiss, Nicole avoided him the rest of that day and most of the next. Avoiding him was easy. She simply attended to matters in the kitchen or kept to her own room.

She was embarrassed at having precipitated the scene. She had wanted somehow to make him know his scarred face made little difference to anyone who cared for him. Her reaction had been as natural, as spontaneous as a mother's need to kiss away the hurt for a child.

But there had been nothing childlike in the fierce need of his response! The answering need in her own body—a primal, instinctive reach for fulfillment—came as a profound shock to her. She had been kissed before. She had been physically aroused before, but never to the point of losing control. Never like this.

Coward! she accused herself as she spent her free afternoon hours in her own room staring blankly at an open book. *Now* who was behaving in a craven manner, fearful of another's reaction? She wanted to be with him, to touch him, but she could not bring herself to face him. What must he think of her? Did he see her now as a lusty widow eager for a tumble with the lord of the manor?

She was vaguely aware of a good deal of activity among the principals of the Thornwood estate that day. She attributed the increased traffic to the marchioness's

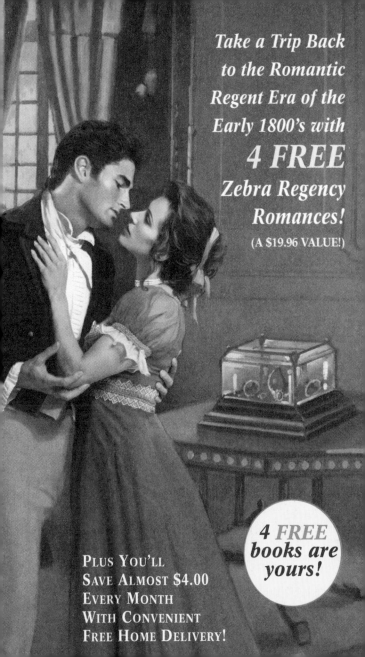

We'd Like to Invite You to Subscribe to Zebra's Regency Romance Book Club and Give You a Gift of 4 Free Books as Your Introduction! (Worth $19.96!)

If you're a Regency lover, imagine the joy of getting 4 FREE Zebra Regency Romances and then the chance to have these lovely stories delivered to your home each month at the lowest prices available! Well, that's our offer to you and here's how you benefit by becoming a Regency Romance subscriber:

- 4 FREE Introductory Regency Romances are delivered to your doorstep

- 4 BRAND NEW Regencies are then delivered each month (usually before they're available in bookstores)

- Subscribers save almost $4.00 every month

- Home delivery is always FREE

- You also receive a FREE monthly newsletter, which features author profiles, discounts, subscriber benefits, book previews and more

- No risks or obligations...in other words, you can cancel whenever you wish with no questions asked

Join the thousands of readers who enjoy the savings and convenience offered to Regency Romance subscribers. After your initial introductory shipment, you receive 4 brand-new Zebra Regency Romances each month to examine for 10 days. Then, if you decide to keep the books, you'll pay the preferred subscriber's price of just $4.00 per title. That's only $16.00 for all 4 books and there's never an extra charge for shipping and handling.

It's a no-lose proposition, so return the FREE BOOK CERTIFICATE today!

Say Yes to 4 Free Books!

Complete and return the order card to receive this
$19.96 value, ABSOLUTELY FREE!

If the certificate is missing below, write to:
Zebra Home Subscription Service, Inc.,
P.O. Box 5214, Clifton, New Jersey 07015-5214
or call TOLL-FREE 1-888-345-BOOK
Visit our website at www.kensingtonbooks.com.

FREE BOOK CERTIFICATE

YES! Please rush me 4 Zebra Regency Romances without cost or obligation. I understand that each month thereafter I will be able to preview 4 brand-new Regency Romances FREE for 10 days. Then, if I should decide to keep them, I will pay the money-saving preferred subscriber's price of just $16.00 for all 4...that's a savings of almost $4 off the publisher's price with no additional charge for shipping and handling. I may return any shipment within 10 days and owe nothing, and I may cancel this subscription at any time. My 4 FREE books will be mine to keep in any case.

Name _____

Address _____ Apt. _____

City _____ State _____ Zip _____

Telephone ( ) _____

Signature _____ RN070A
(If under 18, parent or guardian must sign.)

Terms and prices subject to change. Orders subject to acceptance by Zebra Home Subscription Service, Inc.
Offer valid in U.S. only.

ll...l...lll...ll.l.l.l.l..l.l..ll.l.l..l.l.l..ll.l.l..l

REGENCY ROMANCE BOOK CLUB
Zebra Home Subscription Service, Inc.
P.O. Box 5214
Clifton NJ 07015-5214

PLACE
STAMP
HERE

taking her leave in midmorning. Now that her son was on the mend, Lady Moresland was returning to her own home and her husband. When Jenkins ordered the kitchen staff to produce a more elaborate than usual tea tray in the afternoon, Nicole assumed Lady Thornwood and Miss Jessica were entertaining callers.

The evening meal had been served and the washing up was in progress. Nicole was making mental notes about tomorrow's menus and setting out the utensils they would need when Jenkins appeared. "His lordship would like to see you in the library, Mrs. Buford."

She tried to conceal her panic as she removed her apron and patted stray wisps of hair back under the cap she always wore in the kitchen.

"You wished to see me, my lord?" she asked on entering the library. He was standing near the fireplace.

"Yes. Please have a seat." When she had taken the chair he indicated, he took one opposite her. He gazed at her silently, and she thought he seemed as nervous as she felt. Finally, he said, "I missed you today. I regret that my conduct has made you uncomfortable."

She felt herself blushing, but she had to be honest. "Sir, it was not *your* behavior that gave me pause, but my own!"

He considered this a moment, then gave her a tentative smile. "You have nothing about which to upbraid yourself."

"But I never should have said those things to you. It was not my place, I know. I have always been a trifle impetuous, I am afraid."

"I admit your challenge angered me." He brushed his hand through his hair, ruining Rogers's efforts to keep him looking stylish. "I lay awake most of the night trying to justify my attitude." He paused. "I could not do so."

"Well, I do not concede I was *wrong* in what I said, merely that it was not my place to tell you."

This brought a quick laugh from him. "I see. Hold to your opinion, do you?"

She nodded and raised her chin. The levity had eased the tension, though.

"Well then, you will be glad to know I sent over to Fitzgibbons this morning to invite Marsten and Wilson to visit this afternoon. I even apologized for turning them away yesterday. We had quite an agreeable chat."

She felt a warm glow of pleasure at this news. "Oh, I am so very glad, my lord!" She knew what an act of courage it had been for him to face his friends.

"So. You were right, and I thank you for bringing me to a realization of the error of my ways." This was said lightly, in a mockingly pompous manner, but she recognized an undertone of utter sincerity.

"Quite all right, my lord. Anytime you feel in dire need of a set down, you may call upon me. What else are friends for?"

He laughed, then sobered. "That is what we are, is it not, Nicole? Friends?"

She felt a warm thrill at his use of her name. "Yes, I hope so."

"Then you will forgive my lapse in decorum?"

"There is nothing that warrants forgiving."

In the days following, Nicole had cause to regret the changes her own actions had brought, for now Thornwood spent many an afternoon playing billiards or cards with his friends. Occasionally, Captain Marsten's sister made a fourth for card games.

When one of the parlor maids made a casual observation about Miss Marsten's interest in Lord Thornwood, Nicole experienced a profound pang of sheer jealousy.

But what had she expected? She reminded herself she was, after all, the *cook*. Had she not already enjoyed extraordinary freedoms for one of her position in a household?

She had come to Thornwood on a lark. The wager was but another instance of harmless rivalry between her and Edward. It simply had not occurred to her she might form an attachment for her employer or the new household. Oh, she had not doubted she would get on well enough. All her life she had made friends easily. But all her life she had been straightforward, open, and honest.

Her position in Thornwood Manor was based on deceit.

In another two weeks the lark would be over, the game finished. Now when she thought of Mrs. Hankins, Lady Thornwood, the kitchen staff, and all the others with whom she worked so easily, guilt threatened to engulf her. How would they feel knowing they had been instruments in an elaborate hoax?

It was not intended as a hoax, Nicole argued with herself.

No, but the hoax was there all the same, an unforeseen, unwelcome—and inevitable—auxiliary to her joking competition with Edward.

More than all the others, she dreaded revealing herself to Adam Prescott, Earl of Thornwood. She admitted to herself that her feelings went beyond friendship, but the friendship, with its shared interests and easy laughter, had grown and blossomed. Would it now wilt under her own deceit?

Nor was this deception the only one to weigh on her conscience. The elder Jamisons and her father, the beloved Monsieur Thibaud, all believed her to be visiting a fictive friend from her school days, a certain N.—for Nancy—Buford, a relative of the Earl of Thornwood. Her weekly letters to maintain this illusion were harder and harder to write. Her father's letters disturbed her greatly, but she thought she had allayed his worries.

Thus it came as a profound shock when Jenkins sought her out one afternoon with the news that she had a visitor. "Mrs. Buford, there is a French gentleman waiting to speak with you."

"A . . . a Frenchman?" Nicole felt a stab of panic. "Did he give his name?" But she knew who it was.

"Calls himself Monsieur Thibaud. Seemed a cut above the ordinary by his dress and manners. I put him in the anteroom off the foyer, though normally you should receive your guest in the servants' hall, you know."

"Thank you." Nicole recognized this as a great concession from Jenkins, who was a stickler for propriety. Divesting herself of her apron, she hurried to the small room set aside as a reception room for unexpected guests.

"Monsieur?" Through the partially opened door, she saw him standing at a window, looking out at the spacious green lawn and circular driveway at the front of Thornwood Manor. A traveling cloak, his hat, and his gloves lay on a nearby chair. She quickly crossed the room to embrace him. "Papa!" she said softly.

He hugged her tightly, then stepped back to look at her disapprovingly. "Nicole, my only love. What is happening here? The butler did not recognize your name. Only when I mentioned your friend Mrs. Buford did he seem to have any understanding at all."

As had long been their custom when they were alone, they both conversed in French.

"Oh, Monsieur," she said, automatically using the form of address he had insisted upon for over a decade, "it is a long story."

"I should like to hear it. And to know precisely why you are dressed so unfashionably."

She recognized the stern tone he used when he absolutely would not be put off. She twisted her hands in front of her.

"Well . . . you see, I . . . I made this wager with Edward . . ."

"Go on."

"I criticized the food that is often served at *ton* functions. Edward asked if I really thought I could do better. I said of course I could. So we set this wager, you see, and . . . well . . . I am doing so!"

"Explain yourself more clearly, if you please."

"I . . . I . . . have charge of Thornwood's kitchen. I am the cook here." Oh Lord, she thought, this is worse than I imagined.

"You are *what?* Nicole, my darling girl, what you are saying? It cannot be true." Surprise and dismay echoed in his voice.

"I *am* sorry to distress you, but truly I am enjoying the work," she said, trying to placate him.

"This will never do," he said in the same stern voice he had used when she misbehaved as a child. "You must come away with me immediately."

"Please . . . allow me to stay."

Something in her voice or expression had touched him, for his own tone was more gentle as he replied, "Ah, Nicole, you must not. You will ruin all our plans."

"Please. Just give me a little more time. Then I will come with you."

"How much time?" he asked grudgingly, and Nicole knew she was getting a reprieve.

"Two more weeks," she said, so softly it came almost as a whisper.

"No! Never so long. Out of the question!"

"May we discuss this another time, then?" she pleaded, mindful of her duties in the kitchen.

"I am staying at an inn in the village. I shall come

back tomorrow and we will settle this business. But, Nicole, you must come with me, my love." He caressed her cheek.

"We shall discuss it tomorrow. I must go now." She hugged him again and rose on her toes to kiss his cheek. "Please, do not worry about me."

As she left the room, she was confronted by Lord Thornwood, leaning on his walking stick and looking through a stack of visitors' cards on a table in the foyer.

He gave her an enigmatic look. Had he overheard the conversation with her father? *Oh, please, not like this. It cannot end like this,* she prayed silently.

"Good afternoon, Mrs. Buford."

"My lord." Her heart in her throat, she felt her father's presence behind her and stepped aside. In English she said, "Allow me to present Monsieur Thibaud. He is . . . that is, he was my guardian before I came of age." Oh, dear—had that introduction been innocuous enough to satisfy the curiosity of both men?

"Welcome to Thornwood, sir." The earl extended his hand.

"Thank you, my lord. You have a beautiful setting here." He, too, had switched to English. He took the proffered hand and looked from the earl to his daughter.

"I must return to my duties," Nicole said, trying to hint her father out the door.

"Ah, yes." Monsieur Thibaud glanced from his daughter to the earl again and seemed about to say something more. But then he merely donned his hat and pulled on his gloves. "I shall see you tomorrow, my dear."

"Yes. Tomorrow."

She saw him out the door and down the steps to the waiting carriage, waved to him, then turned toward the kitchen. Her eyes locked momentarily with Thornwood's. Was it really pain and suspicion she saw there, or did her own guilty conscience project such feelings onto him?

"Mrs. Buford? Did your visitor upset you?"

"Upset me? Oh, no, my lord."

"I will not tolerate having a member of my staff needlessly distressed. If there is a problem, I should like to help, if I can."

"There is no problem. Please do not refine upon it, my lord. Now, if you will excuse me, I must return to the kitchen."

With that, she made her escape, but she knew the respite was temporary at best.

SEVEN

Adam gazed after her for a moment, then ran his hand through his hair and stamped into the library, hitting his cane emphatically on the marble floor with every step. He poured himself a snifter of brandy, gulped it down, then poured another and sat to drink it more slowly as he mulled over what had just transpired.

Who *was* this Frenchman? Adam had understood enough of the conversation to know the man was urging Nicole to run away with him. Good God! He was old enough to be her father!

True, she seemed reluctant to do as he wished, but the fellow seemed to have some sort of hold over her. Clearly she felt a great deal of affection for him, and he for her.

Adam was amazed at his own reaction to this discovery. He found himself in a murderous rage of jealousy such as he had never known. Victoria's determined efforts to arouse his jealousy by flirting with other men had merely amused him, and Victoria had been his affianced bride. But the idea of a committed relationship between his cook and the man she had introduced as her erstwhile guardian tied Adam's stomach in painful knots.

Guardian, indeed.

And what business is it of yours, Prescott? She is a

grown woman and, as a widow, is fully independent. Afraid you will lose your cook? he sneered at himself.

No! That was not it at all. If Nicole left, she would take something vital out of his life.

He brooded in this vein for some time, finally coming to a decision. He would fight like the very devil to keep her near.

The evening meal was a sumptuous affair, even though only Adam, his grandmother, and his aunt were at table. Lady Thornwood and her sister both praised the meal as being very tasty, but five minutes later, Adam could not have said what he had consumed.

He retreated to the library to ponder yet again the events of this day. He'd been spending less time in Nicole's company than he had before renewing his friendship with Marsten and Wilson. But in this case, out of sight definitely did not equate to out of mind. No matter what he did, where he was, or who his companions were, her image haunted him: Her brown eyes laughing, teasing, thoughtful, or concerned. The way she bit her lower lip in concentration, or tilted her head when she asked a question.

Most of all, he dwelled on her response to his embrace. Surely no other man could lay claim to that passion. *Your wanting something to be so—no matter how vehemently you wish it—does not ensure it will be,* he admonished himself.

But why was there this fierce need? True, he had been without a woman for a good many weeks. This, however, was not a question of the physical need for a woman, any woman. No. His body demanded, his heart ached for this *particular* female.

Good God! Was he in love with her? That had to be it. How had the great Adam Prescott, impervious as he was to real involvement with women, allowed this to happen? And when?

The answers came quickly enough. He'd had no choice, had not even realized it was happening until now. When? Of course. When she was bullying him to get well.

The cook? You are in love with your cook? How will that go over with other members of the House of Lords? Not to mention their wives or such notables of Society as the patronesses of Almack's.

Then Mason's image floated across his mind. "Adam, old man! After all we've been through, is that an important consideration?"

No, by God, it was not. In every way that mattered, she was eminently right for *him*.

Now, if he could only convince *her*—and possibly her Frenchman.

After one of the most fretful nights of his experience, and a meager breakfast—if several cups of coffee qualified as a bona fide breaking of the fast—Adam sent to the stables for a mount. He would have liked to take the black and ride like the wind, but not yet trusting his leg to stand up to the demands of controlling Vulcan, he settled for a more docile horse.

Still questioning his decision, but determined to carry on, he made his way to the only inn in the village. Having asked for Monsieur Thibaud, Adam was shown into a private parlor, where the Frenchman languished over a late breakfast and a newspaper.

"My lord," Thibaud greeted his unexpected guest, "may I offer you some breakfast? Perhaps a cup of coffee?" He indicated a seat.

"Thank you, no." Adam sat and eyed the man for a moment. Where to begin now that he was here? "I have come, Monsieur, on behalf of my cook, Mrs. Buford."

"Mrs. Buford?" The Frenchman seemed momentarily

confused, but quickly recovered and said, "Your cook. Yes?"

"Yes." Adam decided to face the issue head-on. "She seemed alarmed or upset by your visit yesterday."

"Did she?"

"Yes. She did." Adam made an effort to temper his disapproval. "And as she is an important member of my staff, I find it to be in my own interest to ensure her well-being. I confess I overheard some of your conversation yesterday. I should take it very much amiss if you, sir, managed to coerce her into leaving my employ."

"I see." Thibaud studied his visitor carefully and seemed to understand more than Adam had said. "Is your interest in my former ward solely in keeping a capable cook in your kitchen, my lord?"

The question conveyed only curiosity, no hint of challenge, but Adam felt himself strangely defensive. He hesitated, then replied, "Is that not reason enough for my concern?"

"Possibly. But you have not answered my question, my lord." Again, the tone was not challenging, but his gentle determination refused to be gainsaid.

"Nic—Mrs. Buford—is well-liked in my household. We should not like to see her ill-used—by anyone. Even a former guardian."

"I assure you, my lord, I have only the highest regard for your Mrs. Buford. Her interests are of utmost importance to me, and I would never condone *anyone's* using her ill." Now there *was* a challenge in the Frenchman's tone.

"Have I your word, then, you will not use extraordinary pressure to persuade her to leave Thornwood Manor?"

The Frenchman sat in thought for a moment, chewing absently on his lower lip, a habit that triggered a vague unease in the back of Adam's mind. Finally, Thibaud said, "I give you my word that when Nicole leaves her current position, she will do so of her own volition." Before Adam could expel a sigh of relief, Thibaud added, "However, I shall endeavor to persuade her to do so sooner rather than later."

Adam stood to take his leave. "Sir, I appreciate your frankness. Perhaps my own powers of persuasion will work to some influence over her decision."

"I doubt not they will, my son." They shook hands, and Adam fancied he saw a distinct twinkle in the other's eyes. But, of course, that had to be his imagination.

Knowing her father would return that afternoon, Nicole spent the entire morning silently rehearsing arguments she might use to appease his worries.

In the end, she took him to the garden to seat him in one of the wicker chairs there. She had had a pitcher of lemonade and an assortment of biscuits prepared. She poured glasses of the tangy drink for each of them and nervously took a seat opposite him.

She decided her best course of action would simply be the truth. She reiterated what she had told him of the wager with Edward.

"You know how Edward is, Pa—Monsieur," she quickly amended on seeing his raised eyebrow. "He would never allow me any peace."

"It was a monumental bit of foolishness to begin with, my girl."

"You are right, of course. But it was my fault as much as anyone's and, well, I simply cannot back down now when I am only two weeks from besting Edward."

"If besting Edward is your only reason, I am not convinced you have sufficient cause to stay on here. *Is* that your only reason?"

She tried to still her twinges of apprehension. "There

are other reasons. I confess I did not foresee all the consequences of this escapade. It was always so easy before. Now I need time to prepare the people here. My kitchen staff . . . Lady Thornwood. She has been very kind to me, you see."

"And his lordship?"

"He has been kind as well. Mind you, he can be stubborn and cantankerous, but he has had such hardships to overcome—" She hoped her father would not notice how her voice softened when speaking of Adam Prescott, but she proceeded to give him an account of Lord Thornwood's injuries, his grandmother's plea to do whatever it took to help him regain his strength, and his lordship's progress. "So you see," she added, "I should like to end it with them on as amicable a note as I may."

Sitting in quiet thought, her father struggled for the right words. Finally he said slowly, "You seem unduly concerned for the reactions of persons who are merely your employers."

"But we have become friends as well. Of course I am concerned. He has been through so much."

"He?"

She knew immediately she had revealed far more of her own feelings than she intended. "Lord Thornwood. His physical wounds are nearly healed. But I fear if I should leave abruptly, it would cause him some distress. I must find some way to explain all this to him."

"I see." His tone indicated he saw far too much. "I would not have you hurt, my dear."

She gave an airy little laugh that sounded somewhat brittle to her own ears. "Why should I be hurt? In two weeks I shall be back at the Jamisons' with Edward's twenty guineas in my pocket."

But her father was not through. "If someone of Society recognizes you here in this position, you will be quite undone, my dear. Is your standing—or the Jamisons'—such that you could withstand the inevitable gossip?"

"What could the gossipmongers possibly make of my stay here? Lady Thornwood and her sister have been here the whole time. His lordship's mother was here until a few days ago. And I have Milly with me. You remember my maid, Milly?"

"I remember her and I am glad to know you have her. But mine is still a valid concern," he insisted.

"His lordship rarely entertains. The only visitors he has permitted so far are army officers with whom he served in the Peninsula and Belgium—hardly social lions of the *ton*."

"All right. I give up. Reluctantly. But I shall be very glad to hear you are back with your English family."

"Thank you, Papa." She rose and, throwing her arms around him, kissed his cheek, then laughed to see the color rise in his face.

From a window in his chamber on the second floor, Adam looked down on the scene in the garden. He had not intended to spy on Nicole and her Frenchman, but having caught sight of them, he could not tear his gaze away.

He could not hear a word of what was said, but the way they looked at each other and their gestures told him volumes. Seeing Nicole impulsively kiss the other man sent a searing pain through his midsection. The fact that *she* kissed *him* was not lost on Adam.

Seeing Thibaud take his leave, Adam waited a while, then made his way to the garden himself. He found Nicole still there, her feet propped on an adjoining chair in what his mother would surely have said was a most unladylike manner. He thought it charming. There was an open book on her lap. She seemed to be dozing.

Hearing his step, she jerked fully awake. "You startled me, my lord."

"My apologies, ma'am. You looked so angelic there for a moment, too. I am out for a bit of exercise. Would you care to join me for a turn in the garden? We might lose ourselves in my grandmother's maze."

"That sounds dangerous," she quipped. "Perhaps I should ask Milly to join us."

"Never mind calling Milly," he said in a mock growl. "I shall provide you adequate protection from ogres and dragons."

"In that case, I shall be glad to join you."

They talked lightly, agreeing that yes, indeed, it was a lovely day, and that the book she had been reading was quite entertaining.

Then, attempting to be casual about it, he asked, "Did you enjoy your visit with your guardian?"

"He is no longer my guardian, my lord. Yes, we had a very pleasant conversation. We always do."

"You seem to hold him in very high esteem." Keeping his tone light was an effort as he remembered her kissing the fellow.

"Yes, I do. I have known him longer than any other person of my acquaintance."

"Old friends are best, eh?" Out of the corner of his eye, he caught a glimpse of her tilting her head questioningly.

"I should not think one would have to *compare* one's friends," she said, apparently conscious of her choice of words. "Each is to be valued for him—or her—self."

"You are right," he conceded, cursing himself for his jealousy. "I did not mean to suggest otherwise. So tell me, what do you value in this remarkable Frenchman?"

Her answer was immediate. No choosing special words here. "His wisdom, his generosity of spirit, his kindness, his loyalty. Most of all because he loves *me* unconditionally."

You had to ask, didn't you Prescott? That sick feeling was back, with a large dose of despair.

They had arrived at the center of the maze, in which was located a small gazebo. From every angle one looked on, a green wall and a swath of green lawn surrounded the gazebo. It was like being in a private bower. He steered her to a bench in the gazebo.

"And do you love him—'unconditionally?' " He held his breath for her answer.

"Yes," she said, and a huge fist closed tightly around his heart. Then she added, "But not the way you seem to mean." She twisted on the bench to lock her gaze with his. "He is . . . that is, I love him as I should love my father."

The fist unclenched.

"Then you are not planning to leave Thornwood Manor?"

She looked away. "Not for a while."

"That is a relief."

"Why? Is it not easy to replace a cook?" Was the lightness of her tone forced?

"Not one like you," he said, matching her light tone. "Who else would try to tempt me with salmon soufflé?"

"Salmon soufflé?" she asked dumbly.

He laughed and put his arm casually around her shoulders. "You, my girl, are irreplaceable!" Uh-oh. This was a huge miscalculation, he thought, catching the scent of roses and jasmine. She raised her head to look at him and he was undone.

Pulling her close, he lowered his mouth to hers and positively reveled in his triumph at her eager response. Then she pushed softly against his chest.

"You promised me protection," she chided.

"From ogres and dragons—not pirates." He grinned at her and quickly kissed her again.

"I . . . I must get back," she said. "This . . . uh . . . walk in the garden? It was not very wise, I think." She rose.

"Wisdom comes through experience. For me, this has been a most enjoyable experience."

"I did not say I didn't *enjoy* it, merely that it was not wise. Now, my lord, do show me out of this maze."

He wondered if she caught the double *entendre* of her request.

EIGHT

Nicole knew full well she could not walk away from Thornwood Manor as easily as she had arrived there. She would have to reveal the truth of who she was and why she was there. Her deception continued to eat away at her.

Moreover, the deception her father had perpetrated on the Jamisons began to trouble her with greater intensity. She had always regretted that perversion of the truth.

As a child, she had readily accepted her father's insistence it was necessary. As an adult, she knew her father's one lie had been born of pride and his concern for her. For her, though, the ruse had always rankled. She thought it demeaned her father, whom she admired deeply for the very reasons she had listed for Lord Thornwood.

Now she had herself intensified the deception by deliberately misleading Thornwood about the identity of Monsieur Thibaud. If lying about being a soldier's widow and insinuating herself into his household under false pretenses did not alienate Adam Prescott, surely the falsehood about her father would.

Her dilemma was complicated by the fact that only one of the lies was hers alone. To rectify the other one would betray her dear papa's efforts to launch his daughter properly in Society. In truth, Society's acceptance meant more to him than to her, but it was something *he* had set his heart on. Did she not owe him her support after all his sacrifices?

And now there was yet another complication as she faced up to her feelings for Adam Prescott, Earl of Thornwood. The thought of leaving the Manor and never seeing him again sent her into utter despair.

Many a night her self-recriminations and dreams of what might have been had her weeping into her pillow. Daylight would bring a new determination to make a clean breast of it with the earl and his grandmother.

But day after day, she clutched any available excuse to postpone the event.

Meanwhile, she continued to supervise meals that others told her were the best Thornwood Manor had ever tasted. Because Adam had mentioned it particularly, she produced the salmon soufflé again. Another hit was *escalope du veau,* veal in a cream sauce. She outdid herself on tempting desserts, which especially pleased the palates of Lady Thornwood and Miss Wainwright.

Every afternoon she slipped away from the kitchen to spend time with the earl. They never actually made an appointment to meet in the garden, weather permitting, or in the library if it did not, but neither failed the meetings now that Marsten and Wilson had returned to their own homes. These hours became the highlight of the day for Nicole and she thought they were for him, too. Realizing the idyll must end soon, she treasured their time together all the more.

Nicole knew the entire household was aware of the extraordinary amount of time she and the master spent together, but no one said anything. Occasionally, she caught Lady Thornwood eyeing her rather speculatively, but even her ladyship seemed content to leave things as they were for the nonce. The ladies would remove to London for the Little Season in the autumn, and the earl—by then surely fully recovered—would go with them.

There were no more kisses. It was, Nicole thought, as though both of them deliberately held back from such intimacies, perhaps for fear of destroying something fragile and precious. They took long walks together, sometimes talking animatedly, sometimes strolling in comfortable silence.

Nicole found it more and more difficult to deflect his questions about her own background and family. Many times an anecdote he related would spark a memory she longed to share. Sometimes she could alter the details enough to do so, but often she had to squelch her impulse. If he thought it strange she resisted speaking of her own life and childhood while encouraging him to go on and on about his own, he did not say so.

One day he finally talked openly of both his friend Mason and his former fiancée. Mason was, he told her, the most innately honest person he had ever known. And the quality that most appalled him in Victoria had been her willingness to pretend—in effect, to lie and mislead—to get what she wanted. These revelations had Nicole fairly squirming inwardly.

Occasionally their walks took them out to the stables, where Nicole made the acquaintance of Vulcan, Thornwood's favorite mount. His lordship always carried carrots, an apple, or lumps of sugar for what he called his frisky friend. Nicole thought this appellation a gross understatement, for the animal was feared by most of the stable hands.

"Ain't none but his lordship ever been able to handle that one," the youngest groom confided. "Ain't had *anyone* on 'is back since the earl got wounded."

"I hope you are not considering riding that great beast anytime soon," Nicole said to Thornwood as they walked back to the house one afternoon.

"Not until I am more nimble on my feet. Have to get rid of this first." He held up his walking stick.

"Good." There was relief in her voice.

"Don't tell me you were truly worried about me?"

"Not at all," she said tartly. "This entire household has been in a state of suspended animation since your injury. They do not need to have you incapacitated yet again merely because you have an unnatural disposition to court danger."

"I see." The twinkle in his eye belied his exaggerated seriousness. "Your concern is all for Thornwood Manor—never mind Thornwood himself. Is that it?"

"Of course," she said, matching his tone. "Have you not noticed how everyone on this estate watches your every move with only their own interests at heart?"

They paused under a great walnut tree whose heavy boughs hung low, partially obscuring them from view of the house and other buildings.

"To be honest, I care about the interests of only one heart at the moment." He dropped the walking stick and, taking her hand, leaned against the trunk of the tree, drawing her closer.

"My lord . . ." She had longed for his touch again, but, ever conscious she was an impostor, she had been apprehensive as well. However, she glided smoothly into his arms.

"Adam," he insisted softly.

"Adam," she breathed as his lips claimed hers.

Her arms went around his neck and she leaned into him, her breasts pressing against his chest. The kiss began with tentative sweetness, but deepened as his tongue probed and she readily welcomed him.

"Nicole. Nicole. I need you." He rained kisses down her neck, pausing at the hollow of her throat.

She pulled back, but did not disengage her body from

his. "My lord—Adam—I . . . we . . . must not do this."

"Why? You cannot mean your affections are engaged elsewhere. That I could not believe."

"Where my affections may lie is irrelevant, my lord."

"Not to me."

She pushed against his chest and he released her. "You forget who—what—I am." *And when you learn the truth,* she thought, *you will regret this very much.* She turned away so he would not see the tears welling in her eyes.

"So you earn a living as a cook. So what? All I care about is being with you, having you near."

"Oh, Adam. 'Tis impossible. Truly it is." She took a deep breath and turned back to him, but kept her eyes lowered lest he see how much she loved him. "Please, my lord, let us enjoy our friendship while we may."

He took her hand and was silent a moment. Then he sighed and placed a lingering kiss on her palm. "As you wish, madam." He curled her fingers over her palm, patted her hand, and heaved himself from the tree. He picked up the walking stick, offered her his arm, and said in a casual tone, "Shall we go?"

Nicole was devastated by this encounter. She knew he wanted her—now. And, Lord, how she wanted *him!* But she also loved him—and there had been no word of love from him, had there? What was more, he probably would cease even wanting her once he learned the truth. Still, she could not bring herself to destroy the tenuous relationship by telling him.

Two days later the matter was taken out of her hands.

The sky had been overcast most of the day, threatening rain, but never quite making good on the threat. In the afternoon, Thornwood sent to the kitchen to demand

Mrs. Buford—his only available opponent—report to the library for a game of chess. Her kitchen duties satisfied at the moment, Nicole was happy to escape the bickering of two kitchen maids who both had a *tendre* for the same footman.

On reporting to the library she said, "I do thank you for your gracious invitation, my lord."

"Liked that, did you? I have always heard women like to be ordered around."

Well aware he was teasing to get a reaction from her, Nicole merely rolled her eyes heavenward.

"Do you not agree," he pressed, "that strong, masterful males are the most attractive?"

"Oh, yes." Her tone was solemn. "I read once that among baboons and other species of monkeys, the dominant male often exerts his authority by roaring loudly and pounding his chest."

He threw back his head and laughed heartily. "Now that I have you here"—he gestured at the chessboard—"I promise not to roar or pound my chest unless I win."

They were halfway through the second game when Jenkins interrupted to hand his lordship a salver containing calling cards which Adam looked at briefly. "Send them in, by all means." To Nicole, he said, rising, "A young man I met at some sporting events in the spring. He has his sister with him, it seems. Will you mind finishing this game later?"

"Not at all. I should be going anyway." She grinned at him and added, "Do all your gentlemen friends have available sisters?"

He chuckled. "But of course. Makes the trials of the social whirl much easier to bear, you know."

As she neared the door, Jenkins ushered the visitors in. Nicole drew in a sharp breath and cried, "Oh, no!"

"Oh, yesss," Edward and Catherine Jamison trilled together.

"Did we surprise you, Cuz?" Edward asked.

"Well, of course we did—can you not tell?" Catherine answered for Nicole. "But we are being rude to Lord Thornwood."

"Sorry, Prescott," Edward said. "The chit's quite right. May I introduce my sister, the Honorable Catherine Jamison? You already know my cousin."

"Miss Jamison." Adam bowed stiffly in Catherine's direction. "Your cousin?" he asked woodenly.

"Nicole. Nicole Elisa Maria Beaufort. Oh, I say!" Edward finally seemed to comprehend the shock on both Adam's and Nicole's faces. "Nicole, am I to understand he does not know? You have not told him?"

"Told him *what?*" Adam's voice had a dangerous undertone as he leveled a fixed stare at Nicole.

"I . . . uh . . . you see . . ." she stammered.

Edward interrupted. "We had a wager. I bet her twenty guineas she could not last six weeks as a cook." He turned to Nicole and handed her a purse. "Your time was up three days ago, Nicole. Never let it be said I do not pay debts of honor promptly."

Nicole accepted the purse with the same enthusiasm she might have greeted a sack of garbage.

"I see." Adam's expression was unreadable, but the bitter irony cut into her heart as he added, "Well, Mrs. Buford, you have had quite a joke at the expense of the entire Thornwood household, have you not?"

"Please, my lord. Allow me to explain." She reached out to touch his arm, but he brushed her off.

"Jamison just did," Adam said coldly. "Now, if you all will excuse me? I am sure you have *family* matters to discuss."

"Adam, wait—please," Nicole called, but he was already out the door. A vital part of her being had been ripped away, leaving ragged, raw edges. She buried her face in her hands.

Edward stepped near and took her in his arms. "Ah, Nikki, I am sorry. Seeing you here in the library with him, I just assumed he knew all about it. Lord, if I'd had *any* idea . . ."

Catherine looked at her cousin shrewdly. "You are in love with him—with Lord Thornwood—are you not?"

Nicole took a deep breath, and still her voice quavered. "Yes. Yes, I am. And now I have gone and ruined everything."

"Well, we helped, I think," Catherine said. "But surely he will come around."

"I am not certain he will. Not certain at all. He has been through so much, you see."

"Go after him," Edward urged. "You were always able to bring *me* out of a case of the blue dismals."

"I think this goes beyond just feeling blue-deviled," Nicole responded.

At that moment Lady Thornwood came into the library. Nicole quickly introduced the Jamisons, noting that they were her cousins. She waited for the disgust and anger she expected from the countess.

"Your cousins?" her ladyship echoed, observing closely the fashionable apparel Edward and Catherine wore. "Jamison. Jamison. Is your father Viscount Leighton, then?"

"Yes, my lady, he is," Edward responded politely.

"Then what are *you* doing in our kitchen?" Lady Thornwood asked Nicole sternly.

Embarrassed and feeling profoundly guilty, Nicole explained the wager briefly.

" 'Twas all my fault, my lady," Edward interjected. "I should have known Nikki could never resist such a challenge."

"Edward, there is enough blame for both of us, but the greater share is mine," Nicole protested. "I am so very sorry, my lady. I would never have intentionally hurt you or Adam . . ." Her voice trailed off as she saw the countess's eyebrows rise at the cook's use of Thornwood's given name.

Then, to Nicole's surprise, Lady Thornwood chuckled. "So this is why my grandson left the house in such a towering rage a few minutes ago. I do not know when I have seen him in such black looks."

"Oh, dear," Nicole whispered hoarsely. "He . . . he would not allow me to explain . . ."

"He needs some time to cool off, my dear," the countess explained matter-of-factly.

"Are you not angry with me at all?" Nicole asked, awed by her ladyship's calm acceptance of the turn of events.

"I suspected from the outset you were from a much higher level of society than you admitted to. Education and breeding have a way of asserting themselves," Lady Thornwood replied. "When I saw what you had done for Adam, I could only be grateful. And . . . I think he still needs you."

"Go after him, Nikki. Do." Catherine added her voice to her brother's urging. "Edward and I will stop at the local inn to await word from you."

"No," Lady Thornwood said. "You will, of course, stay here. I shall have rooms prepared for you, and *we* shall have a nice tea." She turned to Nicole. "My grandson was headed for the stables when I saw him last. As a little boy he would go off to sit by the lake in the southeast corner of the property. You will need to procure a mount from the stable yourself. You do ride, do you not?"

"Yes, I do," Nicole said. Impulsively, she kissed the older woman's parchment-like cheek. "Thank you, my lady."

NINE

Adam Prescott, tenth Earl of Thornwood, was in a rare taking. He was furious with Nicole, who had played him for a fool. Even as he was allowing himself to feel again, to be once more vulnerable to genuine emotions, she had been merely engaged in a giant joke, a hoax. As angry as he was with her unfeeling behavior, he was even more furious with himself for having been suckered into her game.

She had played it well, he had to give her that. Why, he had even fancied himself in love with her. Hell! Bloody hell! He *was* in love with Nicole, as he had never been in love with Victoria. And that, of course, made Nicole's betrayal infinitely more insidious.

After leaving the library, he went first to his own chamber, where he paced the room for a time, swearing and berating himself for being so gullible. Then, abruptly, he changed into riding clothes and dashed out to the stables with as much speed as his fury and his lame leg allowed. He ordered Vulcan saddled, overriding the stable hands' concern with nothing more than a dark, furious glare.

"Shall I come with you, my lord?" one of them asked tentatively, giving him a hand up.

"No. I do not need—nor do I want—a nursemaid! That means no chasing after me, either. Is that clear?"

"Yes, my lord."

With little urging, perhaps sensing the rider's agitation, the black stormed across the countryside at a pace the devil himself might have envied. Adam tried to clear his mind of all but the wind in his face and the horse beneath him, to no avail. No matter how fast he went, *her* face—those enchanting brown eyes—rose to haunt him.

Unaware of actually directing his mount, Adam had no destination in mind, but Vulcan seemed to. Ahead of them was Adam's favorite childhood retreat. The lake, with its rocky outcroppings and overhanging trees, had been a marvelous playground for him and Mason. How many red Indians had they fought off, the two of them, against overwhelming enemy forces? This peaceful refuge had also provided solace for childish hurts and adolescent woes.

He patted the horse's neck. "You knew where we were going, didn't you, old fellow?" The horse snorted in response. Adam dismounted, tied the reins loosely to a bush, and found his favorite spot looking out on the water, made a deeper blue today by the leaden sky.

Stupid. He had been a right proper cods-head, an addle-cove, as Mason would have said. Had there not been clues enough that Nicole was not what she seemed? Her reluctance to speak of her family or her past should have tipped him off. Her knowledge of history, literature, even court matters. Her accent, for God's sake. How many English cooks spoke with the refined tones usually gained in a girls' finishing school or from a conscientious governess?

How *could* he have overlooked such clear indicators of who and what she was—and was not? Had he been gulled by a pretty face and an enticing body? He recalled how her eyes were mercurial in changing with her emotions. He remembered the feel of her in his arms and cursed himself that even now his own body stirred at the memory. Her response to his kisses—had that, too, been part of the grand joke?

Nicole found him seated on a huge boulder, apparently oblivious to everything around him. Without pausing to change her clothes or even grab a shawl, she had rushed out to the stables, where the grooms needed little persuasion to find her a suitable mount once they understood her mission.

She had to find him. She had to make him understand. These thoughts beat a cadence in her mind in tune with the hoofbeats of her horse.

She was nearly on top of him before the sound of her approach seemed to penetrate his musings. As she pulled up and slid awkwardly to the ground, he rose to face her.

"What are *you* doing here? Come to gloat, have you?"

"No. I came to explain—and to apologize."

"What persuades you to believe I would find your explanation credible," he sneered, "or that I would welcome an apology—which is likely to be as false as everything else about you?"

"Not everything about me is false." She walked toward him until he was almost within arm's reach.

"Hah!" He turned away from her, his body rigid with anger. "I have no need to hear anything you have to say, so you may as well go."

"But I need to tell you—to explain . . ."

Turning back, he cut her off. "Can you not understand? I am not interested in any more lies, my *dear* Mrs. Buford—but that, too, is a lie, is it not? You were never Mrs. anyone, were you? The soldier husband never existed, did he?"

"No," she said softly. "We—I—thought it would be easier for a widow to secure a position."

"One more lie would make little difference, eh?"

"Please, my lord. You are making this very difficult. I never intended to hurt anyone."

"Ah, bless you for your good intentions." His voice fairly dripped with sarcasm. "You do recall that good intentions are said to be the cobblestones of the road to hell, do you not?"

"I see," Nicole said, anger finally overriding her guilt, "that you still spend much of your energy focusing on yourself. You feel so sorry for poor Adam over what you perceive to be my perfidy that you cannot even bring yourself to consider an explanation or accept my sincere apology. Very well, my lord, I shall leave you to wallow in your self-pity." She whirled back toward her horse.

He raised his voice. "You lied to me, to Gran, to Aunt Jess, to my mother—to my entire household!"

Slowly, she turned toward him again. Her voice was calm, matter-of-fact. "Yes, I did. And I was profoundly sorry for doing so even before Edward blurted out the truth." She raised her eyes to hold his gaze. "But how important was it, my lord? Indeed, your grandmother has already forgiven me. I doubt not the rest will at least try to understand. It . . . it seemed so harmless at first . . ." Her voice trailed off in the face of his continued silence.

Finally, he said, "Everything was just a harmless mismanagement of the truth—a lark, is that it?"

"Not *everything*." She made no attempt to keep what was in her heart from showing in her eyes. "In the beginning it *was* a lark—not unlike previous challenges Edward and I have tossed at each other." Her mouth softened in the beginning of a smile at memories, but then she sobered. "But this time, it was different. I never expected . . ." She looked away.

"Never expected *what?*" He took a step toward her and grasped her shoulders to make her face him. "Never expected what?" he repeated harshly.

"I never expected to fall in love with you," she stated bluntly. "There. Now you know. The last triumph is yours, my lord." She gave a bitter little laugh and jerked away from him.

He was too quick and too strong for her. He locked her in his arms. "Say that again."

"Why?" She held herself stiffly, trying to quell the longing as every fiber of her being welcomed his embrace. "Why? So you can throw it back in my face?"

"Say it," he demanded savagely.

"All right!" She pushed against his chest, but he refused to release her. "I love you. And *that,* my lord, is not a lie! You win." Her voice caught on a sob.

Stunned, Adam lifted her chin and stared into her eyes. What he saw there completely obliterated the pain and despair he had felt only moments before.

"Ah, Nicole—" He gathered her closer and kissed her fiercely, his mouth assaulting hers, demanding, probing. She responded in kind, bringing her arms up to encircle his head and hold him close. He gave a low groan in his throat and his lips softened to caress and nibble. "Oh, God, Nicole. I love you, too. I could not stand the idea of losing you—what we had together."

She leaned back in his arms. "Then you forgive me for deceiving you?"

"At this point, I could forgive you almost anything."

"Almost?" she teased.

"Well—yes. I still have lots of questions. Happily, I do not need to know about a husband—but what about that blasted Frenchman?"

"Frenchman?" she echoed.

"Thibaud." His voice was impatient. "For a *former*

guardian, that fellow seems to have an inordinate interest in you."

Nicole giggled. "And so he does." Then she was serious. "Oh, Adam, you needn't be jealous of Monsieur Thibaud. Truly you need not."

"I am *not* jealous." It was a gruff denial of the obvious.

"Really? Now who is telling a lie?"

"All right. I admit it. I want you only for myself. I absolutely refuse to share."

"Your wish is my command, oh lord and master," she said through a joyous laugh and kissed him lightly.

"Since when?" His grin belied his disbelieving tone, and he caught her lips in another deep kiss that successfully changed the subject. Then he said, "This *does* mean you will marry me, does it not?"

"Is that a proposal, my lord?"

"It was meant to be. Now—*will* you marry me?"

"Yes. Yes. A thousand times, yes!" After another lingering kiss, she said, "We must get back. Everyone is worried about your being out here alone on that great black beast."

"You mean my friend, Vulcan? But he's a pussycat."

"Oh, I am sure." Her voice was heavy with irony.

"He is. See for yourself." He tossed her onto Vulcan's saddle and, leading the black over to the boulder to use as a mounting block, he climbed on behind her. He leaned down to catch the reins of the other horse and, hugging Nicole to him, urged Vulcan in the direction of the stables.

On the return ride, Nicole felt herself as happy as she had ever been in her life. Their conversation was punctuated by a kiss now and then, but she explained fully about the wager and answered questions about her life with the Jamisons. In the back of her mind, however, there was still the one great lie she had not cleared up for Adam—Monsieur Thibaud's true identity.

"So—do I apply to Viscount Leighton for permission to marry you?" Adam asked. "Is he likely to refuse me? In which case, my love, I would be forced to abduct you and carry you off to Gretna Green."

Nicole laughed. "He would not refuse you. Uncle Jamison has never refused me anything I wanted—ever. And I *do* want you, Adam Prescott." She kissed him and then added, "In any event, it is a moot question, for I *am* of age, you know. We need no one's permission to marry."

"Still, I would do the polite thing," Adam insisted. "I would not wish to incur resentment or hard feelings in your relatives."

Nicole bit her lip. This was the perfect opening to tell him, but since that secret belonged to her father as much as—or more than—to her, she could not share it until she had written Monsieur Thibaud news of her engagement.

"We will sort it out later, I am sure," she said.

At that point, they arrived back at the Thornwood stables, where the grooms were visibly relieved to see the master's return—and not a little curious to see him riding double with Mrs. Buford. Curiosity gave way to carefully subdued amusement when Nicole's mount was seen to be suffering no lameness or other injury.

Adam chuckled as he and Nicole strolled toward the house. "The servants' hall will be abuzz tonight, my dear."

She elbowed him playfully in the ribs. "And you will not be there to share the brunt of their curiosity with me."

"Nor will you be there ever again. Starting now—to-night—you take your meals at *my* table."

"May I please oversee the preparation of meals, my

lord?" she asked with exaggerated meekness. "At least the next few?"

He agreed, but first there was the matter of informing Edward and Catherine, Lady Thornwood, and Aunt Jess of their news. They found these four in the drawing room languishing over the remains of afternoon tea. None of them seemed overly surprised.

Amidst the congratulations and best wishes, Lady Thornwood ordered up champagne to toast the engagement. Then Adam accompanied Nicole to the kitchen, where their news—in the way of servants' grapevines—had preceded them.

"Oh, miss, how wonderful. Does this mean I may go back to being a lady's maid?" Milly asked. "I do so hate the washing up in the kitchen."

Nicole and Adam laughed. He winked at Milly and said, "Yes—and you can stop playing chaperon, too."

The next two days passed in a whirlwind of idyllic bliss for Nicole. She dispatched letters to her father and to the elder Jamisons, and she knew Adam had written his mother. Adam would have had the wedding immediately by special license, but he was persuaded to wait. It would take place at Thornwood's own village church—after a proper reading of the banns.

Meanwhile, Nicole would return to the Leighton estate with Edward and Catherine. The Jamison family, along with a number of other guests, would descend on Thornwood Manor in a matter of weeks.

TEN

Three weeks later, the Thornwood drawing room rang after dinner with the laughter and conversation of upward of a dozen people. Nicole had returned, bringing her aunt and uncle Jamison, Edward and Catherine, and Monsieur Thibaud with her. In addition to Lady Thornwood and Aunt Jess, Adam's family gathering had swelled to include his mother and her husband and his two sisters and their spouses.

Adam wondered privately at the inclusion of the Frenchman, but, secure in his knowledge of Nicole's love, he did not bring it up as an issue. If she wanted the man there, so be it.

The talk was, of course, all of the wedding, with each woman offering detailed suggestions and each man commiserating with Adam over the fuss and ceremony required for a man to be properly leg-shackled.

Adam's mother delighted in being the highest-ranking woman in the room. The marchioness had suggestions for every aspect of the wedding, considering it nothing less than her due when Nicole and Adam accepted her ideas and pouting prettily when they did not. Whenever she spoke, the marchioness managed to command everyone's attention.

"Your father and I had a marvelous wedding trip to Rome," she said to Adam, ignoring her husband's rather chagrined expression. "You would do well to do the same, my son."

"I am taking my bride back to her native country for a visit. We shall travel to Paris via Reims," he replied in a firm voice which discouraged further discussion of that point.

"Oh, well . . ." His mother gave an elegant shrug and went on to another topic. "Since that Mason boy is no longer with us, you should ask the Duke of Claremont to stand up with you, Adam." Oblivious to her son's pain at the mention of Mason, she went blithely on. "Claremont wields a great deal of power in Parliament. Asking him would be a clever move on your part."

"Perhaps it would, Mother—*if* I were interested in using my marriage to make some sort of political statement. But I am not. I have asked Captain Marsten to act as groomsman. He and his sister will arrive tomorrow."

"Oh. I see. Well." She turned her attention to Nicole. "And who will give the bride away? I assume it is to be the Viscount Leighton, though your Cousin Edward could perform that service just as well, my dear Nicole. Or, should you prefer it, I am sure Moresland would agree to perform as surrogate father."

Adam looked at Nicole with a sympathetic twinkle. She seemed momentarily taken aback, but she answered his mother calmly.

"I do appreciate your concern about this matter, my lady, and I thank the marquis for his willingness to perform such a service for me, but it will not be necessary to impose on him so."

"So, which is it to be? The viscount? Or his son?" the marchioness persisted.

Nicole cast a worried look at Adam. She and the Jamisons had arrived only that day. She and Adam had had precious little time alone together and had spent little of what they did have discussing wedding details. He saw her glance from him to Monsieur Thibaud, and the Frenchman suddenly looked distinctly alarmed.

"Neither," Nicole replied to the marchioness.

"Neither? Then who?"

Adam marveled that his mother could sound haughty and rudely curious at the same time.

The Frenchman gave Nicole a silent "no," but she ignored him and turned her gaze to lock with Adam's.

"I thought to ask my father to give me away," she said, her voice soft, but clear and determined.

"Your father!" several voices questioned and expostulated simultaneously.

"Your father?" the marchioness repeated. "But I . . . we understood your father was deceased."

"My father." Nicole's voice was stronger now as she took the arm of Monsieur Thibaud. "Allow me to present my father, Monsieur Jean-Pierre Armand Beaufort, *le comte* D'Arcy."

"Nicole, my dear, we agreed—" the newly acknowledged *comte* said, but Nicole interrupted him.

"No, Papa. *You* agreed—but I refuse to go through the rest of my life living with your invention, no matter how well-meaning it once was. You are my father, and I love you dearly." Tears shimmering in her eyes, she hugged him tightly.

Adam moved to stand near her. "You little minx," he said softly. "You let me go on believing . . . why, I ought to . . ." His voice lowered to a whisper for her alone. "Never fear, my love, I *shall* devise a most exquisite punishment for you. No need to be jealous, indeed!"

She smiled at him tremulously as he offered one

hand to Beaufort and slipped the other around Nicole's waist.

"Welcome to Thornwood, sir," Adam said. "I must say, I like you better as her father than as the erstwhile guardian."

"Thank you, my lord." Beaufort's eyes twinkled merrily.

"Oh, Adam," Nicole said, "I was so very afraid you would be angry. I wanted to tell you, but I felt I had to discuss it with Papa first. Truly—I swear to you—this is the last lie between us." Her voice trailed off.

Adam squeezed her waist more tightly for a moment and whispered into her hair, "We will discuss it later, my darling. Right now, we must deal with this bombshell you have dropped." He released his hold, but remained standing next to her.

"I cannot believe this." Catherine's voice held more wonder than resentment. "You held this from Edward and me all these years?"

"And here I thought she could never keep a secret," Edward said with a laugh. "Your eyes always give you away, Nikki."

"Lord Leighton," Beaufort said, "I feel I must apologize to you and offer you an explanation."

"No need, Beaufort. I am glad it is finally out in the open."

"You *knew?*" His niece and his two children spoke in unison. His wife smiled complacently.

"Yes. I am sorry, Thibaud—uh, Beaufort. I had you investigated soon after you brought Nicole to us. She is the image of her mother, so there was no doubt Nicole was my sister's child. But we did wonder about the fate of her father. I learned the entire Beaufort family, save one younger son, died in the Terror. There was no trace of *his* death, and his description fit you, so . . . I did share the information with my wife, but we agreed to respect your privacy."

"I thank you, sir," Beaufort said. "You are as generous in spirit as ever your sister—my dear wife—said you were. I regret I did not confide in you."

"A *comte*. Oh, how nice," the marchioness gushed, thus breaking the tension. "Adam, darling, your bride has rank equal to your own."

"Rather surprising for a cook, eh, Mother?"

"Oh, well. Least said of that, the better," his mother said dismissively.

"Mirabelle!" Lady Thornwood's impatience was clear. "Do try not to be such an inveterate snob." The countess came to Nicole and hugged her. "I liked you just fine as the cook. You gave me back my grandson."

"Thank you, my lady," Nicole said softly.

The rest of the evening passed in a haze for Nicole. She heard her father explaining his refusal to trade on a French title that had little meaning in England. He had not wanted to join the ranks of French aristocrats eking out their useless existence dependent on the largesse of English connections.

Yes, he earned an honest living as a chef now. His quiet pride and his adoration of his daughter had brought the entire company around. Finally, late in the evening, the drawing room group broke up.

"I would have a word with you before you retire," Adam said quietly to Nicole. "Please meet me in the library after you have said your good nights."

Curious and a little apprehensive, she reported a few minutes later as he had requested.

"You wished to see me, my lord?"

He enfolded her in his arms. "And hold you," he murmured against her neck. "But you must stop 'my lording' me, love. You sound like a servant." He kissed her, caressing her back and drawing her closer.

"Yes, my lord—I mean Adam," she said, obviously teasing with her mistake. "But I am—that is, I *was* the cook."

"Was. Gran found a replacement."

"That easy, was it? And here I was laboring under the impression good cooks were hard to find."

"They are." He chuckled and steered her to a chair in which he sat, pulling her down on his lap. "Gran stole our new cook from the Duchess of Renlynne and is paying her an exorbitant salary. But Gran thinks it a great coup over an old rival. The Duchess is apparently very temperamental—abused the cook."

"Oh, dear. I hope the *cook* is not temperamental, too."

"I do not think she is, but why should it matter as long as she supplies us with decent meals?"

"Because, my lovable dense one"—she took his face between her palms and brushed a kiss across his lips— "I would be immensely unhappy were I to find myself unwelcome in the kitchen. I truly love to cook, you know. I should hate to give it up entirely."

"You may do as you wish, my dear." He ended a long, passionate kiss by tickling her in the ribs. "Now, about this 'Monsieur Thibaud' business . . . you put me through hell—well, purgatory, anyway."

"Adam, stop." She giggled. "Stop now. I am not responsible for your jumping to conclusions."

"Nor did you disabuse me of them. And believe me, woman," he said seductively, "you will pay for that bit of deceit."

"Promises, promises," she whispered. "In a few days, I shall be glad to pay the debt in full."

"Never. It will never be paid in full. 'Tis indeed a

tangled web you weave. I intend to stay caught and demand payment forever."

"Good. Then I can give up my practice to deceive."

Nicole's Salmon Soufflé

For four servings:

3 tbsps butter or margarine	1 can (7-8 oz) salmon
3 tbsps flour	1 tbsp finely chopped
1/2 tsp salt	shallots
dash of white pepper	1 tbsp finely chopped
1 c milk	chives
6 egg yolks	6 egg whites

Melt butter in saucepan over medium heat. Stir in flour, salt, and white pepper. Add milk and bring to a boil, stirring until thickened. Remove from heat.

Beat egg yolks until thick and lemon colored. Slowly add the hot white sauce to the egg yolks, stirring constantly. Stir in salmon (flaked, skin and bones carefully removed), shallots, and chives.

Beat egg whites to form stiff peaks. Carefully fold into the fish mixture. Pour the resulting blend into an ungreased 1 1/2-2 qt. soufflé dish.

Bake at 325 degrees F about 45 minutes—or until a knife inserted in center comes out clean.

Note: You may substitute canned lobster, crab, or tuna for salmon and parsley for the chives. The six egg *yolks* may be reduced to three, but do *not* reduce the egg whites.

Mushroom Sauce
for Nicole's Salmon Soufflé

2 tbsp chopped shallots
2 tbsp butter or margarine
2 tbsp flour
1/4 tsp salt
dash of white pepper

1 1/4 c milk
1 small can sliced
mushrooms
1 1/2 tsp fresh snipped
parsley

Sauté chopped shallots in butter or margarine until shallots are translucent. Do not brown them. Stir in flour, salt, white pepper, and milk. Cook over medium heat, stirring constantly until thickened. Stir in mushrooms and fresh snipped parsley.

Note: You may substitute dill for the parsley.

NOT HIS
BREAD AND
BUTTER

by

Jo Ann Ferguson

ONE

"Are you ready for me, my lord?"

Percival Dunstan stirred in his bed and smiled at the delicate voice sifting through the dream that had not quite disappeared. The voice created new fantasies to flitter into his mind as he was poised between sleep and waking.

"Yes, I am ready for you." His smile widened. Her soft tones had been enough to take care of that, for they would rouse even the most oblivious of men.

"Where would you like to have this?"

Ah, her voice was lovely. "Here would be fine."

"But, my lord, it is so hot."

"Then disrobe and—"

At a gasp and the clatter of china, he rolled over and sat up to see the determined sway of a gray skirt and white apron sash heading toward the door. Dash it! He leaped off the bed and after her.

"Meredith!"

For a long moment, he thought she would not pause. Then she faced him, her arms folded in front of her, but he could see her trembling fingers. Her raven hair was pulled back in a demure bun, save for a trio of strands that, as always, had slipped out to follow the length of her neck. Her eyes, the same deep gray as her simple gown, sparked with anger.

"I am sorry, Meredith," he said.

When she averted her eyes, he looked down to see he wore no more than his nightshirt. He pulled on a pair of breeches and motioned for her to come away from the door. "I did not mean to suggest anything I shouldn't."

"You did not *suggest*. You were quite clear."

Dash it! She was not going to allow him to apologize and get out of this gracefully. He would like to have laid the blame for all this at his father's feet, but he could not. Yes, the previous Lord Westerly had let Westerly Manor fall into disrepair and had let most of the staff go while he took to his deathbed. Yes, his father had allowed those who remained free rein to speak their minds in a way unheard of among the Polite World.

But this was not his father's fault. He should not have let Meredith's soft voice tempt him into voicing what he had kept hidden since she first brought him his breakfast tray earlier this week. No woman should have hair so black and eyes such a lustrous silver. Not even the drab uniform of the servants could lessen the color in her cheeks, which was higher because of her vexation with him, or the gentle curves beneath the gray gown.

"You are correct, Meredith." He motioned toward the tray. "Will you be so kind as to set out my breakfast before I do something else to send you flying up into the boughs?"

She smiled and crossed the room to where she had left the tray—so loudly—by the settee, where he liked having his breakfast while he read the local newspaper. On rare occasions, a copy of one of the London papers was included for his enjoyment.

"You did sound as if you were half asleep, my lord." She poured coffee into a cup and fixed it as he preferred it.

He had not had to remind her once that he wanted a

little extra sugar in his first cup of the morning. Taking the cup from her, he sat on the settee so he could watch as she arranged his breakfast plates on the low table. He chuckled. "I was at least half asleep. I do believe I was quite lost in my dreams and speaking to you from them."

"A dream of Lady Brattlestone?"

He chuckled. "By Lord Harry, don't wish that virago on me, even in jest." He refilled the cup and watched as she lifted the top on the covered plate. "What has Cook made for me today?"

"Cook has prepared eggs and potatoes as you favor, my lord." She hesitated, then lifted the top of another plate. "And there is fresh cinnamon bread."

"Cinnamon bread?" His eyes widened. "Now there is a rare treat I haven't enjoyed since coming back to Westerly Manor. I shall have to thank Cook for putting aside her assumption that only biscuits should be served at breakfast."

"Yes, my lord."

Something in her tone caused him to set his cup by the plate and reach for the bread. He did not pause to spread butter on it. Instead, he took a bite. He smiled as he savored the sharp flavor that mixed so perfectly with the bread's sweetness.

"This is excellent."

"Thank you." She continued to place the dishes on the table in front of him.

"Your recipe, Meredith?"

"Yes.

"You should have said as much."

She straightened and locked her hands behind her. The pose nearly made him choke on his second bite of bread, for it emphasized those enticing curves even more.

Meredith Tynedale realized her mistake instantly and shifted so her hands were clasped in front of her. Good heavens! No one else had ever made her as self-conscious as Lord Westerly did. When she had been hired just before his father died, she had not fretted about every word and every action. Now she acted as awkward as a young girl who had years remaining in the school-room.

It might have been easier to be serene if Lord Westerly did not have those brilliant blue eyes and that tawny hair that curled along his nape. His jaw was firm, matching the muscles that accented his every motion. Although he was not tall, he possessed a strength of will that would draw eyes in any crowd—at least her eyes.

She could hear Andrelina, the most outspoken of the kitchen maids, teasing her about her infatuation with Percival Dunstan. *If you want him to notice you, you need to stop being so blasted demure.* Why did Andre-lina's absurd advice always tempt her when Lord West-erly was near?

"It would be unseemly to boast, my lord," she said quietly.

He laughed, and she could not help smiling as she went to open the double doors leading to the balcony that ringed the upper level of Westerly Manor. She really liked the sound of his laugh. It was unrestrained and utterly sincere, reminding her of his young brother Jere-miah, who had just celebrated his fifth birthday.

"Such humility is refreshing, but you should not hide your special talents, Meredith. Cook has been here at Westerly Manor since my father was married the first time, and I doubt if she has varied the menu twice in all those years." He raised the bread in her direction as if it were a glass of fine wine. "I salute your skill."

"Thank you, my lord." She hesitated, then asked, "Will there be anything else?"

"Yes."

She faltered, about ready to leave. Had she done

something wrong to linger like this? She could not take her leave when he continued this conversation.

"Do not look so dismayed, Meredith." He smiled, and she relaxed. It would be impossible for her not to react to that smile, which glittered in his eyes. "I only wish to hear you accept my apology for putting you to the blush."

"You need not apologize, my lord. One cannot be held responsible for what one says or does while asleep."

"But I wish to apologize, and I would like to hear you accept that apology."

"It is accepted." She could not imagine what else she might say.

Meredith did not wait to hear anything further. When she had closed the bedchamber door, she rushed across the sitting room, where gold on the plaster friezes glittered in the morning sunshine. She smiled automatically at Struthers, the baron's valet. The rangy man seemed held together by fraying string that might break at any moment.

Her smile faded when Thorpe came into the room just as she reached the door to the corridor. She stepped out of the imperious butler's way, not doubting he would walk right over her if she did not. She eased around a marble-topped table decorated with fresh flowers from the garden.

"Why are you loitering here?" Thorpe asked sharply. "You should have left minutes ago."

"Don't chide the lass." Struthers jutted his pointed chin at the butler. "She cannot take her leave before Lord Westerly dismisses her."

Dismay struck Meredith. She had scurried away without waiting for the baron to send her on her way. If Thorpe discovered that . . . Raising her own chin, she said, "Lord Westerly had some questions for me."

Thorpe's scowl deepened. That she refused to be in-

timidated by him had infuriated the butler, because
Thorpe saw himself as master of the belowstairs household. "If you have answered them, be on your way, girl."

Meredith nodded, then hid her grin when Struthers
winked at her. The valet could avoid the majordomo, so
he was not as daunted by Thorpe as were most of the
staff.

Slipping out of the room, she went to the kitchen at
the back of the house. The scents of the food being
prepared for the other meals of the day had already over-
mastered the aromas left by breakfast.

"How was *he* this morning?"

Meredith sighed. She should have guessed Andrelina
would be lying in wait for her, but had hoped to have
a chance to gather her wits before being subjected to
her questions.

"He seems to be in excellent health, as always," she
replied.

"And how did it go?"

"It was as to be expected." She reached for the bucket
of flour so she could begin mixing the rolls for tonight's
meal.

"Your expectations or his?" Andrelina giggled, her
pixie freckles making her look as young as Jeremiah,
although Andrelina must be a year or two older than
Meredith. Certainly her thoughts were obsessed with the
very adult issues of flirtations and seductions. If a lad
did more than glance at one of the serving maids, Andrelina knew about it as soon as the maid did. She loved
gossip and was miserable nothing of interest had developed between Lord Westerly and Meredith.

"He was very pleased with me this morning,"
Meredith said, keeping her head down so Andrelina did
not see her smile.

"Was he?" Excitement bubbled through Andrelina's
voice. "How do you know?"

"He told me I should not hide my special talents."

"He *said* that?"

"Yes."

"Oh, my goodness!" Andrelina's eyes were round as she bent to whisper, "And what special talent did he refer to?"

"My cinnamon bread."

"You spoke only of your cinnamon bread?" She frowned. "Oh, Meredith!"

Spooning flour onto the table, she laughed. "What more do you expect?"

"Your cinnamon bread?"

"He said it was a nice change from what he is accustomed to."

"So he likes a bit more spice in his mornings?"

Meredith rolled her eyes. "Andrelina! It amazes me how you can reach that conclusion when I've told you over and over nothing has happened out of the ordinary."

"You would reach the same one if you were not so bamblusterated by him that you cannot see him as anything but the fine lord. He is a man, Meredith, and a man the *on dits* say appreciates a pretty lass. You are pretty, so why not take advantage of what he could do for you?"

"You are the one being skimble-skamble." She shook her head as she reached for a ladle of water. "I have no interest in an *affaire de coeur* with anyone in Westerly Manor. My parents—"

Andrelina's smile vanished again. "Do not say that again. I know your family was once of the gentry, but you are what you are now."

"Exactly."

Muttering something, Andrelina walked away.

Meredith bent to her work and smiled. It was never boring here, especially when her heart thudded with the memory of Lord Westerly's smile as he leaped out of bed to gather to him the woman of his dreams. Yet she knew it never could be Meredith Tynedale.

TWO

"Good afternoon!" Meredith peered into the shadows gathered beneath the low ceilings of her parents' home. Although she had become accustomed to the splendor of Westerly Manor in the year she had been there, she was certain this would always be home.

Her mother rushed to the door and hugged her. Each time Meredith called, her mother's hair was whiter, but her welcoming smile never changed. "We had hoped you would be visiting us soon."

"Cook gave me two hours to call." She held up a loaf of bread. "She thought you might enjoy this for lunch."

"Your cinnamon bread, Meredith?"

"Yes."

"I am certain they love your recipe for this at Westerly Manor."

"Yes." She drew off her bonnet and hung it on the wooden peg by the door. In doing so, she could hide her face from her mother, not wanting to let Mama guess how unsettled she was. As she walked into the sanctuary of the cozy parlor, she let her sigh sift through her teeth.

"What is amiss, daughter?"

Meredith looked at where her father was coming to his feet from his small desk by the hearth. "Papa! I didn't expect to find you here at this hour." She gave him a quick hug, again hiding her face. She must be cautious about what she said. To Mama she could speak frankly, but Papa took offense too easily.

"Sir Norman is afraid of becoming ill," he answered with a jovial laugh that shook his widening belly and made the few remaining hairs on his head bounce.

"What frightens him this time?" She smiled, because the baronet was well-known for fearing any ailment that came into the shire. He would lock up his house, turning away all callers, when the ague swept through the countryside.

"I am not quite certain, although his friend Lord Campbell broke his leg trying to take a fence last week."

"Broken legs aren't catching."

He chuckled again. "Mayhap not, but Sir Norman, as you know, takes no chances with anything. As he prefers the house quiet and empty while he avoids taking to his sickbed, I thought it prudent to do my work here." He motioned for her to sit on the settle on the other side of the hearth. "You didn't answer my question, Meredith."

"Nothing is amiss, Papa. I am just glad to be visiting here where I do not need to worry about making an error, as I do at Westerly Manor." How could she be lathering her father with such out-and-outers? She was guarding her words more closely now than she ever had at the manor house.

"Take care." Papa sat and tapped his fingers on the leather top of his desk. "I would not have agreed to let you go into service there if I had guessed Lord Westerly would be taken and his son would come home to oversee the household."

"The present Lord Westerly is not the problem."

"Then what is?"

Her mother's laugh saved Meredith from answering. "Mr. Tynedale, must you pelt the girl with questions each time she calls?" She set a painted tray on the sideboard in front of the room's only window. Offering the plate with slices of cinnamon bread to her husband and then to her daughter, she said, "You should be enjoying Meredith's call."

"Which I do, Mrs. Tynedale." He smiled as he took a bite of the bread. "Your cooking skills continue to improve, Meredith."

"Now, now," chided her mother with a smile. "Listen to you. One would think she had been a horrible cook before she went to Westerly Manor."

"She still could learn much from you." He patted his full belly. "I was thin as an anatomy, Meredith, when I met your mother. Did I ever tell you how she won my heart with her cooking?"

Meredith laughed. "You may have mentioned it once or twice."

She listened as her parents continued to jest and talk about events at the baron's estate of Haremede Park. This teasing was what she had missed most since she had gone to Westerly Manor. She had friends among the staff there, but she always enjoyed coming home.

Especially today.

Meredith tried to ignore that thought. It refused to be dislodged during lunch and while she helped her mother clean up as they left Papa to his work. She thought she had done a good job of hiding her disquiet until her mother asked her what was wrong. Quickly she explained about how Lord Westerly had unsettled her when she brought him his breakfast.

"Ask Cook to send someone else." Mama put the cleaning cloth on the table in the middle of the kitchen, which seemed so tiny in comparison with the one at Westerly Manor. "Or I can speak with Mrs. Montgomery."

"No!" She could not imagine the to-do it would cause if her mother petitioned Westerly Manor's housekeeper on her behalf. That was not true, either. She *could* imagine it. She simply did not want to.

"Meredith?"

"It will be all right, Mama," she said much more calmly. "Lord Westerly is not the problem. I am."

"You are intrigued by him?"

She nodded. "He makes me laugh. He challenges me with the most peculiar questions. And when . . ."

"When what?" Her mother's face grew pale. "You have not let him persuade you to forget what you have been taught, have you?"

"Certainly not." She dropped to a stool by the hearth. "As I told you, 'tis my reactions to him that cause the problem. He has been a gentleman, doing nothing untoward. Yet if his fingers brush mine when he hands me his breakfast tray . . ." She sighed. "I cannot explain."

Her mother sat on a backless bench and faced her. "And there is no need for you to explain, for I understand what you mean."

"Good."

Mama shook her head, her white hair billowing like a cloud. "No, Meredith, it is not good. If you were speaking of one of the lads in the stable or of a footman, I would be rejoicing with you at having your heart touched. But you are not. You are speaking of Lord Westerly, a baron who has the good fortune to have plump pockets. He need not marry a wealthy lass, it is true, but he will be seeking a titled lass to be the mother of his heir."

"I know that."

Putting her hand against Meredith's cheek, she said, "I know you know that. I do not want you to forget it when you are in his company. Your father's family once—"

"I know!" Meredith surged to her feet. From her earliest memories, she could recall the endless retellings of the misfortunes visited upon this family by her paternal grandfather's obsession with gambling, which had eaten any inheritance he had been given as the third son of a marquess. That had left his son with only his wits to provide for himself and his family.

Her mother rose and put her hands on Meredith's shoulders. "Just take care, child. You are on a road that can lead only to ruin or heartbreak."

"I know," she repeated in a whisper. She had known the truth before she came home. Hoping to find a different answer here had been silly. Mama was right. If she continued to be fascinated by Lord Westerly, she might soon need to choose between the ruin of her reputation and a broken heart.

The choice would be easy, for she would not do anything to shame her family—but knowing that would not lessen the heartache.

Percy put down the box of toy soldiers and gave his young half-brother a frown. Since their mutual father's death, Jeremiah had become a boisterous, outrageous child who refused to remember the manners even a five-year-old should know. The little boy flitted about like a frightened young bird, never lingering anywhere long.

Percy had sympathy for the child, who had lost his mother only a year before his father died, but his patience was growing thin. The child showed no signs of slowing down in his pursuit of whatever it was he was seeking. Quite to the contrary, he seemed to be gaining more speed every day.

His hope that giving Jeremiah this puppy would help curb the child's unfitting behavior had seemed to create the opposite effect. Now both Jeremiah and the shaggy pup Rex were constantly on the run, as well as continuously underfoot.

Putting the box on a shelf where the other toys should be instead of tossed around the nursery, he said, "Jeremiah, do sit still."

The little boy frowned, but dropped to the closest chair. His feet swung wildly, kicking at the rungs. The pup dropped, panting, beside him.

Percy offered his brother a smile, but got only a frown in return. Wishing his sister Nancy would return from her calls, because she could calm the child better than he could, he said, "You need to stop bouncing about like a stone being shot across the water."

"Let's go and play ducks and drakes!" the little boy crowed. "The pond is—"

"Not where we need to be just now." He heard the door click open. "Ah, here comes your tea."

"Oh, boy!"

Percy stepped aside as Jeremiah bounded off his chair and ran toward the door with Rex at his heels. His smile vanished as neither the little boy nor the puppy slowed as the door opened wider. "Watch out!"

He leaped forward as Jeremiah hit the tea tray in Meredith's hands. Gripping it, Percy cursed as the flowered teapot wobbled. The tray tilted as she suddenly released it. Was she out of her mind? The food erupted off the plates, flying in every direction.

"Are you mad?" he shouted, wiping cream from his waistcoat. He plucked a cake from his sleeve. "You should take more care. If—"

"Hush," she said.

"Now see here. You . . ." He realized she was speaking to Jeremiah, who was crying. She was kneeling and drying the little boy's cheeks with the corner of her apron as Rex licked up the spilled cream.

"You aren't hurt," she continued as if the baron had not spoken, "but you could have been. You must take more care, Master Jeremiah, and watch where you are going. The tea could have burned you badly."

"If you hadn't pushed him aside?" Percy asked.

Meredith did not look at him as she held up a napkin so Jeremiah could blow his nose. "I am sorry, my lord, that the teapot is broken, but I did not want it to fall on him."

"Of course not." Percy squatted. "Jeremiah, go and ring for help to clean up this mess." As the little boy raced to the bellpull, clearly not having learned a lesson about slowing down despite his brush with disaster, he added, "Are you hurt, Meredith?"

"I am fine." She looked at him, and her mouth grew round. "Oh, my lord, your waistcoat is ruined." She dabbed at the spots left by the cream. "I am so very sorry."

He clamped her hand against his chest. Did she have no idea of the effect created by her efforts to atone for this accident? She was making it impossible for him to recall his resolve and ignore how her eyes glittered in his dreams.

Dash it! He should not be thinking this way about one of the kitchen maids. Although other lords still considered the servants a source of private entertainment, too much else should be occupying his mind—the estate's current financial state, his sister's hints she was going to announce her own plans as soon as a proper length of mourning was over, as well as young Jeremiah, who would soon be needing a tutor. Instead, he found his thoughts drifting off, anticipating the next time he might have a chance to see Meredith.

"You have no need to apologize," he said, ignoring Jeremiah's shout as he and the puppy raced out onto the balcony.

"I do feel a need, and I would be grateful if you would accept my apology."

He chuckled as she reminded him of his own words earlier today. Was she using them for the same reason he had? To allow this moment to last just a bit longer? "Then I do accept your apology, Meredith."

"Thank you." She drew her hand away from him and bent to gather up the spoons that had scattered across the nursery carpet.

"No, thank you for saving Jeremiah from his own want-witted enthusiasm."

"He is just a little boy. Little boys get excited easily."

"They do, don't they?" His fingers were brushing her cheek before he could halt them.

He watched as her eyes grew round, and a smile curved along his lips. She had such lovely eyes—not just their color, but how they changed with each emotion even as they glowed with intelligence. She had depths to her he wished to explore, but for now he would be satisfied to savor what he could with a single kiss. Her eyes widened even farther as his hand curved beneath her chin to bring her mouth toward his.

"Is this where—oh!"

Meredith came to her feet and whirled to see Andrelina standing behind her. Andrelina's mouth gaped as she stared at them.

How could I be so stupid? Meredith wondered. She had spoken with Mama not two hours ago about how Lord Westerly made her think the most inappropriate thoughts. Mama had urged her to curb those thoughts before they betrayed her. She *had* listened . . . until Lord Westerly's tender caress against her cheek pushed all good sense from her head.

"Thank you, my lord," she said, hoping her voice sounded more normal to their ears than it did to hers. "I do believe that piece of sugar missed hitting me in the eye."

Lord Westerly's eyes twinkled as he said, " 'Twas my

pleasure. I did not want you to be hurt when you saved Jeremiah from his own silliness. You are quite the heroine, and I thank you." He looked past her and smiled. "Jeremiah, I believe we shall take tea in the small parlor this afternoon."

"I will have it sent to you," Meredith hurried to say.

"Thank you." He took his younger brother's hand and walked out of the room. The puppy wagged its tail, then raced after them.

Andrelina dropped to her knees and began to pick up the broken pieces of the teapot. "A piece of sugar? Am I supposed to believe that was all he was looking for when he had your face cupped in his hand?"

"Are you calling Lord Westerly a liar?" Meredith asked, taking a cloth and rubbing at the stain on the carpet. She doubted if all signs of the tea splattered on it would come up.

"No, rather I would consider him jobbernowl for not taking advantage of the situation."

"The situation was that young Master Jeremiah nearly was scalded by the tea. Lord Westerly was quite upset."

"So I saw." She chuckled. "I wonder what might have happened if I had delayed a moment longer in opening the door."

So do I! Meredith did not speak that thought aloud as she bent to scrub. No matter how hard she worked, she could not escape the memory of pleasure whirling through her at his touch. Somehow she must. She simply had no idea how.

THREE

"Percy! Oh, Percy! Please say yes."

Percy swung down off his horse as his sister Nancy rushed up to him. She was almost five years younger than he, but she looked younger still as she put up her hand to keep her straw bonnet from bouncing off her head. The mousy hair he had tugged when they were both children now was a vibrant brown that shone in the sunlight.

"Say yes to what?" He handed the reins to a groom and put his arm around Nancy's shoulders, which were covered by her favorite lace shawl. She must be returning from her day's calls.

"Bryant is going to be calling this evening."

"Now there is a surprise." He chuckled when she grimaced.

"Do receive him, Percy."

"I have never turned him—or anyone else—from my door."

She tugged on his coat and laughed. "Don't jest with me now. Just please say yes."

He steered her toward the house. "By your expression, am I to assume our good neighbor Sir Bryant Truby is about to make his intentions known?"

"Percy! I asked you not to tease me!"

"I will assume that is an affirmative. So all I need to say is yes when he asks for your hand?"

"Please, Percy, do tell him yes."

He grinned. "I will listen to his offer. I promise you that."

"Oh, Percy! Stop teasing me."

"All right, Nancy." He paused and turned her to face him. Every day, Nancy looked more and more like the portrait of their mother which hung at the first floor landing of the main staircase. In spite of that, he had a difficult time not thinking of her as a child.

Now she wanted to wed. It seemed impossible, but she was of an age and apparently of an inclination to leg-shackle herself to quiet Sir Bryant. "I *will* listen to his offer, and I will give my blessing if it is in your best interests."

"You are taking your responsibilities as Lord Westerly so seriously!"

"As Father despaired I ever would."

Her smile dissolved. "Oh, Percy, you were not truly a disappointment to Father. He spoke of you often in the days before he died, always with the hope you would be worthy of the title you would receive."

"I will look forward to speaking with your Sir Bryant this evening." He kissed her on the forehead. "Go and make yourself pretty for him."

"He will not be here for at least four or five hours."

"That gives you plenty of time, then, to make yourself presentable."

With a feigned growl, she slapped his arm before rushing into the house.

Percy let his light expression fall away. *Hope you would be worthy of the title you would receive.* Father had not expected he would be worthy. His father had urged him to go to London to enjoy a young man's entertainments. Yet when Percy had spent the whole Season there and returned to London for the next, his father had decided Percy was a wastrel, intent on besmirching the family honor. Nothing Percy had done would change his father's mind, and the one thing he had left undone had condemned him even more in his father's eyes.

Upon walking into the house, he handed his hat to a serving lass. He paused in the kitchen to let Cook know Sir Bryant would be calling this evening.

"I will have just the perfect thing made," Cook said, her grin warning that the whole household must already suspect the reason for this call. "Can I help you find something, my lord? Have you lost something?"

Percy shook his head, although he wondered if he had lost his mind. He should not be peering around the kitchen like an eager lad watching for his lady fair. "No, I haven't lost anything."

"Then I shall set the girls to making a special treat for you and Miss Dunstan and Sir Bryant."

"Thank you." He heard muffled giggles as he went out of the kitchen. A glance over his shoulder gained him nothing, although he saw the maid who had come to the nursery to clean up the ruined tea last week. Egad! Mayhap his father had been right. He was making a muddle of his role of the respected baron.

Turning on his heel, he walked back into the kitchen. It was time he took control of things . . . now!

Meredith hummed lightly to herself. She seldom had the chance to be alone like this, even in a house as big as Westerly Manor. Even though she loved music, she knew her voice had a tendency to wander from the proper note. That had not mattered when she was young and singing in an empty meadow. Now she did not want to inflict her singing on anyone else.

As she reached up to a high shelf to take down the

pieces of silver stacked there, she heard footfalls coming along the hall beyond the silver room door. Hastily she bit off her song in mid-note. Had Cook sent someone to help her with this huge task? It would be wonderful to have another set of hands, but she had been enjoying this moment alone.

"So you are the one making all the clatter."

She whirled from the shelves as she heard Lord Westerly's laugh-laced voice. "I am sorry if I disturbed you, my lord."

"Quite the contrary. With Nancy taking young Jeremiah down to the pond to terrorize the ducks, the house is oddly quiet." He walked in and smiled as he picked up the bottle of wine from the table in the middle of the crowded room. Setting it back, he peered into the pan where she had mixed wine with finely ground chalk and hartshorn. "Why are you polishing silver instead of cooking?"

"Cook needed extra hands today to do this, so I offered mine." She put another tray on the table. Her fingers brushed the raised pattern of the filigree on its edge.

She had not guessed she would see this design of irises and grape leaves here at Westerly Manor. This must be a twin to the tray she had seen in her grandparents' house. She could not have been much more than a toddler the last time Grandmother had used it. She did not wonder what had happened to it. She knew. It had been sold, like everything else.

"Meredith, I am so very sorry."

She looked up at him, startled. "You have nothing to apologize for." She reached for a piece of soft leather and dipped it into the mixture, then spread it across the silver tray.

"But I do. I have heard what is being said."

"Said?" she choked. Why hadn't she realized before

now that his footfalls had been coming from the kitchen, instead of the main part of the house? She knew what he must have heard, because Andrelina had wasted no time in spreading her gossip among the servants.

Oh, heavens, she hoped he had not heard what she had this morning—that she was about to be installed in the baron's private rooms as his convenient. She had chided the ones repeating the rumor and the ones listening, but she doubted if anything she said or did would slow its retelling. Such intriguing gossip would spread through the house until something even more interesting replaced it.

Lord Westerly took a silver goblet down from a shelf. Rubbing dust from it, he tilted some of the wine into it, then sat on the chair she had brought in so she could reach the highest shelves. Taking a sip, he said, "You should know by now the rumble of rumors do not stay belowstairs. They find their way into every corner of the house."

She shuddered. "As long as they go no farther."

"And reach your family?"

"It would greatly disturb my parents to hear what I have heard." She began to rub the pattern along the edge of the tray. "Papa is determined that our family's honor never be blemished again."

"I would be glad to reassure him that—"

"No!" She realized her tone was as sharp as when her mother had suggested speaking with Westerly Manor's housekeeper.

"No?"

"My lord, don't you realize that your calling on my parents will just give countenance to the whole of this silliness? Even those I have persuaded not to share the half truths will wonder why you are making such an unexpected call."

He arched a brow as he took another sip. "You seem

to understand human nature very well, Meredith. Are you a student of such?"

"It behooves a serving lass to watch closely everyone around her, so she might not make a mistake that would embarrass her employer."

"Such as repeating gossip?"

"I do not heed it or repeat it, my lord. That could cause the very humiliation I try to avoid."

"I suspect it is more than that. You seem always to be watching others, as well as yourself." He raised his hand. "I did not mean to put you to the blush, Meredith."

She started to raise her fingers to her hot cheeks, but drew them back, for they were covered with the mixture to remove the tarnish from the silver. Bending to her task, she waited for him to realize she did not want to speak of such things and to take his leave. She was aware of his gaze on her hands as she wiped away the shadows along the pattern on the tray.

"How often do you have to do that?" he asked.

Meredith swallowed her sigh. He was not going to leave, and she could not ask him to go before someone chanced to walk by and see this cozy conversation. "Once a week is best," she replied.

"You do all this silver once a week?"

She could not help smiling at his amazement. "I told you Cook needed extra hands to deal with this."

"And she will need more. I shall have to talk to Mrs. Montgomery about hiring more help before the wedding."

"Wedding?" Her head jerked up and her voice came out in a squeak. She had not guessed Lord Westerly was planning to wed. But then again, what did she know of his life beyond his jesting with her when she brought him his breakfast or his tea?

"Nancy has let me know Sir Bryant Truby will be calling to offer for her this evening."

"Congratulations, my lord. It will be deemed an excellent match, and she will not be far from Westerly Manor, so you shall see her often." She scrubbed harder against the tarnish. Had he noted her reaction? How could he have missed it? She was grateful he was being a gentleman and not mentioning it. She had to stop being foolish and letting the rumors around the house convince her Lord Westerly thought of her beyond her service to the household.

"Yes, it is a good match." He stood and set the goblet on the table. "It shall mean opening up rooms of this house that have been closed since before my father's death." He clasped his hands behind him. "Nancy has been waiting impatiently for that mourning to end, I can tell, so she might have her dashing Sir Bryant."

"He is a fine gentleman who is well respected throughout the shire."

His nose wrinkled. "You do not need to dissemble. He is a bumpkin, but his weakness, fortunately for my sister, is for horses. She never will have to worry about him chasing another woman's skirts, although she may become quickly bored with his delight in breeding the ultimate race horse." With a laugh, he said, "But I am not the one marrying, so I leave it in her most capable hands to decide how best to handle Sir Bryant."

"A very wise decision."

"As I would like to leave some of the preparations for the wedding in yours."

Meredith set down the tray. "In my hands?"

"Why not? You have proven your skill with pastries and breads is superior to anyone else's in Westerly Manor, mayhap even in this part of England."

"Thank you."

" 'Twas not a compliment. 'Twas a fact."

Smiling, for she could not hide her pleasure with his generous praise, she said, "I would be delighted to help make the wedding dessert, my lord."

"You misunderstand. I want you to oversee the whole of the wedding breakfast."

"Me?"

"Cook assures me you will do a fine job."

"But I have never done something like this."

His smile became roguish. "Something I can imagine you have often thought in my company when I say something outrageous to bring that pretty color to your cheeks, although you have not said it to me before."

Meredith lowered her eyes before she became enthralled by the invitation in his. Andrelina's voice rumbled through her head. *If you like the lord, let him know. He could give you a taste of the life you will never know otherwise.*

"So do you agree, Meredith?"

She almost cried out yes, she would agree to whatever he wished. Keeping the words from surging forth, for she knew he spoke only of his sister's wedding, she said, "I am honored to offer my help, my lord."

FOUR

Meredith was sure someone was watching her. The sensation of a steady gaze aimed at the middle of her back had been taunting her since she had begun gathering the materials to make dinner rolls for the evening meal.

The others in the kitchen were all intent on their work. No one was looking in her direction. They had become adept in the past two weeks at pretending not to stare at her as they bent to whisper.

She could not scold them for heeding absurd gossip, although she thought the rumors would come to an end when Lord Westerly asked her to oversee the preparations for Miss Dunstan's wedding breakfast. That should have proven he thought of her as nothing but a kitchen maid. Instead, his request seemed to fuel the gossip, sending it flitting about the house until Mrs. Montgomery had taken her aside to demand the truth.

She sighed, knowing Mrs. Montgomery might have given her her congé if Lord Westerly were not planning on her to handle the wedding breakfast. What a bumble-bath this was!

Someone *was* watching her.

Every instinct warned her of that. Putting the bucket of flour on the table, she reached for the scoop as she glanced surreptitiously over her shoulder. Something moved in the shadows by the stillroom door. Acting as if nothing were amiss, she put the scoop down and turned to reach for the salt cellar.

With a quick motion, she reached into the shadows and pulled out—Master Jeremiah!

"What are you doing lurking here?" she asked, kneeling so she could meet his eyes.

He squared his narrow shoulders in a motion that reminded her of his father, even though the previous Lord Westerly had been sickly by the time she started working here. Only his golden hair brought his older brother to mind, for she had never seen such a furious frown on the present Lord Westerly's face.

"I can go where I wish!" he announced with an arrogance amusing in such a young child.

"True, but how much fun is it to sit in the corner and just watch people?"

"I wanted to see what you had done with it."

Meredith fought not to frown. "With what, Master Jeremiah?"

"With Percy's eye. Is it in your apron pocket?"

"Pardon me?"

He folded his arms in front of him and regarded her as if she had no sense whatsoever. "I heard Nurse tell one of the nursery maids how you had caught Percy's eye. Where do you have it?"

Meredith sat back on her heels. Heavens, how was she to explain this to this very literal child? Anything she said could be the very worst thing. Quietly, she asked, "When did you hear Nurse say that?"

"Yesterday."

"Have you seen your brother since then?"

"Yes."

"Did he have both his eyes?"

Jeremiah pondered that a moment, then nodded, clearly disappointed. "Yes."

"Nurse was just teasing when she said that."

He shook his head. "Nurse *never* teases about anything."

"Mayhap your brother asked her to."

"Mayhap." Again he considered it intently. "Percy likes to hoax me and Nancy."

Meredith smiled. This had been the right way to persuade the child not to heed the gossip of his elders. She struggled to keep her smile in place as she wondered how she could keep him from hearing any more such tittle-tattle. Going to Mrs. Montgomery might convince the housekeeper to turn her off without a recommendation in order to keep peace in the household.

She needed some time to figure out how best to deal with this. Coming to her feet, she asked, "Master Jeremiah, would you like to help me prepare the rolls for tonight's supper?" When she saw him start to frown, she hurried to add, "No, I think it might be best you do not. You would not want to get your good clothes all covered with flour. Making bread can be very messy, you know."

"Can it?" His eyes lit up just as she had hoped they would.

"That is why it would be better that you do not help."

"But I want to help."

She almost laughed, but kept a pensive expression on her face. Tapping her finger against her lips, she said, "If I were to get you an apron to put over your clothes, then I suppose you could help."

He bounced from one foot to the other as she tied an apron up under his arms. Even so, it brushed the floor, so she refolded it and tied it again. He quickly pulled a chair across the uneven floor, drawing the attention of everyone working in the kitchen.

"My helper," Meredith said with a strained smile. If one person said the wrong thing, this reprieve could come to an immediate end.

Jeremiah clambered up onto the chair and grinned at the bucket of flour. He reached in with both hands.

She plucked them out and shook her head. "This has to be done just right. We have to count the scoops to make sure it is right. Can you count to twenty?"

"Of course!"

Her smile became genuine as he regarded her with five-year-old pride. "Good. Then you can count twenty scoops of flour into the bowl while I get the rest of the ingredients."

Meredith did not go far as she listened to the little boy solemnly count out the proper amount of flour. When Cook smiled and winked at her, Meredith chuckled. Cook had complained more than once about Master Jeremiah's always being underfoot in the kitchen in hopes of getting a treat.

As she came back to where she would mix the bread, Jeremiah continued counting, "Eighteen . . . nineteen . . . ten-teen?"

Meredith laughed. "It should be ten-teen, shouldn't it? But it's actually twenty."

"Twenty," Jeremiah said, rolling the word around as if trying to sample every flavor of the syllables. "Nineteen, twenty."

"Perfect." Meredith placed the other ingredients that had been kept warm by the hearth into the bowl and picked up a wooden spoon. "And now we stir it all together. Would you like to try it?"

"Can I?"

"If you are careful. Stir it slowly until the flour gets caught by the water."

He whirled the spoon through the bowl. A white cloud burst out of it. She could not help laughing as it flew over her and the little boy. Wiping it away from her eyes, she froze as she heard a much deeper laugh.

Lord Westerly leaned his hands on the other side of

the table. Trying not to look past him to see the others watching them, she swept flour away from her face with her apron, then did the same to clean Jeremiah's face.

"I'm helping, Percy!" he announced as he held up the dripping spoon.

"Keep it in the bowl." Meredith steered his hand back to the bowl and showed him how to mix the flour, yeast, and water with the other ingredients without making a mess.

"I see how much you are helping." Lord Westerly laughed again and winked at Jeremiah. "Now we know what Meredith will look like when she is old and white-haired."

"Like Gran-gran?"

"Just like the portrait of your great-grandfather." He got a cloth and dipped it in a bucket. When he held it up, she gasped as he wiped her face instead of the boy's. "Only far prettier."

"If you say so." Jeremiah bent to his task. "This is getting harder to stir."

"Good," Meredith said, ducking away from the cloth Lord Westerly held. "That means you are doing it right. Keep stirring."

"May I speak with you a moment?" Lord Westerly asked quietly. "Alone."

"Of course." She poured some flour onto the table. "Keep stirring, Master Jeremiah. I shall be right back to help you with the next step."

Every eye in the kitchen was on her and Lord Westerly as he opened the door leading to the kitchen garden. As she stepped out into the warm sunshine, she risked a look behind her. Cook was shooing all the servants back to their work.

She sighed.

The wrong thing to do, she realized, when Lord Westerly asked, "Is something amiss, Meredith?"

"No, of course not." She could not explain to him how he was adding another layer to the gossip already swirling through the house.

"That sigh sounded very unhappy."

"Why did you want to speak to me, my lord?" She would not lie to him, but she could not tell him some of the truth without revealing all of it. It would be unseemly for her to tell him how uncomfortable the rumors made her. Nor must she speak of how she regretted Mrs. Montgomery's decision that Meredith no longer bring Lord Westerly's tray to him in the morning so there would be no hint of impropriety, even when none existed.

He led the way along the curving path between the beds of vegetables and herbs. By the ancient well set in the far corner, he paused. "I wanted to tell you how much I have missed having your cinnamon bread, Meredith."

"But I have been preparing it several times each week. I can make you some for this evening."

"The evening seems so long to wait."

"You're saying that only because you want a piece of warm bread," Meredith said with a chuckle.

"That is not what I want." He took the damp cloth and ran it along her cheek again. His single fingertip beneath the cloth outlined the curve of her cheekbone before pausing at the corner of her mouth.

She gazed up at him, waiting for him to speak the words that would delight her heart and shatter it at the same time. All the jesting, all the hesitant conversations—everything, she feared, had led to this moment.

"What do you want?" she whispered.

"I should say I want to thank you for your kind attention to Jeremiah today. He has been so unhappy since Father died."

"As you have."

He smiled sadly. "I did not realize it was so obvious."

"Yes, my lord." She dared not add that Andrelina would never have taken note of anything but his eager glances. Yet ignoring the grief dimming the corners of his smile had been impossible. "I did not know your father well, for I came to Westerly Manor only a few weeks before he died. However, I have seen how the others here reacted. They respected him deeply, and it hurt them when he was gone. I cannot imagine it would be any different for his sons, save that it would be even more difficult."

"You have a unique way of looking at families."

"What do you mean?" She knew she should edge back a step as he moved to lessen the distance between them, but she could not. She wanted to remain so close to him that every breath was flavored with the herbs put in his armoire to keep his clothes fresh.

"You see my family as close-knit as yours is."

"I can judge only what I witness."

He chuckled. "And you see me trying to keep up with young Jeremiah."

"As well as being concerned about your sister's marriage and future. That suggests family members who care deeply for each other."

"Or simply are fulfilling their obligations."

She shook her head. "An obligation would not require you to do all you have. You know secrets do not stay secret long in a house like this, and things spoken of openly are known almost as soon as the words leave one's mouth. I have heard how you questioned Sir Bryant for nearly an hour to be certain he would be a good husband for Miss Dunstan."

"A fact I hope my sister does not know." He chuckled. "She was vexed that it took so long for me to make my decision to give the match my blessing. If she had any idea why it required that amount of time, I fear she would fly right up to the boughs in an unrelenting pelter."

"She should—"

"So *this* is where you are!" Miss Dunstan rushed up to them. She ignored Meredith as she scowled at her brother. "Do you have any idea where Jeremiah is? His nurse is frantic that she cannot find him."

Lord Westerly put his hand on his sister's arm. "Calm yourself, Nancy. Jeremiah is helping Meredith with making the bread for our meal tonight."

"What?" Her eyes widened as she turned to look at Meredith. "Then where is he?"

Meredith smiled. "In the kitchen, where I left him stirring the flour and yeast together." She curtsied quickly. "Thank you, my lord, for answering my questions. I will check into that immediately after I help Jeremiah knead the bread." She knew she was babbling, but she could think of nothing but putting an end to this. How want-witted she had been to chat with Lord Westerly as if they were equals! "Good day, my lord, Miss Dunstan."

Percy started to call after Meredith to halt her, then glanced at his sister, who wore a puzzled expression. Even as he watched, her lips turned downward. He knew that scowl was aimed at him when she said, "Really, Percy, I had thought even you would be more circumspect."

"Do not accuse me of a crime when I have not committed one."

"Haven't you heard what is being said about you and that kitchen maid?"

"Now you sound like an old tabby, Nancy." He smiled to soften his words. "I had thought you, of all people, would comprehend how seriously I take my duties here. If thanking Meredith for her attention to Jeremiah is a mistaken thing, then I am guilty."

"You could have thanked her in the kitchen."

"True, but I have learned that complimenting one of the staff in front of the others is bound to create dissension and jealousy."

Her shoulders lowered from their defensive pose. "I never considered that."

"You should, for soon you will be running Sir Bryant's household. I know he likes things peaceful, and you would be wise to make every effort to keep tranquillity in the house."

"It is something I must give some thought to."

"When you can pull your mind from thoughts of your betrothal ball."

She gasped, "How did you know of that?"

"I *do* heed some of the rumbles spiraling through the house." Putting his arm around her shoulders, he walked with her toward the back gate because he wanted to avoid the kitchen just now. "Why don't you tell me what you have in mind?"

As his sister outlined all the guests she planned to invite and the food she wanted to have served, he glanced back at the kitchen door. He was amazed to see Meredith standing there, but, as his gaze caught hers, he was glad he had asked his sister what she had in mind before Nancy could ask him the same about Meredith.

His answer would have to be that he did not know, but he was eager to find out.

FIVE

Meredith was sure she had never seen anything more beautiful than the reflection of the guests' glorious clothes in the mirrors along Westerly Manor's ballroom wall. She smiled to herself as she held out a tray of glasses of wine to one of the footmen, so he might deliver them to the baron's guests.

Even two days ago, she would have called anyone who had said this ballroom could be cleaned and readied for this evening a widgeon. Now it glistened more beautifully than the day it had been built, for the wood friezes were honey gold with their age and a recent polishing.

Tonight, the formal announcement of the wedding plans between Sir Bryant Truby and Miss Nancy Dunstan would be made amid this incredible assembly. Although it would be a surprise to no one, the guests were sure to toast the match with champagne and many cheers, and their conversation would reach deep into the night toward dawn.

She listened to the music wafting over the heads of Lord Westerly's guests, who seemed oblivious to it. Mozart, she was certain. Papa had insisted she study music, much to Mama's delight. It had strained their tight budget to pay for a music instructor, but Papa had been adamant. The granddaughter of a marquess's youngest son must have a decent education, even though she would have little use for it as a kitchen maid.

"Why are you loitering here?" Thorpe asked in his most disdainful voice.

Meredith knew the best answer would be a polite nod and hurrying off to get more glasses of wine. Yet even as she thought that, she said, "I truly love Mozart."

"Mozart? Why are you babbling about your personal life when you have work to do?" His nose wrinkled. "I don't recall a Mozart among the guests or the household staff."

She laughed. Pressing her hand over her mouth as his gray brows lowered in a deeper scowl, she whirled away before he could explode. That laugh was going to be costly. As soon as Thorpe realized what she meant and how silly he had sounded, he would focus his outrage on her for humiliating him within the hearing of others.

Hurrying back to the kitchen, Meredith kept herself busy and out of the butler's sight. It was not difficult, because all the last-minute details were making Cook frantic. When Cook, who was usually the most even-tempered person in the house, threw a ladle at a footman, Meredith gathered up a tray and headed for the ballroom.

How was she ever going to handle all the details for the wedding breakfast? Yesterday, Miss Dunstan had approved the menu, making a few changes so the tarts would be raspberry instead of strawberry and asking for sweet buns to go with the hot chocolate the ladies would be drinking.

Meredith had been confident she could contend with anything until this morning, when Miss Dunstan had sent more changes, some of which contradicted her comments yesterday. This afternoon, there had been more. Mayhap Cook had ceded this task to her because Cook had not wanted to do it.

Meredith chided herself. Cook was going to be busy with all the meals for the guests during the days before and after the wedding. It behooved Meredith to tend to this single meal without complaint.

Her mood took a turn for the worse when she handed the tray to Orel, one of the newest footmen. He took the tray, but grasped her arm. When he bent forward to suggest where they might meet after dinner was served and what they might do when they were all alone in the shadows of the garden, she yanked her arm out of his grip. She raised her hand to slap his impertinent smile from his face, but turned and walked away instead. She did not want to draw more attention to herself tonight.

"Why are you wearing such a dreadful frown?" Andrelina asked as she popped out of one of the rooms along the hall.

"Orel . . . he . . ." She muttered a curse under her breath and kept walking.

Andrelina stepped in front of her, forcing Meredith to halt. "So he asked you to join him in the garden after the guests go in to dinner?"

"You knew about his plans? Why didn't you warn me?"

"Warn you? Meredith, how can you be so silly?" She sighed. "I was just trying to help."

"By defusing the rumors? Do you think creating new ones is the way to do that?" With a shudder, she wrapped her arms around herself. "Orel was shameless in suggesting what we might do. He certainly is no—"

"Gentleman?"

"Exactly." Meredith sighed.

"When are you going to realize you are a kitchen maid, not a fine lady? You can't aspire to be with a gentleman like those in the ballroom." Andrelina chuckled. "Of course, most of those who claim that distinction are as rakish as a young footman."

"You know what I meant."

Andrelina tugged on her arm and drew her through a door out onto a terrace. The summer heat had vanished with the sun, and the gentle breeze was a tender caress. Overhead, the full moon peeked through the highest branches of the trees at the edge of the rose garden.

Meredith gasped when she realized they were on the terrace just outside the ballroom. Her friend must have lost every bit of her good sense to think they could have a discussion of anything here. If they were seen, there would be perdition to pay.

"Have you ever seen anything more wonderful?" Andrelina giggled like a little girl as she looked into the ballroom, where the music had changed to a waltz. "I wish I could be one of those pretty ladies being twirled about on the hand of a fine gentleman."

"Maurice would be glad to dance with you."

She laughed. "He would be much happier to do something else with me." She shook her head and chuckled brightly. "Meredith, you have to stop blushing every time someone mentions anything about men and women and what brings them pleasure."

"We shouldn't be speaking of such things here."

"Why not?"

"Lord Westerly's guests—"

"Like to discuss enjoying the very same thing. Where do you think heirs and by-blows come from?"

"Andrelina!"

"Don't take that horrified tone with me! I know you think the baron is a perfect gentleman and would never entertain such immodest thoughts, even though he seems to have created them in your head." She giggled again. "And certainly you have heard the story about Lord Westerly and—"

Meredith folded her arms in front of her. "Andrelina,

I try not to listen to gossip. You know how little of it is actually true."

"This was. I had it confirmed by . . ." Andrelina's eyes grew as round as the moon overhead, and she gulped loudly.

"What is wrong?" Meredith asked.

"I suspect I am what is wrong." A warm, rich laugh came from behind her.

Lord Westerly! If he thought she was partaking in this scan-mag with Andrelina, he must be sure she had been false with him when she had assured him she did not heed gossip. If he had heard what she and Andrelina had been saying just moments ago . . . She wanted to run back to the kitchen and hide in the back storage room.

As Andrelina mumbled something, curtsied, and rushed away, Meredith faced Lord Westerly. She hoped the dim light would hide the flush she was certain was brightening her cheeks.

"Don't look so chagrined by your friend's candid enthusiasm with discussing matters that should be more private," Lord Westerly said with a smile, motioning toward a bench by a rosebush that had grown up over the stone wall at the edge of the terrace. As she sat, he did as well, leaving a polite distance between them. "I have told you myself rumors are pervasive in a house like Westerly Manor."

"How do you endure hearing your name muddied?"

"I know what I have been guilty of, and I know as well what I have not done." He shrugged. "I shall be guilty of nothing more than my due."

"Oh."

"May I say you look astonished, Meredith?"

"I am. My father would never be so forgiving of someone speaking about him."

"Nor would mine." He rested his arm on the back of

the bench, but did not touch her. She was torn between being relieved and being disappointed. "And may I say you look very lovely here in the moonlight?"

"Better than in the daylight?"

His laughter burst from him. "You are constantly amusing, Meredith. Your friend would have tittered like a drunken bird and batted her eyelashes at me if I had been foolish enough to offer her such a compliment. You, on the other hand, debate each word like a politician in Westminster."

"My lord, I didn't mean—"

"Of course you did." He laughed again. "And that is why it is so delightful to spend time in your company. You do not treat me with anything save with the respect you feel I deserve. That is refreshing."

Meredith regarded him with bafflement. He was mistaking her disquiet at his compliment for wit. She did not want him to guess, especially now, how distressed she was at his admiration. Because he had owned some of the gossip about him was true—and which part was the truth?—she must take care she did not become another of the incidents of which he was guilty.

"You look puzzled, Meredith."

"I am." *I am puzzled why you seek me out so often and why I wish it was even more frequently.* Silencing the rebellious comment that came directly from her heart, she added, "I am curious why you are out here instead of inside with your guests."

"Again that honesty." He took a deep breath and let it ease out slowly. "There are many things I have come to enjoy about London and its whirl, but endless gibberish that pretends to be witty conversation leaves me filled with *ennui.*"

"If you do not wish to talk, you could dance."

"I could, couldn't I?" He came to his feet. "Will you do me the honor of standing up with me, Meredith?"

"Me?" She had not smelled strong spirits from him, but he must be fuzzy to be asking *her* to dance.

"Why not you? You don't have another partner for the next quadrille, do you?"

She rose. "You know how unlikely that would be. I have duties, my lord, that I have ignored for too long. I should return to them before Thorpe notices how long I have been away."

"Where did your honesty go? You know Thorpe is not the problem."

"You can say that because you do not have to answer to him, my lord. He—" She put her hand over her mouth to silence the words that would heap umbrage on the butler and mayhap even on Lord Westerly himself. How could she forget herself? Again!

"You cannot tell me anything about Thorpe I have not already heard from my valet and from Mrs. Montgomery. Thorpe is learning, I assure you, that he is not the master of Westerly Manor." His eyes narrowed. "At least, he has changed his ways toward me. Your comments suggest he has not been as prodigious in changing his ways toward the staff. You can be assured I will speak of this matter at the earliest possible moment to Mrs. Montgomery."

"Lord Westerly—"

He put his finger to her lips as she had moments ago, and the searing heat that erupted through her made her gasp. A hint of a smile curved along his mouth as he said, "I will not speak to anyone of who brought this matter to my attention." Stepping back, he held out his hand. "So shall we dance, Meredith? The first movement of the quadrille is already half over."

"I shouldn't."

"Why not? Don't you know the steps?" He cocked his head toward the ballroom. "That tune is one that has been about this area since before either of us was born.

I have seen folks dancing to it at the church fair as well as here at Westerly Manor."

"Yes, I know, but I shouldn't dance."

"Again I ask why not."

She hesitated, then knew she could hold back the truth no longer. "My lord, there have been too many who have taken note of the attention you have paid to me."

"Is that so?" He stepped toward her.

Backing away, she yelped when she bumped into a planter. She turned to make sure the flowering bush did not topple off the terrace. When Lord Westerly reached past her to brace the planter, she held her breath. To move in any direction would mean touching him. To touch him . . . she dared not think of what might happen.

"It seems," he murmured, his breath sliding along her nape like a gentle caress, "to be far steadier than you, Meredith."

"I am fine. I should—"

"Dance with me."

When he held out his hand, she bit her lower lip. Slowly she raised her fingers to place them on his. The fierce pulse rushed through her again, as heated as when he had brushed her mouth with his fingertip.

Slowly, he led her into the pattern of the dance. It was a lighthearted dance, without the seductive strains of a waltz. Her feet must have found the steps on their own, because she could not look away from his eyes, which burned her as if the sun were rising within them.

While she stepped away and back toward him again to the rhythm of the music, she wondered if he could hear the much more frantic beat of her heart each time he took her fingers and twirled her about.

The melody came to an end. She dropped into a curtsy as the ladies had in the ballroom. Looking up, she realized he was not bowing as the gentlemen were. His finger under her chin brought her to her feet and closer to him. She could not tear her gaze from his, even as every alarm within her shrieked for her to leave *now.*

"You dance beautifully," he whispered, "although I would expect nothing less from you. You make even rushing through the house on Cook's errands look as exquisite as a feather floating on the gentlest breeze."

"Thank you, my—"

"No," he said as quietly, "do not say *my lord.* Do not acquiesce to me simply because of who I am." His fingers curved along her face, tipping it closer to his.

With a cry, Meredith drew back. "I cannot forget that, my lord."

"Why not?" He ran a single finger along her ear.

She fought her knees, which seemed to be made of uncooked dough, as she stared at him in astonishment for a moment before backing away toward the hallway door. *You have not let him persuade you to forget what you have been taught, have you?* Mama's voice resounded in her head.

But, Mama, she argued silently as she ran back into the house before she succumbed to the temptation glowing in his eyes, *why did you never warn me how sweet the persuasion could be?*

SIX

The house was quiet, but the walls seemed to be too close. Meredith had come into the kitchen garden to prepare beans for cooking and to escape the knowing glances aimed in her direction. She had no idea if someone had seen her dancing with Lord Westerly last night or been a witness when he had tried to kiss her. Someone must have, because she heard the whispers.

Why didn't the gossips leave her alone? What had happened between her and Lord Westerly was no bread-and-butter of theirs.

A bean snapped out of her fingers and flew across the stones of the kitchen garden path. She paid it no mind as she reached for another. It too popped into pieces and careened away from her.

She sighed as she set the pot on the steps and went to retrieve the beans. She could not let her gloom unsettle her to the point that she would be useless. That would give Thorpe the very excuse he needed to turn her out. She would not give him that pleasure.

Putting the beans in the pot with the others, she went to the well and drew water to clean them. She poured the water into the pot and carried it back to where she had been sitting. Gently, she scraped the last of the dirt from the beans.

A shadow slipped over the pot, dimming the eye-burning brightness of the sun's reflection. She did not look up. There was no need. She knew Lord Westerly stood there. What connected them in this way that mixed delight and despair?

"I think," he said, "it would be wise to speak of what happened."

"There is no need." She continued to wash the beans. When his hand dipped into the pot to capture her fingers, she gasped. She started to pull away, but the pot rocked. She could not let it topple over. Did he put her into these positions intentionally? Last night, the planter. Today, the pot filled with water.

"You are seldom wrong, Meredith, but you are so very, very wrong now." He drew her to her feet as his damp hands encircled her face. She was sure the water would sizzle away in the heat spreading from his skin to hers. When he tipped her mouth toward his, she drew back hastily.

"My lord, you mustn't."

"I mustn't?" His fingertip traced her cheekbone, then along her cheek to her lips. "Why not, Meredith?"

"I have work to do." It was a weak excuse, but it was the sole one she had when she truly wanted to be right here in his arms.

"You are always so busy."

"Westerly Manor has many tasks for us."

He chuckled. "For all of us."

"With your sister's upcoming wedding, we are determined Westerly Manor will be glorious and welcoming to your guests."

"You have changed the subject, Meredith."

She looked back down at the beans in the pot. "I thought that would be wise."

"Mayhap, but must you always be wise? Have you never wished to be caught up in a most foolish moment?"

Meredith bent and picked up the pot, holding it in front of her to keep some space between them. "I do not have the luxury of being foolish. My grandfather—"

"Nonsense!" He plucked the pot from her fingers and set it back on the steps. Taking her hand, he drew her along the path toward the secluded well by the back wall. "You cannot live your life forever in the shadow of events that happened before you were born."

"You do!"

"Me?"

"My lord, you said yourself rumors do not stay belowstairs. Neither do they stay abovestairs. It is well known you savored your time in London before your father died."

"I shan't deny it."

Meredith blinked back hot tears. What else had she expected him to say? To deny the rumors as having no more truth than the ones about him and her?

"What does that have to do with anything?" he continued when she did not answer.

"It would deeply hurt my family if I were to act in an unseemly manner in your company."

"Act in an unseemly manner in my company?" His laugh was terse. "How is it you can make something as charming as a kiss sound as onerous as one's most frightful obligation?"

Her breath thudded against her ribs as if she had raced across the fields between her parents' cottage and Westerly Manor. The very thought of his lips on hers was intoxicating, but she must not.

She did not realize she had said the last aloud until he replied, "Yes, you must."

His hands on her shoulders brought her closer. She had no time to protest—even if the words would have formed in her mind and fallen from her mouth—before he captured her lips with a groan that told her he had longed for this as she had.

His lips were gentle as they explored hers. When she could not keep her hands from rising to his shoulders, he tugged her against his strong chest. She gasped as overmastering pleasure captured her when his fingers sifted through her hair. Slowly, his kiss deepened until her breath strained against her mouth.

Her fingers clenched on his shoulders when his mouth caressed her neck as his hands slid down her back. The tip of his tongue outlined her ear, and she could not silence the soft moan of delight that bubbled out of the fiery cauldron roiling within her. He laughed with obvious satisfaction before his mouth slanted across hers again.

"Meredith!" Cook's voice rang across the garden. "Where are you, girl?"

Meredith pulled herself out of Lord Westerly's warm arms. She knew exactly where she was. Half out of her mind.

She did not say anything to him as she went to answer Cook's call. She tried not to think what she would have done if this interruption had not come.

Or what she would do when he sought her out again . . . as she feared he would. As she *hoped* he would.

"Lord Westerly?"

Percy breathed a sigh of relief as he closed the account book on his desk. His father had possessed many good intentions, but he had had no skills with overseeing this estate. These account books had not been updated since his father had let his clerk go last year. Westerly Manor needed a competent clerk immediately.

Would Meredith's father consider accepting a position

as estate manager here? A smile teased the corners of his mouth. Meredith would be so grateful for the advancement for her father, and if she were grateful . . .

"Lord Westerly?"

He pushed those beguiling thoughts from his head as he replied to his impatient butler, "Yes, Thorpe?"

The butler's pinched expression warned he was disturbed. At what? Percy had done nothing to set the man off, unless Thorpe had gained the sudden, unsettling skill of reading his mind. He could not guess what he might have done to vex Thorpe now. Dash it! Mayhap his conversation with Mrs. Montgomery and Cook had come to Thorpe's attention, and the butler had rightly guessed that Percy was inquiring about his treatment of the lower staff.

"There is a gentleman here who wishes to speak with you, my lord," he said in his precise tones.

"A gentleman?"

"A solicitor, my lord."

Percy smiled. This might be just the dandy! Whatever had brought the estate's solicitor to Westerly Manor might be the very thing to lure his mind to set aside thoughts of Meredith Tynedale. He tapped his finger on the book as he wondered why Austin had not sent his usual note telling of his plans to call at Westerly Manor.

"Shall I bring him in, my lord?" Thorpe's voice took on a censuring coolness.

"Of course."

Percy stood and stretched. When he saw the sun had passed its zenith, he realized he had been perusing these blasted account books for at least three hours. No wonder his back was as stiff as an old man's. And he had gotten little done because his mind refused to think about the rows of numbers when he wanted to think only of the soft texture of Meredith's lips while he held her in his arms.

The door opened. A gray-haired man with a pair of spectacles perched on the very tip of his long nose walked in. His drab clothes identified him as a solicitor, but they were as wrinkled as if they had been crushed beneath a wagon wheel.

Percy paid the man's appearance no mind, for this was not Austin, his family's solicitor. He did not know this short man who was striding toward him with the determination of a man who had a job to do and wished to have it completed with all possible speed.

"Lord Westerly?" he asked.

"Yes."

"I am Goodman, solicitor for the Marquess of Satterfield."

Percy searched his mind. Satterfield? Not even the name was familiar. "Welcome to Westerly Manor. How may we be of assistance to you, Mr. Goodman?"

"I understand you have a Miss Meredith Tynedale working here."

Meredith! This had something to do with her? Egad, he was unable to escape the constant reminder of how she intruded in his thoughts, but what would a marquess want with a kitchen maid from Westerly Manor?

He almost laughed at such a question. Certainly he knew what *he* wanted with her. That kiss they had shared in the kitchen garden had confirmed it.

"Yes," he said, trying to conceal his curiosity about why a solicitor would be asking about Meredith.

"May I speak with her?"

"Of course." Looking past Mr. Goodman, he motioned to Thorpe. "Will you have Meredith brought here?"

Mr. Goodman cleared his throat and frowned.

"Yes?" Percy asked, exasperated that the man did not speak plainly.

"I would rather speak with the young lady where she is most comfortable."

In my arms? Percy was glad the question had been heard only in his own head. Gesturing toward the door, he said, "Certainly, Mr. Goodman. If you will come with me . . ."

Thorpe was frowning again, but Percy ignored his butler. It might be inappropriate for a baron to escort a solicitor to speak with a kitchen maid, but his curiosity demanded satisfaction. The only way to gain that was to witness Mr. Goodman's discussion with Meredith.

Every effort he made to engage Mr. Goodman in conversation brought Percy only the tritest responses. Either the man was as uninteresting as a stone, or he was determined to say nothing that might reveal why he had come to Westerly Manor.

The kitchen became silent when they entered. Cook looked up from the hearth, wiping her hands on her apron, an uneasy expression on her face.

Percy wondered what *his* face revealed. Or was it simply the funereal silence that seemed to billow from around Mr. Goodman?

Walking over to where Cook stood, he asked, "Where is Meredith?"

"In the back kitchen, my lord." She lowered her eyes as her voice cracked, showing her disquiet. "Do you wish me to call her?"

"No," he replied, glancing at Mr. Goodman, whose foot was tapping impatiently against the stone floor, "we shall speak with her there." He motioned toward the arch at the far side of the kitchen. "This way, Mr. Goodman."

A buzz of whispers followed in their wake, but Percy pretended not to hear them. He could not fault the kitchen workers for their curiosity when his own was plaguing him.

As he stepped past the arch, he forgot about everything but the delightful sight in front of him. Meredith was kneading the bread he suspected would be for his breakfast tomorrow, because the scent of cinnamon tickled his nose. Strands of her hair accented the enticing curve of her cheek before dropping across the even more beguiling curves beneath her bodice. He wanted to banish Mr. Goodman and the kitchen staff from here while he drew her up against him once more. This time, he would not let her escape his arms with a single kiss.

Mr. Goodman brushed past him and asked, "Are you Meredith Tynedale?"

She wiped flour from her hands. "Yes. May I help you, sir?"

Mr. Goodman smiled broadly. "Quite to the contrary. I am here to help *you.*" He chuckled. "I suggest you consider how best to inform Lord Westerly of the termination of your employment here."

"Termination of her employment?" Percy scowled. "You must be mistaken, Mr. Goodman. There is no good reason why Meredith should leave Westerly Manor." *And one very good one why she should stay.*

"What I have to tell her will provide a good reason." He continued to smile.

"I don't understand," Meredith said. When she looked at him, Percy wanted to draw her to him and assure her none of this was his doing. "Why would I ask to be released from my duties here?"

"Because your father's circumstances have taken a turn for the better." He paused, his gaze flickering between her and Lord Westerly. "It is not right you should be working in a kitchen, *Lady* Meredith."

SEVEN

"Lady Meredith?"

Was that Lord Westerly's voice? It could not have been Meredith's, because no words formed in her paralyzed brain. *Lady Meredith!* She was simply Meredith Tynedale, daughter of Ewan Tynedale and his wife.

"Daughter of Lord Satterfield," the man announced, sounding as delighted as if the whole had been his idea.

Lord Westerly said quietly, "Meredith's father is a clerk for my neighbor—"

"No longer. With the death of his great-uncle's cousin, he is now a marquess. And that makes Miss Tynedale now Lady Meredith."

"Oh, my!" *That* was her voice, although she was not sure how she had devised even those two words in a row.

A hand cupped her elbow. Lord Westerly's hand! She could not be so overwhelmed, even in the midst of this madness, to mistake his touch for any other's. When she was steered to a bench by the closest hearth, she sat gratefully. She closed her eyes and tried to breathe.

"Are you all right, Meredith?" he asked.

She nodded, still not trusting her voice. Papa was now a marquess? Her jolly, hard-working papa disdained the *ton* because he believed they were all licentious gam-

blers like the ones who had led his father astray and
ruined the family's good name. Now he was one of them.

And so was she!

"This is all so unfathomable." Again that was the
truth. She would have asked herself if she were asleep,
but she never would have dreamed of *this!*

Mr. Goodman pulled some pages from under his coat
and handed them to her. Even reading seemed beyond
her, but she forced herself to focus on the ornate writing
on the page. It confirmed everything Mr. Goodman had
said. Papa was to be the next Marquess of Satterfield.

"Forgive my appearance, my lady."

Meredith's head jerked up at Mr. Goodman's words.
How long would it take her to accustom herself to being
called that? A lifetime?

"Our carriage," he continued with a warm smile that,
if it was meant to reassure her, failed, "was halted last
evening by some rogues who relieved all the passengers
of everything save the clothes we were wearing." He
tugged at his wrinkled coat. "I fear I am making a poor
impression after sleeping in these clothes."

She rose and placed the papers on the table where she
had planned to make bread. "Mr. Goodman, that is horrible! Did the authorities offer you any help?"

"None." He regarded her intently, so intently that she
wanted to hurry back to the storage room and hide.

Instead, she faltered as he pulled out a chair and motioned for her to sit again. She was sure every servant
in Westerly Manor must be lurking just out of view,
watching this . . . watching her.

"Thank you," she whispered.

"My pleasure, my lady."

She winced, unable to halt her reaction. This must be
a dream. No, a nightmare, because she could not ignore
Lord Westerly, who was listening in silence.

"May I?" Lord Westerly asked, pointing to the papers.

"Please." She knew desperation had filled her voice when he gave a bolstering smile. It succeeded where Mr. Goodman's had not, and she let her stiff shoulders sag, knowing Lord Westerly might understand this better than she did.

His brows arched as he set the papers back on the table. "It seems congratulations are in order, Meredith."

"My lady," Mr. Goodman said, scowling at Lord Westerly, "I think it would be prudent for you to leave now to call on your parents, so that this might be explained more fully."

"Leave?" she gasped. "But I can't go."

Mr. Goodman's scowl now was aimed at her. "What reason do you have to remain here, my lady? You are no longer in service."

"I promised Lord Westerly I would oversee the preparation of his sister's wedding breakfast."

Lord Westerly's face tightened as Mr. Goodman's blanched. She understood what neither of them had to say. As a marquess's daughter, she had no place in a baron's kitchen.

Coming to her feet, she took a deep breath before saying, "Lord Westerly, I would be glad to offer any advice I can in order to make your sister's wedding as lovely as she wishes." When Mr. Goodman opened his mouth to protest, she added, "I know my father would wish that, as we are still neighbors."

"That is very generous of you," Lord Westerly replied, his voice taut. "I am sure Nancy will appreciate your help, although I know she will understand, as I must, that you shall be extremely busy with your family's sudden change in fortune. The move to Satterfield Park alone will be time-consuming."

"Move?" She could not keep her hand from pressing over her heart, which pulsed with a sudden ache. Leaving here she had not considered. Leaving Westerly

Manor, yes, but not going so far she would not have the chance to see Lord Westerly again.

"There are many things you must consider, my lady." Mr. Goodman herded her toward the door. "Your life is going to change in ways you cannot imagine now."

She *could* imagine ways it would change, and she did not like any of them. As Mr. Goodman steered her through the door where the kitchen staff was listening, wide-eyed, she looked back at where Lord Westerly had been standing.

She was sure her heart would break completely when she saw him walking in the opposite direction without a glance in her direction. Had he put her out of his life so swiftly?

She wished she knew how, because she could not guess how she would be able to put him out of her heart.

"Meredith, we have a caller," her mother said as she came into the small room under the eaves. It had barely enough room for Meredith's narrow bed and the wash-stand.

Folding a blanket to put in the trunk at the top of the stairs, she kept her eyes on her work. "Who?"

"You know who." Mama crossed the room in a pair of steps and put her hand on Meredith's arm. "Child, I have seen you peeking out each time a person arrives at the house. I have seen your disappointment when the caller is Mr. Goodman or another of the men who are helping your father. You are not wearing that expression now. You know who has arrived."

Meredith's fingers trembled as she set the blanket on the foot of her bed. "Mama, I think it would be best if I remain here. I don't know what to do or say to Lord Westerly."

"He must be as unsettled by all of this as you are. If

he has taken the time to call, you should not add to everyone's distress by avoiding him. After all, didn't you tell me you had offered to assist with Miss Dunstan's wedding if he needed your help?"

"Yes, but—"

"There cannot be any 'buts.' You have promised to help him with the wedding. You cannot break that pledge now simply because you are confused at your sudden change of station."

She could not argue with that. She *had* promised Lord Westerly she would help with his sister's wedding plans, but when three days passed, then four, then a week, she had given up hope he would call. And if he was calling now simply for assistance on the wedding . . . no, she did not even want to think that.

Taking only a moment to check her appearance in the glass by the washstand, Meredith followed her mother down the tightly curving stairs. She hesitated in the doorway to the parlor. Her mother's gentle shove forward kept her from escaping up the stairs.

Lord Westerly turned to face them. Dressed for a ride, he looked dashing in a navy blue coat, light blue striped waistcoat, and buckskin breeches that accented his sturdy strength. Even in the memories stored in her heart, she had not recalled the brilliant glow of the sunshine on his golden-brown hair.

He wore no more expression than the logs on the hearth. Bowing his head toward her mother, he said, "Good afternoon, Lady Satterfield. I trust you will forgive my uninvited call."

"Of course." She glanced at Meredith, then away, before saying, " 'Tis such a lovely afternoon. Meredith, why don't you take Lord Westerly out into the garden while I gather some refreshments?"

"My lady, that is not necessary." Discomfort eased

the tension on his face. "I should not be asking you to—"

"Some things can never change. It has always been my pleasure to offer hospitality to guests in this house." Mama smiled. "Nothing shall change that." Again her elbow bumped Meredith in the back. "Meredith will be pleased to show you the garden, my lord."

"Thank you." He offered his arm.

Meredith put her hand on it. Mama was right. Avoiding Lord Westerly would gain her nothing. This must be resolved. Nothing would be as it had been, she knew, but she was curious as to what would happen now.

Pausing only long enough to get her bonnet, Meredith walked with Lord Westerly out into the garden. The sunshine was warm, but she shivered.

"You can't be cold," he said.

She wanted to laugh with delight at the familiar teasing sound in his voice. "Just nervous, my lord."

"It would not be inappropriate now for you to call me Percy."

"But—"

"Do you intend me to address you as Lady Meredith?"

She smiled. "I have to own I never gave the idea any thought."

"I have. I have given it much thought." He put his hand over hers on his arm. "It seems very strange to have someone else bringing me my breakfast tray each morning."

"Everything seems strange."

He withdrew a folded sheet from under his coat. When he handed it to her, he said, "I hope you will consider attending Nancy's wedding."

"As a guest?"

"It would be unthinkable to ask you to resume your duties in the kitchen at this point." He chuckled.

She smiled. "All the way from Westerly Manor to

here, Mr. Goodman rang quite a peal over me for even offering to help." She hesitated, then said, "If your sister needs any suggestions . . ."

"I have informed her of your generous offer, but do not be annoyed if she does not ask. She is so horrified to think she might have offended you in some way while you were at Westerly Manor that she will do all she can to avoid doing the same again." He tapped the sheet of paper. "Do try to come, Meredith. It will be a good way for you and your parents to be introduced into the Polite World in this shire. The attention will be focused on Nancy and her *beau,* so you can enjoy the festivities."

"Do you think that? What if our presence is disruptive?"

"You will be my guests. Let me, as host, worry about that." He led her across grass dappled by shadows from the trees. Looking back at the small cottage, he asked, "How long are you staying here?"

"Papa arranged with Sir Norman to live here until everything is settled with the courts about Papa's new title."

"Then you will go to Satterfield Park."

"They say it is beautiful," she replied, not meeting his gaze. He might see how desolate she was at the thought of leaving the only home she had known before going to Westerly Manor . . . and leaving him.

"Your parents must be ecstatic with the change in their fortune."

"You would think so, but Papa has long hated what he has derided as the wild ways of the *ton.*"

"Now he is part of the Polite World."

"Yes."

He drew her down to sit on a painted bench amid the daylilies at the edge of the garden. "So are you."

"Yes." She laughed, thrilled that now they had begun talking, she was not so anxious. "Thank heavens I am too old to be sent to London for a Season. From what I have heard of that whirl, I would tire of it before the first week was out. I cannot be so concerned with what I am wearing and what everyone else is saying and doing that I forget everything else. How did you tolerate it?"

She had expected him to offer her a jest in return, but his voice became somber as he said, "Quite the contrary, Meredith. You are not too old for a London Season, and you are now obligated to give your father a male heir."

Heat surged around her, and she feared she was blushing. "My lord—"

"Percy, if you would, Meredith."

She nodded. Arguing would be silly when she did not want to drive him away. She wanted him to be sitting here with her, hoaxing her, enticing her as he had when she had been his employee. "Percy, there are things I find disconcerting still."

"Like being here with me?"

"You know me too well."

"I would say it is quite the opposite. I don't know you well enough." His fingers rose to twist a vagrant lock of her hair about them. "So many times when I tried to get to know you better at Westerly Manor, we were interrupted."

"I had duties then that precluded me from enjoying a conversation like this."

"Conversation is not what I am speaking of."

"That is quite clear." Papa's voice intruded before Meredith could answer.

Percy came to his feet. "Lord Satterfield, I called to extend my congratulations to you and to invite your family to join us at Westerly Manor for my sister's wedding. If—"

"Now that you have done your duty, you need not feel obligated to remain."

"Papa!" Meredith gasped, shocked at his cold tone. "Mama is bringing refreshments for us to enjoy in the garden."

"I think not."

She looked at Percy, wishing she could explain her father's odd behavior, but unsure what to say when Papa stood right beside her. The amazement in Percy's eyes slowly became anger, but he simply bowed his head to her father.

"I bid you a good afternoon, my lord." Turning, he took Meredith's hand and bowed over it. He raised his head. When his gaze caught hers, she saw the longing for more than this chaste touch. "And to you, Meredith. I trust you will consider my invitation."

Although she wanted to ask if he meant the one printed for his sister's wedding or the beguiling one in his eyes, she said quietly, "I will."

He smiled, and she knew he understood what she could not say. If only she understood, too . . .

Papa waited for Percy to walk to the gate, where his horse stood, then turned to Meredith. "I have heard a most distressing thing, daughter."

"What?" She could not guess what he might find so upsetting that he had so rudely sent Percy away. Looking past her father, she watched Percy mount and ride toward Westerly Manor.

"Rumors of you and Lord Westerly and of how you and he were seen more than once in an embrace."

"Papa, 'tis not what you are thinking," she said, wondering which rumor had reached his ears. She had been so certain no one had taken note of the kiss Percy had given her in the kitchen garden. "The tray had fallen, and he was helping me gather up the broken china, and—"

He took her arm. Leading her back toward the house,

he said nothing while he glanced about as if fearing someone was eavesdropping on them now.

"Are you telling me, Meredith, that hideous slur is the truth? You were in that man's arms?"

She clasped her hands in front of her. "Papa, why are you asking? You know I worked in Percy's kitchen. We often were together. The tray fell when I was taking tea to Jeremiah's nursery."

"I heard nothing of anything in the nursery." His lips pursed with outrage. "I speak of you being in his bedchamber."

"Papa, things were different then. I had my duties."

He grew ashen, but held up his hands to halt her explanation. "A marquess's daughter should never be in the rooms of a man who is not her family or—"

"Papa! Be sensible! I was not a marquess's daughter then. It was my duty to bring Percy his breakfast tray."

"It was nothing more than that?"

It was so much more. He made my heart sing with laughter before he made it delight at his touch. Swallowing harshly, she said, "Papa, one thing I learned in Westerly Manor is people will do anything to have good gossip to share, even make up stories."

"I am glad to hear it was nothing more than that. In that case, I think it would be very wise for us to attend this wedding as our firing-off into the *ton*." He patted her shoulder and walked away.

She leaned her head against the shutters. She could find many words to describe going to the wedding, but not a single one was *wise*.

EIGHT

Meredith paused and clutched the reticule that matched her gown as she stepped into Westerly Manor's foyer. She never had entered the house this way before, because she always had used one of the side doors when she had lived here. The view of the curving staircase rising from the pattern of the parquet wood floor would have taken her breath away if she had not been holding it so tightly. So many times she had come through this foyer, but she had not paused to notice how the sunlight splashed through the upper windows to pool in the very center of the space, a welcome to all guests to Westerly Manor.

Ahead of her, her parents were speaking with a footman. Orel, she realized with a flush of dismay as he turned to greet her. When he lowered his eyes and hurried away, she knew he recalled, as she did, what he had suggested they might do the last time Westerly Manor had hosted the Polite World at the betrothal ball.

Mama smiled kindly while she motioned for Meredith to join them.

Meredith took a single step, but paused as a man came down the stairs. She had known this meeting with Thorpe was certain to take place, yet had hoped to delay it for as long as possible.

Thorpe smiled graciously at her parents and hurried

toward them. "My lord, allow me to show you and your family to the garden where the guests are waiting." He glanced at Meredith and away as hastily as Orel had.

She waited for the pulse of pleasure she had expected to relish at this meeting, but there was nothing save uncertainty. Enjoying Thorpe's discomfort would make her no better than the officious butler.

Walking along the corridor leading to the garden, she wondered how everything could seem so familiar and so strange at the same time. There was nothing familiar about being introduced to the other guests. She struggled to keep a smile in place as she tried to match faces and names. Several of the guests she recognized from the betrothal ball, but she guessed none of them recalled how she had been dressed in simple gray that evening instead of the delicate yellow-sprigged gown she wore today.

Letting her reticule hang from her wrist by its strings, she took a glass of chilled wine from a tray held up to her. Thanking the footman by name, she edged toward where a waterfall sang beneath the conversation. She stood beside a rosebush and watched her father greet the other guests and talk with them as if he had done this all his life.

"Amazing, isn't it?"

Meredith did not turn at Percy's voice. "I thought he hated the *ton*."

He came around the rosebush to stand beside her. Her breath caught, and she stared at him in his black coat that, somehow, remained pristine even outdoors. His dark breeches contrasted with the perfection of his white shirt beneath a silver waistcoat.

He must not have noticed her stare, for he continued to watch her father. "Sometimes it is easy to hate what one is envious of."

"That is cynical, Percy."

"It is, isn't it?" He smiled as he faced her. "But I would wager every flower in this garden hates you, for today you are lovelier than all of them combined."

"Thank you."

"Thank you?" he repeated, his smile wavering. "That does not sound like the Meredith I know, who would have chided me for trying to change the subject with a compliment."

"The Meredith you know may be gone."

He shook his head. "Just because your father is a marquess now instead of a clerk is no reason for you to change what you are."

"A kitchen maid?"

"You know that is not what I mean. I mean the quick-witted woman who so often reminded me that an accident of birth should not rule one's life."

"I reminded you of *that?* How?"

He laced his fingers through hers. "By treating me as a person, not simply a title. A favor I shall return to you now."

She drew her hand out of his as she noticed glances in their direction. "Mayhap that was a mistaken thing to suggest."

Percy followed Meredith's dismayed gaze and cursed under his breath. He had not wanted to believe the new marquess and his family would overshadow his sister on her day, but mayhap Meredith had been correct about that, too, for too many eyes were focused on them.

Gesturing to a passing footman, he took a glass of wine and sipped it as if nothing were amiss. He used the time to scan the guests. More and more were looking at them and bending to whisper. He could guess the course of the conversations, for both Nancy and his valet had warned him what was being said about the kitchen maid who had been raised so high so quickly.

"It is all bizarre," Meredith murmured, drawing his

gaze back to her lovely, heart-shaped face that was as colorless as the white roses. "When last you held a gathering here, I hid on the terrace and peeked in to watch the dancers."

"And now you are a guest. I don't doubt this is unsettling to you." He tilted his head toward where Thorpe was watching with a frown, which vanished as the butler noticed Percy looking at him. "Your being here seems to have a peculiar effect on the whole of my household."

"I knew it would not be wise to come here."

"How could you stay away? Jeremiah has been so anxious to see you."

"He has?"

"Nearly half as anxious as I have been."

Meredith set her glass on a low stone wall that separated the garden from the pool that collected the waters from the waterfall. "Offer your brother my regrets."

"Your regrets?"

"I think it would be best if I returned home. I don't want to ruin your sister's wedding."

"Meredith, would you leave me to all of this alone?" He grimaced as he pointed to the satin draped over the chairs that awaited the guests in front of the arbor where the wedding would take place.

She smiled, then whispered, "I cannot risk allowing the rumors you know are being repeated to become *on dits* throughout the Polite World."

"Because the rumors could ruin you?"

"Because the rumors could ruin my family."

He frowned as he stepped closer. "You worry too much about your family's honor."

"Why shouldn't I? My father has endured the shame of being ostracized once."

"Through no fault of his own."

"Yes, but—"

"He endured it and survived it."

"Will he survive being ruined by his own daughter's mistakes?" Her eyes became luminous with tears.

"What mistakes?"

She regarded him for a long minute, then sighed. "This has become too complicated."

"Then do not make it more complicated by fleeing at the first hint of innuendo. If you have learned nothing else from me, Meredith, learn that you should not take on the guilt heaped on you by others unless you justly deserve it." He brushed her cheek with the back of his hand.

A foolish thing to do, he knew, when the longing to taste her lips consumed him. He gave her a smile, then excused himself. Nancy would be outraged if he were late in walking her down the aisle to marry her baronet.

The house was oddly quiet as he climbed the stairs and knocked on the door of his sister's room. A maid opened it only a crack, then wider to let him in.

Nancy whirled from where she was being buttoned up. Her Abigail muttered under her breath, but moved to keep at her task of doing up all the small buttons on the back of the wedding dress.

"Percy!"

"Calm yourself, sister." He chuckled as he put his hands on her arms to keep her still. "You never will be dressed in time if you hop about like oil on a hot pan."

"Are they here?"

He smiled. "Sir Bryant greeted me on my way in to check on you. He—"

"Not Bryant. Them! Lord Satterfield and his family!"

Percy noticed how the room instantly became as hushed as the rest of the house. Every ear was waiting for his answer. Every eye was gauging his reaction to his sister's question.

"All the guests are eagerly waiting for you, Nancy, but none more than your fiancé." When she frowned at him and opened her mouth to ask another question, he halted her by saying, "The marquess and his family will be seated near the front, just as you requested."

The room burst into a buzz of conversation, and Percy smiled. This was going to be a very interesting afternoon.

"Would you like a glass of something cool?"

Beneath a tree whispering in time with the music from the orchestra, Meredith turned from the woman whose name she could not remember. The woman had been trying to impress her for the past hour, so Meredith was happy with any interruption.

Her eyes widened as she smiled more sincerely. "Andrelina! I had hoped to see you today." To the woman, she added, "Excuse us for a moment."

"Yes, yes, of course," the woman said, clearly flustered as she went to find someone else to speak with.

"I am so glad to see a friendly face," Meredith said as she took the tray and set it on a nearby table.

"If Thorpe sees—"

"I shall glower at him."

Andrelina laughed, then put her fingers to her lips. "He was quite put out by your father's becoming a marquess. I do believe he thinks it all happened just to vex him."

"And the others?"

"Everyone is pleased for you. Nothing like this has ever happened at Westerly Manor before." Andrelina hesitated before saying, "I want you to know I am not repeating any of the gossip that has been flitting about the house and beyond, Mer—my lady."

"You have always been a good friend." She smiled. "Even though I irked you often when I did not heed your advice about men."

"Oh! I shouldn't have suggested—"

Meredith could not keep from laughing when Andrelina blushed as brightly as she had caused Meredith to so many times. "Andrelina, you gave me advice you thought was good."

"I did." She squeezed Meredith's hand before taking her tray and stepping back as Jeremiah rushed up, his puppy Rex at his heels.

"Where have you been?" the little boy demanded.

"At home." She bent to scratch the dog behind the ears and was rewarded with a wagging tail and a widemouthed grin from the pup.

"Your home is here."

Although she longed to agree with him, Meredith shook her head. "Not any longer."

"I want you to stay here so we can make more bread together." He held up his hands. "Cook lets me knead the bread sometimes, but she doesn't believe I can count to twenty all by myself."

"Would you like me to speak with her about that?"

He grinned. "Would you, Meredith? Would you really?"

"I would be delighted to." She squatted so she could look him straight in the eye. "You have to forgive Cook. Sometimes it is not easy for us to understand how people grow and change."

"That is most definitely the truth," said Percy from behind her. He held out his hand to draw her to her feet. "Too often, we are seen as what we were, not what we are."

Before she could reply, Jeremiah tugged on her dress. "Will you talk to Cook now, Meredith?"

"Jeremiah," Percy said quietly, "you should address her as my lady or Lady Meredith."

"Nonsense." Meredith smiled. "Jeremiah is welcome to call me Meredith as he always has." She ruffled the little boy's hair. "We're cooking bosom-bows, and cooking bosom-bows always call each other by their first names. Right, Jeremiah?"

"Right." He giggled.

Percy chuckled. "Meredith will take you to speak with Cook a bit later. Just now, she is going to stand up with me."

Jeremiah's nose wrinkled. "Dancing isn't as much fun as kneading bread." He rushed off, Rex barking behind him.

Meredith's smile wavered, but she kept it in place as she said, "The wedding ceremony was lovely, Percy. Your sister should be very pleased."

"I believe she is pleased it is over." He laughed again. "I know I am."

"You had no reason to be nervous."

"Except in anticipation of asking you to dance with me." He smiled as the violins began the first notes of a waltz. "You will dance with me today, won't you, Meredith? You need not worry about Thorpe reminding you of any duty. You need only be a pleasant guest and allow your host to enjoy a few minutes in your company."

"Thorpe would prefer to chide me still, I think."

"Mayhap you are right, but why are you thinking of my arrogant butler when you should be thinking of how much fun we could have dancing to this waltz?"

Meredith had no answer to that, because he was offering her what she had dreamed of. When she nodded, he drew her into his arms, but did not step toward where the others danced.

"I thought you wanted to dance." Her voice cracked as her dismay returned.

"Meredith—"

"Or mayhap it would be better not to be seen together.

We don't want to ruin your sister's wedding by giving new life to all the rumors."

His hands framed her face. "Meredith, listen to me."

"I know it has been most uncomfortable to—"

"Listen to me. Please."

When she opened her mouth to reply, he claimed her lips, kissing her until she softened against him. His arms slid around her as he drew her even closer until she shared every breath with him. This was what she wanted, where she wanted to be, where there was no pretense, only joy.

Meredith cried out in horror as her arm was grasped and she was pulled away from Percy. She swallowed her angry words when she stared at her father's furious scowl and her mother's dismay.

"So the rumors are true!" thundered her father. "You *have* done more than serve this man his breakfast."

Percy slowly drew Meredith's arm out of her father's grip. "My lord, you are creating undue interest in our conversation."

"Then let the conversation be over." Papa motioned to Meredith. "You are excused, Lord Westerly. I shall not allow you to continue to lead my daughter astray."

"If you think I will step aside and allow you to bully Meredith, who has done nothing she needs to be ashamed of, you are mistaken."

Although each word was bitter on her lips, Meredith said, "It might be better if I speak with my parents alone, Percy."

"So your father can intimidate you into feeling and doing nothing for fear anything you do or say or feel might be what he deems shameful?"

She recoiled from his fury. "Percy, please. You have tried to make your family proud of you since your return from London."

"Is that what you thought? That I have worked this

hard simply to atone for mistakes I may have made in London?" His eyes drilled her. "Mayhap you need no help being led astray, Meredith, because you certainly have let your own assumptions based on the gossip you have swallowed lead you so far astray about this." His anger tightened his jaw. "I trust you will enjoy the rest of your stay at Westerly Manor."

"Percy!" she gasped, but he turned on his heel and walked away. She rounded on her father. "How could you?"

"How could *you?* A marquess's daughter should have higher aspirations than a baron with a questionable reputation."

"How has Percy done himself harm in your eyes? He was generous to continue my employment here at Westerly Manor after his father died, and he has never treated me with less than respect."

She raised her chin and looked past her father to her mother, who was wringing a handkerchief nearly to shreds. Wishing she did not have to say these words when they might cause her mother pain, she could withhold them no longer. "Papa, listen to yourself. You have become the very thing you hate. Don't let that hate keep me from having a chance at love."

"Love?" He sniffed. "Has that raffish rogue said anything to you of love?"

She started to answer her father, then turned and walked away before he could hear how her heart was breaking . . . again.

Even though Meredith had guessed her parents would insist on leaving the wedding celebration posthaste, she saw her father caught up in an intense conversation with Sir Bryant. Apparently his hatred of Lord Westerly did not extend to the baron's brother-in-law.

A small hand tugged on her dress. She tried to find a smile for Jeremiah.

"You said later," the child said. " 'Tis later now."

She glanced back at the wedding celebration, then nodded. Going with Jeremiah would give her time to compose herself before facing Papa again.

Before she could say anything, Rex jumped up and grabbed her reticule. It fell from her wrist. He raced toward the front stairs, holding it firmly in his teeth.

"I'll get it back," Jeremiah cried.

"Be careful!"

She wondered if he heard her as he ran up the stairs after the dog. She gasped when she realized they were headed for the balcony along the second floor. That was too dangerous for them when they were racing with reckless abandon.

Lifting her skirts higher, Meredith sped up the stairs after them. Her shout not to go outside went unheeded as Rex ran out the double doors at the top of the stairs.

"Jeremiah!" she called. "Come back before you slip and fall!"

He paid no more attention to her than the puppy did. Rex barked, wagged his tail, and raced away with Jeremiah in pursuit. Wishing someone was nearby to help, but guessing everyone was outside with the wedding celebration, Meredith chased after them. If they did not slow down, they could crash through the railing.

She held her breath as they careened around the corner. Jeremiah's giggles and Rex's yips let her know they had negotiated the tight turn with ease. Following them, she gasped when she saw a door open almost directly in front of the puppy.

Rex could not stop in time. He slid into the door, jumped back and shook his head with a startled bark, then ran into the room. Jeremiah let out a whoop and ran after his dog.

Meredith ignored the lilt of music from the garden and hurried after them. She faltered when she entered the room. Except for what came through the door, there was no light within. The drapes must still be drawn. The shadows seemed thicker when her eyes were accustomed to the day's bright sunshine.

"Jeremiah?" she called, blinking in hopes she could peer through the dusk.

"He's not here now."

She whirled as the door shut. "Percy!" She took a step toward him, then halted, still lost in the darkness. "Percy, you need to stop them before they get hurt."

His hand curved around her shoulder, guiding her toward him. Amusement filled his voice. "They will be fine. I sent them back to the garden to get something to eat." He pressed her reticule into her hand. "They dropped this, which I believe is yours."

As her eyes slowly adjusted, she looked down at the silk bag now covered with dirt and other things she did not want to think about.

"If it is ruined," he continued, "Jeremiah will do some extra chores to earn the money to replace it."

"That is not necessary."

"I think so."

She wished they were not speaking with the politeness of strangers. Gripping the strings of her bag, she said, "Thank you for halting them. I should . . ." She gasped as she stared past him.

She could not mistake the grand bed or the settee with the table in front of it where she had placed his breakfast tray each morning. Whirling, she reached for the door to the balcony.

He put his hand over hers on the latch. "That would not be wise, Meredith. If someone were to see you skulking out of my room—for the wedding celebration has a clear view of this room—think of the gossip that would engender."

"If I go out the door to the hallway—"

"You are certain to be seen as well." He rested one shoulder against the door and smiled. "It seems you finally have proven your father right, Meredith. You have been led astray, although not by me. Who would have guessed Jeremiah and Rex would be the culprits to bring about your ruin?"

"Did you plan this?" She held her breath. If he had, he was not the man she had believed him to be.

He smiled. "I would like to take credit for it, but, to own the truth, you are simply a victim of happenstance. It happens to all of us sooner or later."

She forgot her own circumstances as she heard regret in his voice. How had she mistaken this grief for cynicism? "Tell me, Percy. What was it you did to turn your father against you?"

"It was rather what I refused to do."

"Please tell me." She put her fingers on his arm. Even though staying here a minute more increased the chances of her being discovered in his private chambers, she could not let this moment pass.

His hand curved along her face. "I refused to kill a man."

"What?" she cried, horrified.

"You are so innocent in so many ways, Meredith. If you were to be sent to London for a Season, you would see all the greatest beef-heads in the kingdom gather there. Gossip there is a true art form, and it is often confused with the truth until no one knows what is real and what is just an embellishment."

"I don't understand."

He smiled wryly. "A friend believed a rumor suggesting I had taken up with his mistress. Even though I assured him it was not true, he refused to believe me and challenged me to a duel. I refused."

"That was the wise thing to do."

"But as you have seen, my dear, wisdom has as many guises as truth. My father saw my refusal to kill my erstwhile friend on the dueling green as a sign of dishonor. From that moment, he believed I was worthless."

"That is ludicrous!"

"Is it? It is any more ludicrous than the fact I could not speak to you of my feelings for you when you were a servant here?"

"Feelings?"

"Meredith, you bring such joy into my life. Yet I could not say that when you worked here, because it would have been assumed I wished only to bed you."

Heat flashed up her face. "I know."

"It *is* ludicrous. Just as it is ludicrous that your name is blemished now because you stand here with me where we have stood before."

She closed her eyes and sighed. "Percy, is there any way I can leave with my reputation intact?"

"Yes."

"Tell me."

"I would rather show you."

She gasped when he tugged her into his arms. The sound disappeared beneath his fervent kiss. The reticule fell from her fingers as she wrapped her arms around his shoulders. If she were to be condemned as a harlot, she might as well enjoy this kiss. That thought faded along with every other one but rapture as he etched heated kisses across her face.

"Stand up with me," he whispered against her neck.

"The dancing is—"

He raised his head and caught her face between his hands again. "Stand up with me not to dance, but in front of the minister."

"In front of the minister?"

He smiled. "Why do you look so baffled, Meredith? I'm asking if you will be my wife."

Again she could only repeat, "Your wife?"

"My wife. I think I have loved you since the very first morning you brought me your cinnamon bread. You chided me then for the dreams you thought were of someone else." He kissed her swiftly. "Even then, all my dreams were of you."

"Yes, I will marry you."

"Today?"

"Today?" she gasped.

With a laugh, he took her hand and drew her around the bed to the door to the outer chamber. He swung back the door and laughed as she stared at the crowd waiting there. His sister and her new husband, her parents, Jeremiah—who sat on the floor with a panting Rex on his lap—even Andrelina stood there with the minister waiting in the very middle of the crowd.

"A special license is easier to get than I had suspected," he murmured. "We can get married right now."

Mama stepped forward and smiled as she motioned to her husband. "Meredith, both your father and I have given Percy our blessing on this match. Right, Mr. Tynedale?" She flashed Meredith a conspiratorial grin before adding, "I mean, right, my lord?"

Sure she had never seen her father look so chagrined, she could not help gasping when he said, "Of course, my dear. It seems this man's intentions toward you were quite honorable, Meredith."

"Yes," she managed to reply as her mother drew her to one side and brushed her hair back behind her ears from where it had come loose while she chased Jeremiah and his dog. "How did you persuade Papa?" she asked while Percy went to speak with the minister.

"I reminded him how my father had not wanted me

to marry a titleless man from a family awash in ruin, but that I had not heeded my father because I loved your father."

"And Papa listened?"

She laughed. "After a while. I do believe he accepted the inevitable when I reminded him you are now a grown woman. I told him as well that, if you love Percival Dunstan, you should marry him, and your life is none of your father's bread-and-butter."

With a laugh, she hugged her mother before going to where Percy held his hand out to her. She put hers in it as they turned together to face the minister.

EPILOGUE

"Are you ready for me, my lord?"

Percy stirred in his bed and smiled at the delicate voice sifting through the dream that had not quite disappeared. The voice created new fantasies to flitter into his mind as he was poised between sleep and waking.

"Yes, I am ready for you." His smile widened. Her soft tones had been enough to take care of that, for they would rouse even the most oblivious of men.

"Where would you like to have this?"

Ah, her voice was lovely. "Here would be fine."

"But, my lord, it is so hot."

He smiled as he rolled onto his back to look up at Meredith. Her ebony hair still cascaded down her back, tangled from his fingers in it during the night, and her eyes were soft from the sleep they had found late in the night after she had given life to his fantasies of holding her in his arms.

Locking his hands behind her nape, he gently drew her down to him for a lingering kiss. Even his fantasies had not been as wondrous as the rapture they had found together last night.

She drew back and whispered, "It is getting cold."

"You are quite mistaken." He offered her a lascivious grin. "I would say it is getting very pleasantly warm, my dear Lady Westerly."

With a curtsy, she laughed. "My Lord Westerly, your breakfast awaits."

"My breakfast?" He pushed himself up to sit. When she placed a tray by him on the bed, he lifted the top of the closest plate. "Cinnamon bread? When did you have time to make this?"

She sat beside him and broke the topmost piece of bread in two. "I didn't. Jeremiah did—with Cook's help—as a wedding gift for us." She offered him the bread.

Taking it, he put it on the tray. Then he set the tray on the stand by the bed. With a laugh, he pulled her into his arms and leaned her back in the pillows.

"Jeremiah will be insulted if we don't try his bread," she whispered as she combed her fingers through his hair.

"We will, but later." He brushed her lips with his. "I understand cinnamon bread is good cold, too."

"I suspect we will find out. Later. Much later." Her laugh vanished as he captured her lips as she had captured his heart.

Meredith's Cinnamon Bread

Bread:

2 packages yeast
3 1/3 c warm water
1/4 c sugar
1 tbsp salt
3 tbsps butter-flavored shortening
7 to 8 c flour

Filling:

1/3 c sugar
3 tsps cinnamon (or to taste)

Stir yeast into warm water. Add sugar, salt, and shortening. Stir. Add 5 cups of flour and mix together. Add enough of the rest of the flour to make the mixture silky. Knead on a floured surface until no longer glossy (about 5-8 minutes).

Put mixture in a lightly greased bowl and let rise in a warm place (not hot) for an hour, until bread has doubled in size.

Punch down dough and divide in half. Flatten out in approximate width of bread loaf pans. Mix sugar and cinnamon together. Dampen bread with water and sprinkle sugar/cinnamon mixture atop it. Roll up, seal edges, and place in lightly greased bread pans. Let rise in a warm place until double (about an hour).

Heat oven to 400 degrees F. Spread butter lightly on top of loaves, taking care not to punch down, if you wish. It makes for crisper crusts.

Cook for 30-35 minutes or until desired brownness and loaves have a hollow sound when tapped. Cool on a wire rack.

Enjoy!

More Zebra Regency Romances

Celebrate Romance With Two of Today's Hottest Authors

Meagan McKinney

__In the Dark	$6.99US/$8.99CAN	0-8217-6341-5
__The Fortune Hunter	$6.50US/$8.00CAN	0-8217-6037-8
__Gentle from the Night	$5.99US/$7.50CAN	0-8217-5803-9
__A Man to Slay Dragons	$5.99US/$6.99CAN	0-8217-5345-2
__My Wicked Enchantress	$5.99US/$7.50CAN	0-8217-5661-3
__No Choice But Surrender	$5.99US/$7.50CAN	0-8217-5859-4

Meryl Sawyer

__Thunder Island	$6.99US/$8.99CAN	0-8217-6378-4
__Half Moon Bay	$6.50US/$8.00CAN	0-8217-6144-7
__The Hideaway	$5.99US/$7.50CAN	0-8217-5780-6
__Tempting Fate	$6.50US/$8.00CAN	0-8217-5858-6
__Unforgettable	$6.50US/$8.00CAN	0-8217-5564-1

Call toll free **1-888-345-BOOK** to order by phone, use this coupon to order by mail, or order online at **www.kensingtonbooks.com**.

Name _____

Address _____

City _____ State _____ Zip _____

Please send me the books I have checked above.

I am enclosing	$_____
Plus postage and handling*	$_____
Sales tax (in New York and Tennessee only)	$_____
Total amount enclosed	$_____

*Add $2.50 for the first book and $.50 for each additional book.

Send check or money order (no cash or CODs) to:

Kensington Publishing Corp., Dept. C.O., 850 Third Avenue, New York, NY 10022

Prices and numbers subject to change without notice.

All orders subject to availability.

Visit our website at **www.kensingtonbooks.com**.

DO YOU HAVE THE HOHL COLLECTION?